"…DV Berkom pens her plots fast paced and smoothly flowing with tons of action, thrills, with characters that are relatable and really likeable. I was thrilled to find that you can go from book to book and not miss a step. A must read for all crime, suspense fans…" - *My Cozie Corner Book Reviews*

"An edge of your seat, page-turning read!" - *I Am, I Said Book reviews*

"…This is a well written series, with good characterization and fast pacing that will have you clicking the Kindle at a rapid fire pace to keep up. Don't read this when you're trying to go to sleep." –*Amazon reviewer*

"The story line was great, when one book ended, it moved smoothly to the next. I read them all in 4 days!" –*Amazon reviewer*

"…Flawlessly written and an author I'm going to have on my bookshelves from now on." -*ZenCherry Blogger/Reviewer*

"…As a stereotypical guy, I usually don't enjoy, or read much of, fiction that has a female as the main character - mainly because I can't relate to them. However, D.V. Berkom is one good storyteller and I am looking forward to reading the continuing saga of Kate Jones." – *Michael Gallagher, Top 10 Amazon Reviewer*

The Kate Jones Thriller Series
Vol. 1

DV BERKOM

THE KATE JONES THRILLER SERIES, VOL. 1
Copyright © 2013, 2016 D.V. Berkom

Published by:

Second print edition. Printed in the United State of America.

ISBN: 0997970804
ISBN-13: 978-0-9979708-0-7

TABLE OF CONTENTS

Bad Spirits

BAD SPIRITS

Something didn't feel right.

Dark.

Dirt floor.

My left side ached, and I could barely swallow. I sat with my eyes closed and tried to recall what happened. The events from the previous night came crashing back into the present, and the fear of discovery threatened to overwhelm me again.

I peeked around the corner of the corrugated steel building. A lone goat munched on some dried grass near a split-rail fence. A few yards away a rooster pecked at the hard, dry earth. An older woman with salt and pepper colored hair and skin like a walnut scattered seed in front of him. She clutched a brown and white serape around her against the early morning chill.

Everything appeared calm, bucolic, even. I leaned back against the metal wall and took stock of my position.

Salazar ruled this little section of Sonora with an iron hand. The woman outside would not help me, for fear of payback. In fact, no one who knew him would be fool enough to assist Salazar's crazy American woman.

Especially when she took something that belonged to him. Something he valued above all else. And it wasn't only his pride, although that would be enough to get me killed.

I opened the canvas backpack next to me to make sure the contents were still safe, that I hadn't somehow lost it all in my mad rush to escape.

The cash was all there. I breathed a sigh of relief. It meant my survival. Without it, I would have nothing with which to bargain for my life, if it came to that. As it was, the stash wouldn't get me the immediate help I so desperately needed. It wasn't like I could call a cab in this part of Mexico, even if I had a phone.

If I knew Salazar, he'd already locked down the small airport a few miles away, and was probably trying to bribe aviation officials in Hermosillo, Obregón and even Puerto Peñasco, although each of the towns lay miles from his hacienda.

I needed to get to San Bruno, a small fishing village on the Sea of Cortez. Salazar didn't have much pull with the ex-pats who lived there. Besides, they'd help a fellow American.

Especially one with a boat load of dinero.

I zipped the backpack closed, stood up, and heaved it over my shoulders. Funny how much money weighed.

Bad Spirits

I waited until the older woman had stepped inside her weathered home, and then I quietly slipped away down the dirt road, careful not to disturb El Gallo as he strutted past the disinterested goat.

I tucked my blonde hair up under a baseball cap to hide it and hitched a ride west on the back of an ancient Ford pickup. The driver looked me over once and waved me into the truck bed to sit with the alfalfa, probably thinking I was some silly gringa on a tourista's adventure. I was glad I had grabbed an older jacket from one of Salazar's bodyguards. All of my clothes were too new, too expensive. I'd be a prime target for bandits. As it was, I was a sitting duck lugging around the cash, paranoid that everyone knew I'd stolen millions of dollars from a notorious drug lord.

What I'd seen last night confirmed my worst fears, and then some. I'd been in denial about Salazar's true nature, and it hit me like a bullet to the brain. His expression held no remorse, even as he sliced through the man's throat—a man who, until that moment, had been a loyal soldier in Salazar's increasingly bizarre attempts to own the Sonoran drug trade. My sense of self-preservation skyrocketed, and I took the only way out.

It seemed like the Hand of God had intervened, and I'm not given to religious hyperbole. I'd abandoned the delivery van a few miles from the ranch the night before, and grabbed as much cash as I could stuff in the backpack. The vehicle had been parked in the drive with the keys and money in it. I simply took the initiative.

I made myself comfortable, and had to inhale great gulps of dusty air to counteract the nausea and shaking as I watched the sun rise in the distance, and the road race away from the back of the pickup.

***

I woke as soon as the pickup stopped. We'd parked next to the imposing white mission of the town of Santa Theresa.

"This is as far as I am going," the driver said in Spanish. I thanked him and asked where I could get a good breakfast. He pointed down a nearby street and indicated the second restaurant I would come to served the best Huevos Rancheros in town.

I sat in the shade under the palm roof, aviator sunglasses on, a can of Fanta in my hand, as the aged Mexican woman prepared my breakfast. A dark-haired boy, about four years old, played hide and seek with her while she cooked. I'd always loved the casual, family-centered vibe of Mexican restaurants. No hurry, enjoy your meal. It didn't matter what you looked like, or where you were from, you were there to share in one of life's greatest gifts: food.

The woman set my plate down in front of me and smiled shyly. The little boy stood next to her and peered over the edge of the table, curious to see how the gringa ate her breakfast. I grinned at him and thanked her, and poured her homemade salsa on my huevos. Then I topped it off with a few jalapeños. The woman walked away and after a moment's hesitation, the little boy scurried after her, giggling.

I finished my soda and had walked to the counter to pay for my meal when a white SUV with smoked windows drove by, slowing as it passed the restaurant. I moved behind one of the roof supports. The truck looked familiar. The woman behind the counter glanced at me, then shoved the little boy underneath the brick counter with a terse admonition.

The SUV moved past us and turned the corner. Not waiting for the change, I grabbed the backpack and ran out the rear of the restaurant, into the alley.

The white SUV sat idling at one end. The passenger side door opened. I heaved the pack over the fence in front of me and scrambled after it, scattering chickens and dogs as I landed hard on my ass. The sound of squealing tires told me I needed to move, now.

I sprang to my feet, shouldered the pack, and sprinted through the backyard, headed for the door of the cinderblock house. The teenage boy sitting on the couch didn't have time to react other than to open his mouth in surprise as I burst through the door and plowed through his living room, knocking over chairs and leaping over plastic toys on the floor.

I skidded to a stop when I reached the front door and eased it open, careful to check each end of the dirt street that ran in front of the house. The SUV was nowhere in sight, so I slipped out the door and started to run.

I heard the SUV before I saw it and veered right. I ignored the heavy pack mashing my kidneys as I ran, determined to escape with both my life and every ounce of the money. I caught a glimpse of the kid from the last house out of the corner of my eye, running parallel to me. If he kept it up, there'd be two dead bodies in the street.

"Get back inside!" I yelled. He continued to match my direction and motioned for me to follow him. I couldn't think of a better plan, so I did. He slipped behind a rusty corrugated building and I tracked right behind him.

The sound of the SUV skidding to a stop on the gravel street, followed by angry male voices spilled over me. I ran like I'd never run before, knocking crates over, oblivious to anything not nailed down in front of me, never once losing sight of the boy's red shirt.

He led me into a rabbit warren of alleyways, jogging first one way, then the other. I was completely disoriented by the time we stopped. I bent over, trying to catch my breath, and let the backpack sag to the ground. He was breathing heavy, too, although not as much.

He held a finger to his lips. I struggled to slow my breathing and listened. A television commercial for a sports drink blared a few doors down. Somewhere a dog barked. There was no sound of Salazar's men or the SUV. I sighed with relief.

"Who are you?" I asked the kid in Spanish.

"Manuel."

Bad Spirits

I held out my hand. "Manuel, I am so happy to make your acquaintance." He smiled and shook my hand, nodding.

"Why did you help me?"

Manuel shrugged. "You were in trouble."

Good enough for me. I inspected the area where we stood. A six foot high concrete wall surrounded us, the space open to the sky. Mismatched plastic chairs surrounded a white plastic table covered with a cheerful flowery table cloth. A metal bird cage hung from a wrought iron stand, with no bird in sight. Two wooden cases of empty Seven-Up bottles stood in the corner.

"How do I get out of here?" I asked.

Manuel frowned. Then his face split into a big smile.

"My Uncle Javier can give you a ride in his truck. He will take you wherever you want to go."

"I have a little money. I can pay him."

Manuel grinned. "Even better. My uncle will do almost anything for money."

***

The panel truck was a tad overcrowded. It appeared that Uncle Javier had a side business that involved smuggling humans.

There were a total of thirty two people besides me in the back. I sat between a young couple from Jalisco and an older, indigenous man dressed in a poncho. I didn't understand his dialect very well, and after a few attempts at communication, I gave up and talked with the younger couple. The smell of excitement and fear permeated the truck. Everyone there had paid dearly for the chance to cross the border into the US, and stories about disreputable 'coyotes,' as the smugglers were called, abounded.

I felt a small measure of safety, since I wasn't taking the same route. Once Uncle Javier dropped his cargo off at a prearranged place, he'd drive me to San Bruno, where I'd be able to find simpatico ex-pats who would help me leave the country.

The rest of the travelers, however, didn't have it as good. The US government had recently beefed up security along the Arizona border, and bandits had flocked to the area, attracted by the easy money of ripping off the migrants, who needed help to get across.

The compartment grew stuffy and uncomfortable, but no one complained. The young couple from Jalisco had dreams of opening a restaurant in a small town outside of Flagstaff, where several of the woman's relatives lived. They asked me many questions about what they could expect, and I tried to give them realistic answers, explaining that Arizona was not what you'd call immigrant friendly. They'd heard about the controversy, but had been told they'd be able to get work visas easily. I told them I thought there was a very long wait for these visas. They remained undaunted.

After a few hours, the truck slowed to a stop. The sound of slamming car doors and muffled voices echoed in the dark. Someone disengaged the handle on the other side of the door and rolled up the panel. Silhouetted against bright headlights, two masked gunmen pointed AK-47s at us.

My hand moved instinctively to a zippered pocket on the backpack. Luckily it was dark, and the gunmen didn't notice. I slid my hand back to rest on my thigh. There was no reason to pull out a gun at this point. I'd be dead in seconds, as would the rest of the occupants in the truck.

"Everyone out!" The taller of the two gunmen waved his weapon to indicate where we should go. People began to gather their things. Husbands wrapped protective arms around their wives as they murmured in fear. I helped the indigenous guy to his feet. His eyes had an intensity I found oddly reassuring. We moved toward the open door. Once ten people had climbed out, the gunmen barred the rest from getting off the truck.

I barely overheard the other gunman's orders as he demanded the people hand over all their valuables, or they would be shot. They opened their belongings and he rifled through, looking for money or jewelry. Once the first group had been robbed, the next ten were told to come out of the truck. The younger couple, the indigenous guy and I stayed behind in the last group. I wouldn't give up my backpack without a fight. I moved to the back of the line, quietly pulled out my gun and shoved it into the waistband of my jeans. It was loaded with a round chambered. Eduardo had taught me well.

We inched closer to the gunmen. Adrenaline took the place of the fear I'd been feeling, and everything appeared crystal clear. I was probably going to die, but would damn sure try to take out the gunmen before they hurt anyone. The thought didn't surprise me. After living with a man like Salazar, I'd never again be the same person who'd traveled on her own to Mexico three years ago.

It seemed like a lifetime.

I watched as the rest of the passengers stepped off the back of the truck. The gunman motioned for the older man to get out. He bent over as though to tie his shoe. Then he straightened and whipped his poncho to one side, revealing a sub machine gun. He let loose with a barrage of bullets, mowing down both of the gunmen. The assault was so unexpected neither of them could get a shot off before the old man's aim found its mark. Miraculously, he hit none of the passengers.

With a sharp cry Uncle Javier ran blindly into the creosote bushes. The old man let him go.

At first stunned, soon everyone clamored to touch his hand and thank him. I slumped against the wall of the truck in relief and closed my eyes against the grisly sight of the dead men.

The young couple I'd been talking with said something to the old man that I didn't catch. He replied and nodded his head. I moved closer to the couple and asked what he'd said.

The young woman had tears in her eyes. "He said he was sent to protect us." She wiped her eyes with her hand. "He said the spirits moved him to come to this place and bring a gun. He also said to tell you to trust no one on your journey."

Apparently. How the hell was I going to make it all the way to San Bruno without trusting someone?

After recovering the items taken from them, a few of the male passengers dragged the dead gunmen out of sight. The older man in the poncho guided everyone else into the back of the truck. His eyes held mine for a moment. He seemed to look through me, as though he knew my mind. The young couple walked up beside me and the woman took my hand.

"He says you are not coming with us." Her expression mirrored the concern on her husband's face. "You must be careful."

The old man murmured something to her and she turned to me.

"He says there are bad spirits surrounding you. He will say a prayer to intercede for you, but you must not rest—not even when you think you are safe. It is for this that the spirits wait." The old man leaned over and pointed at me as he spoke again.

The woman's eyes darkened. "He tells me your destiny is to live looking over your shoulder, never knowing when these spirits will come for you- until you give up everything. Only then will you be free."

Okay then. Well. I'd never been good at taking advice, and tonight was no different.

"Tell him thank you, and that I will consider his warning."

She spoke in rapid sentences. The old man looked up, shook his head and laughed, then walked away. She shrugged and said, "He's an old man," by way of explanation.

I said goodbye to them both and walked over to the gunmen's truck. The keys dangled from the ignition.

I took the initiative.

***

I drove through the night, glad for the anonymity of the darkness. I had to swerve to avoid a small herd of steers somewhere outside of Moctezuma. Otherwise, the trip was uneventful. I stopped for fuel at a tiny roadside station and woke the proprietor, who did not appreciate the interruption.

I'd made it to the outskirts of Hermosillo by sunrise, and decided to try my luck by continuing to drive in daylight. The truck didn't agree.

The four-wheel drive coughed and sputtered its way to the side of the road, and then died. I got out and lifted the hood and checked the belts, the hoses, and whatever filters I could find. I had no idea what was wrong. It had been a long time since I'd worked on a vehicle, and my skills were rusty. Not to mention the truck was a later model, and most of its components were either electronic or impossible to get to.

Bad Spirits

I lowered the hood and reached in the passenger side for my backpack. With a sigh, I shrugged on the pack and started to walk.

The first couple of cars zoomed by me so fast I barely had time to stick my thumb out. The third slowed and stopped just ahead, waiting for me to catch up. It was an old Ford Galaxy convertible—long, low and sea green, with a trunk the size of Manhattan. The driver had a goatee and wore Wayfarer sunglasses, a Hawaiian shirt and a baseball cap with a purple Vikings logo.

I threw the pack in the back seat and sat in front. The gun was still in my waistband, just in case this guy turned out to be a serial killer. Or a Fox News anchor.

"You like the Vikings?" I asked.

"Yeah. They haven't won a playoff in years."

So he was American. I looked more closely at him. He reminded me of someone, but I couldn't put my finger on it. Probably some celebrity. "You from Minnesota?"

"Nope. Virginia. I just like the Vikes. How about you?"

"Minnesota, born and bred."

We drove in silence for a while.

"What's in the pack?"

I tensed. Too personal. The old man's warning flashed in my mind. "Just stuff," I replied.

He snorted. "Stuff? What kind of stuff?"

A feeling of dread swam through me. Just take it easy, Kate. He's a friendly American, that's all.

"Oh, you know, the usual. Clothes and things."

"Looks pretty heavy."

"Well, there are shoes, too." I hoped my smile looked innocent enough.

"What's a pretty thing like you doing out here in the middle of the Sonoran desert?" He glanced in the rear view mirror. "That pickup truck back there on the side of the road yours?"

"I wish. I've been hitching for days."

"You wouldn't happen to know a guy named Roberto Salazar, would you?"

I nearly choked.

He smiled. The scenery reflected off his sunglasses.

"I guess you do." He glanced at me. "Don't freak out. I'm one of the good guys." He reached for the glove box, hesitating until I nodded for him to go ahead. My hand rested under my jacket near the gun.

He pulled out a badge that read Drug Enforcement Administration, Special Agent.

Shit. A backpack full of drug money and I catch a ride with a DEA agent.

My options had just narrowed considerably. The larger question was how did he make the connection? Had news of my escape really spread that fast?

I was torn. If I told him who I was, he'd detain me for questioning, and possibly arrest me since I'd been involved with Salazar. On the other hand, I'd get a free pass to the states, maybe even a new identity if I volunteered information. It was possible he already guessed my identity.

I decided to test the waters.

"I've heard of him."

"What have you heard?"

"That you don't want to get on his bad side."

"Sounds about right. Ever met him?"

"Once, at a party, I think." Better to establish a slight link rather than play completely stupid. "Hey—do I know you from somewhere? You seem familiar." My hand inched toward the door handle.

He chuckled and pushed on the accelerator. The Galaxy's speedometer read sixty-five, then seventy. Alarm shot through me like a lightning bolt, and that old familiar panic returned.

"Why don't you slow down? You're making me nervous."

He sped up in response. "How can a little speed make you nervous? Living with Salazar was so much more dangerous."

I glanced out the windshield. We headed straight toward a bend in the road. I strapped on my seatbelt. His grin reminded me of Jack Nicholson in The Shining.

"Scared, Kate?" He turned to look at me.

"Stop—" The words died in my throat as the Galaxy plowed into the side of the black steer standing in the road.

As if in slow motion, my upper body and legs flew forward from the force of the impact, the center of my body anchored in place by the single strap of the seatbelt. Glass shattered and metal screamed, drowning out the animal's bellow.

A deathly stillness followed the crash. The punctured radiator hissed steam. Dazed, I unhooked the seatbelt and opened the passenger side door, and fell onto the roadside. My gun dropped onto the road with a clatter. I grabbed it, then dragged myself up onto the door to stand, gasping and choking from having the wind knocked out of me.

I felt around for broken bones, but didn't find any. The driver's seat held shards of glass instead of the driver. Warily, I stepped around to the front of the car.

The steer's dead body lay wedged underneath the front wheels. At least it had been quick. My backpack rested a few yards further up the road. It appeared to be intact. I walked over to retrieve it when I heard a moan.

He sat slumped against a mesquite tree on the side of the road. Blood from a head wound stained his Hawaiian shirt a dark red. His left leg canted out at an unnatural angle. The ball cap was nowhere in sight. He watched as I approached, his breathing ragged.

With no cap and sunglasses, I finally recognized him, even through the blood on his face.

I aimed the gun at his chest.

"I thought you said you were one of the good guys."

"You won't make it, Kate. Salazar's got everybody out looking for you, and he didn't say he wanted you alive. I came to find you before they did."

"Gee, thanks John. That was real nice of you." I should have known the square jaw, the aquiline nose. John Sterling was DEA, all right, but not the good kind. He wanted the money, not me.

"Give me your gun." I pointed at his armpit.

He sighed as he slid his hand underneath his shirt to the shoulder holster I knew he always wore. The rhythmic rise and fall of his chest belied the difficulty he had breathing. After a couple of futile attempts, he let his hand drop to this thigh.

"I can't."

Careful to keep my gun out of reach, I leaned over and slid his Glock out of the holster, then stepped back.

He closed one eye and squinted. "You gonna kill me?"

I considered the question for a moment, let him sweat. Then I shook my head.

"No."

He nodded. "Didn't think so."

I turned to go. The backpack felt much heavier than before.

"He'll find you. Salazar never quits."

I shrugged the pack onto my back.

Neither did I.

JUST PASSING THROUGH

Paranoia kept me off the highway. The blisters on my feet burned with each step. There weren't many other transit options in this part of Sonora, apart from the occasional steer. Although I'd left John Sterling broken and bloody by the side of the road, he wasn't the only one searching for the cash, and I needed to be careful, or I'd end up dead.

I wore my jacket even though the temperature had soared. The ball cap I used to hide my blonde hair didn't prevent the sun from searing my neck, and I needed the coverage.

My spine ached from the weight of the money. I limped toward what looked like a small carne asada place that had appeared like a mirage on the horizon. Normally family owned, these Mexican versions of an open-air barbecue joint dotted the countryside along well-traveled routes. Since the highway I skirted happened to be the only one that led to San Bruno, I didn't have the luxury of following a less popular road.

The buff colored hound sleeping in the shade of an ancient station wagon pawed at the air, chasing dream rabbits. The whitewashed structure's silence told me I'd arrived after the lunch hour, with the inhabitants more than likely taking a siesta.

I shrugged off the pack and let it fall to the ground.

"Hello? Anyone here?" I called out in Spanish.

"One moment," answered a man's voice.

A burly, middle-aged man in a white tee shirt and black trousers walked through the door at the back of the restaurant, wiping his hands on a towel.

I glanced at the menu board propped up on the counter. "May I have two tacos and a Seven-Up?"

He nodded, reached into an old cooler for my soda, and set it on the counter.

As he prepared my lunch, I scanned the road in each direction, aware of my vulnerability. Relieved that traffic was light, I took a sip of the Seven-Up and turned back to watch him.

Finished, he placed the plate of tacos in front of me. He glanced out at the dirt lot, a quizzical expression on his face.

"Where is your car?"

I took a bite of my taco. "I haven't got one."

"You're a long way from anywhere. A woman alone needs to be careful."

"When does the bus come by here?"

"Not until tomorrow."

The hound shuffled past me, sniffed at the backpack and, disinterested, wandered off.

"Would you happen to know anyone around here who's trying to sell their car?" It was a long shot, but the least I could do was try. Although the news of a gringa with cash would travel fast, my feet and back screamed for relief.

"I might be willing to sell that car over there." He nodded his head at the dusty old pile of metal.

"As long as it runs. How much?"

"Two thousand dollars. US."

I smiled. He knew an opportunity when he saw it. "No, my friend. The car is not worth nearly that much. Five hundred."

He smiled back, revealing a gold incisor. "But then I will have no car. One thousand."

"Is there enough gas to get to the next town?"

"The tank is half full."

I sighed and made a show of thinking about his reply. I'd give him five thousand if it meant getting my ass to San Bruno faster.

"Seven-fifty. That's my last offer, friend."

He held out his hand and grinned. "Deal."

***

Aside from the cloying cigarette smell and ripped upholstery, the car was perfect. No one would look twice at the ugly brown station wagon, and the cracked windshield obscured the occasional curious glance inside. The car's shelf life would only last until I reached the next town, but I'd be that much closer to San Bruno. I didn't dare keep driving. A bus was my only other option.

I pulled into Los Otros in the late afternoon. A small town within a short drive of the Sea of Cortez, the population consisted of mainly Mexican farmers, with a few ex-pats from the US sprinkled in. Its main street boasted a cantina, a bank, a drug store and a Laundromat. I took a left and parked along the curb on a side street, next to a dental office.

The bank had already closed for the day. My plan to transfer a portion of the money to my sister in Minnesota would have to wait until morning. I'd need to keep the amount small. Anything over ten thousand would attract unwanted attention in the US. The longer I dragged the money around, the more I realized I needed to find a way to unload it. Aside from digging a hole in the middle of the desert and burying it, the only thing that made any sense was to wire it to someone I could trust.

My younger sister Lisa was the only person in my family who had any idea how I'd been living the past three years. I didn't trust the rest of my siblings to appreciate the finer points of making a stupid, life-changing mistake, like hooking up with a ruthless, power-hungry drug lord, and then stealing his money to escape.

I figured I'd transfer a little in each town I traveled through, holding out enough to buy a forged passport and pay my way back to the states.

I walked into the cantina and sat at a table in the corner. A kid of about twelve came over and asked me what I wanted. I ordered a Bohemia and asked him what time the bank next door opened.

"Nine o'clock." He put a plastic basket of tortilla chips on the table.

"Where can I find a place to stay the night?"

He turned toward the kitchen. "Mama! This lady wants to know where she can rent a room."

Mama walked through the doorway that led to the back. Tall and fit, energy radiated off her, belying the dark hair shot through with gray. She eyed me curiously.

"I have a friend, an American woman, who rents out her extra room. Twenty-five dollars a night. It's not far, maybe two kilometers."

She wrote down the address and made a crude map on the back of a napkin. I thanked her, paid for my beer and left, following the map to her friend's place. I looked wistfully at the station wagon as I passed by. I couldn't take the chance of staying with any vehicle for too long, so I left it at the curb, the keys dangling from the ignition.

The adobe house sat on a large rectangular dirt lot. Cheerful yellow curtains dotted the windows. Two lime trees grew next to a small shed. A profusion of lush plants in colorful pots greeted me as I followed the curving walk to the front door. I rang the doorbell and turned to survey the neighborhood. It appeared relatively quiet, with the exception of a stray dog and a kid on a bicycle.

"Yes?" The door opened and a woman with dirty blonde hair and a lived in face peered out, smiling.

"Your friend at the cantina sent me. She said you might have a room available for the night?"

"Yes, yes. Come in. You're American?" I nodded. "Lovely. How long will you need the room?"

"Only for the night. I'm just passing through."

She sighed. "Everyone 'just passes through' here." She glanced at my backpack, then at the walk behind me. "Do you have any other luggage?"

"I travel light."

"Apparently."

She showed me to my room and I slid the pack under the bed. She asked me if I wanted to wash up before dinner. I said I would.

Her name was Lana, and she'd just turned forty the day before. We dined al fresco in her backyard under strings of lights, giving it a festive air. She served fish tacos with rice and had finished her third margarita by the time I'd barely drunk one.

"I came here ten years ago. Followed a man." She shook her head, smiling. "You probably know how that goes." She stared off into the darkness and took another drink. "Girl meets guy, girl falls for guy and follows him to another country. Guy leaves girl in one horse town with no money." She shrugged. "Things a girl will do for love, eh?" She had no idea.

Lana noticed my drink was empty and picked up the pitcher. I placed my hand over my glass.

"I'd better not." I leaned back, trying to relax and enjoy the mild, star-filled night, but that was a thing of the past, now. Alcohol only dulled my senses.

"So what's your story, Miss I'm-just-passing-through?"

"I'm on my way to Mazatlan," I lied. No sense leaving a trail for Salazar. "I have some friends there I haven't seen in a long time."

We talked long into the night, or, I should say, she did. I answered her questions with the truth if I could, lies if she got too personal. Around one she passed out in her chair, her snores cutting through the still night. I wrapped her arm around my shoulders, hoisted her to her feet and walked her to bed. After taking off her shoes, I tucked her in and walked out, closing the door.

I searched through the kitchen, found a box of plastic baggies in a drawer and took them to my room. There I pulled out several stacks of hundred dollar bills from the backpack and stuffed them into the baggies.

Next, I carried the bags outside and set them on the ground alongside the two lime trees. Earlier, I'd noticed a pick and a shovel leaning against the house and went back to get them.

It took all the strength I had to hack my way into the caliche-filled ground between the lime trees and shed. At first I used the shovel, but finally resorted to the pick ax. Once I had a deep enough hole, I dropped the bags of money in and covered them with the remaining dirt. I poured water from the kitchen on the freshly dug earth, knowing it would be dry by morning and the evidence obliterated.

I returned to my room. My backpack was much lighter. I calculated roughly a third of the money now lay in the hole in the yard. Satisfied I'd found a necessary temporary home for the cash, I fell into a fitful sleep.

***

Sunlight streamed through the curtains, and my eyelids snapped open. At first unsure where I was, I remembered and sat up, glancing at the clock on the dresser. Eight thirty. Just enough time to have breakfast and walk to the bank. I hated doing the transfer in daylight, but didn't have a choice.

I brushed my teeth with my finger and some toothpaste I found in the medicine cabinet and washed my face. Then I went out to the kitchen to see if I could get some coffee before I left.

Lana stood at the stove, frying eggs and bacon, talking to a dark haired man sitting at the table. Instinctively, I stiffened. The less people I encountered, the better. Lana turned at the abrupt pause in conversation, and broke into a wide smile.

"You're just in time for breakfast. Jorge dropped by this morning and offered to give you a lift into town." She pointed her fork at me. "Kate, Jorge. Jorge, this is Kate."

"Mucho gusto." Jorge bowed his head, a charming smile on his face. My shoulders released a fraction. He seemed like a nice guy. Salazar's men couldn't have found me so soon. No one knew where I was headed.

We ate breakfast and drank coffee, making small talk. Soon, it was time to go. Jorge held out his hand to take the backpack.

"Thanks, Jorge, but it's not that heavy." He looked slightly offended, but shrugged as we walked out to his pickup.

We drove to town in silence, which was fine by me. I hadn't slept much the night before, having jolted awake with every sound, and didn't want to make the effort at more small talk.

Jorge pulled up to the curb near the bank and I thanked him and got out. I could feel him watch me walk through the bank's doors. The teller at the window smiled and motioned for me to come to her window. I'd already separated $7,500 from the rest of the money in the pack, and reached into the front pocket where I'd stashed the bundle.

"I'd like to make a wire transfer to my sister in Minnesota, please."

As I filled out the paperwork, I resisted the urge to look behind me. I handed the forms back to the teller and smiled. Tiny rivers of sweat ran down my back and under my arms, and beads of perspiration formed on my upper lip. Maybe wiring money to my sister wasn't such a good idea. It left me exposed in public for too long. The game had changed—my penchant for acting on the first idea that popped into my head could now get me killed. I thought about grabbing the money off the counter and leaving, but stopped short as I realized the transaction was almost complete.

Something hard pressed into my back. I started to turn around to see what it was, and stopped cold at the familiar voice.

"Eyes forward, bitch."

A cold wave of dread washed through me. Frank Lanzarotti. Apparently Salazar wasn't the only one looking for the money.

I stared straight ahead and forced a smile when the teller handed me my receipt and told me to have a nice day.

Right.

"Turn around, real slow, and we're gonna walk out that door together with a smile on our faces, got it?"

I nodded and we moved toward the door, Frank's arm firmly around my waist.

As we neared the entrance, the guard smiled at us. I stopped and turned toward Frank.

"Oh, honey, I forgot to pee," I whispered, loud enough that the guard blushed and turned his head. Frank stiffened and his hand clamped down on my waist, hard.

"What the fuck are you doing?" he hissed into my ear.

With no small effort, I pulled away from him, and playfully patted his arm. "Oh, don't be such a silly, sweetheart. We have plenty of time." I turned to the guard who was looking at everything except the two of us. "Sir, could you tell me where the ladies bathroom is, please?"

He cleared his throat and answered, "Of course, Señora. It's down that hallway and through those doors." He pointed toward the back of the bank.

"Thank you. Now, honey, it won't take that long, I promise." Frank's expression was a mixture of cold, white fury punctuated with splotches of red on his cheeks. I turned around, fast, and headed down the hallway before my shaking knees and frayed nerves failed me.

I burst through the bathroom door and scanned the room for an exit. A bank of high windows ran along the wall in back of the two stalls. I kicked open the door to the first one and climbed onto the toilet. The window opened easily, and I hoisted myself up and over the sill, head first.

I fell to the ground and immediately got up and hauled ass. I made it several yards before I heard Frank scream at his guy to bring the car around. A bullet whizzed past me and pinged off the concrete wall of another building. I detoured through an alley and kept running.

Panic welled up inside of me. I didn't know the town, didn't know where to go. I just blindly ran, hoping for inspiration.

I rounded a corner and saw Jorge parked down the road in his pickup. Without thinking, I ran toward him, waving my arms, hoping somehow he could help me.

As I neared the truck, Jorge opened the driver's side door and got out. I called out to him, but the words died in my throat when I realized he had a gun.

A cry escaped me as I skidded to a stop and fell backward. I scrambled to change direction, mid-step. The weight of the backpack threw me off balance and I slammed into the ground. Jorge's bullet barely missed.

I crawled onto my hands and knees, clawing at the dirt to get to my feet when I heard the music. A rusty old Volkswagen Bug kicking up dust roosters headed straight toward me. Classical music blared through the open windows. I dove behind a trash can on the side of the street. The driver of the VW drew parallel with me and slammed on the brakes, stopping in a cloud of dust. A large automatic gun attached to a skinny brown arm appeared at the side window.

The driver pulled the trigger. The staccato burst of repeating gunfire split the air. Then, silence.

I peeked around the side of the garbage can to look. Jorge lay sprawled on the ground, next to his truck. He looked dead.

Behind me, a dark colored SUV flew past the corner and skidded to a stop.

"Get in," the VW driver yelled. With no time to think, I ran around the side of the car and threw myself into the passenger seat.

"Stay down," he barked, as the VW shot past Jorge and his pickup.

I stayed on the floorboards, afraid to look up, waiting for Frank's bullets to perforate the car.

I tried to anchor myself to keep from crashing into the door and the gear shift as the driver, howling like a madman, steered first one way, then the other. I gave up and curled into a fetal position. The car bounced and bucked to the crashing strains of Rachmaninoff. I hoped like hell he didn't drive us off a cliff.

He spun the wheel to the left and crowed with delight as the VW fishtailed out of a spin.

"You bastards'll never catch us," he yelled to no one in particular.

We took a hard right, slowed to a crawl, and stopped. He killed the engine. I lifted my head to see where we were.

"Stay down," he hissed. I did as I was told. After a few minutes, he started the engine, and began to drive. To say the road he chose had a few bumps would be an understatement. I covered my head to keep from banging it to a pulp on the dash. The VW hit one last hole, and then the ride leveled out.

He turned in his seat to look behind us. "We confounded 'em," he chortled.

Bad Spirits

I carefully lifted my head and looked out the window. We were outside of town, driving past scrub and open space on a paved highway. I breathed a sigh of relief and sat up in the seat.

My rescuer appeared to be about seventy. His face looked like old leather, and his hair resembled Einstein's on a bad day. He had on a set of green scrubs and wore a pair of ancient huaraches on his feet. He turned off the tape player and we drove in silence. I did some deep breathing to still my pounding heart.

"Thank you," I said.

He waved his hand at me. "I always hated that prick."

"Enough to kill him?"

He shrugged. "I euthanize sick animals. What's the difference?" He turned to me and grinned, extending his hand. "The name's Ogden. I'm the local volunteer vet."

***

Ogden, or Oggie as he liked to be called, had been a veterinarian in the Midwest for over forty years. He'd grown tired of shoveling Nebraska snow and decided to retire in Mexico when his wife died. He'd lived here ever since.

When I asked him how he came to be the volunteer vet, he banged on the steering wheel.

"One day I woke up and decided I had a moral imperative to help the poor farmers in the area. So I started stockpiling medicine whenever I went to the states. Pretty soon word got around." He grinned. "Keeps me young. And, I'm never bored." He gave me a sidelong glance. "Why was a piece of shit like Jorge after you?"

I sighed and looked out the window.

"Look, if you don't want to talk about it, I won't ask again. I'd just like to know what kind of hornet's nest I stepped in."

I owed him that much. Frank Lanzarotti was Anaya's man, not Salazar's. My life had just become exponentially more complicated.

Still watching the scenery flow by, I said, "Apparently Jorge was working for someone I used to know, Frank Lanzarotti, who works for a drug dealer out of Central America named Vincent Anaya. I was actually running from somebody else and thought Jorge might help me."

Oggie snorted and swerved to miss hitting an opossum lumbering across the road.

"That's a good one. Jorge and the word help have never been uttered in the same sentence, at least, not in recent memory."

"Look, you can drop me at the next town, the next bus stop, hell, the side of the road, even. I don't want to cause you any trouble. I owe you my life. You don't need to be part of this."

Oggie whistled. "Must be some trouble you're in, Miss Kate. Tell you what—" He reached under his seat and brought out a silver flask, unscrewed the top and took a drink. "I'll drive you anywhere you want to go, provided you fill up ol' Bessie's tank." He patted the car's dash affectionately. "But I have to take care of something first." He took another drink and then offered me the flask.

I shook my head. "It's too dangerous. There are some really bad people who want to see me dead, and they wouldn't have a problem killing you to get to me."

Oggie's laugh ricocheted around the car.

"Hell, Kate. I'm so old, dirt's asking me for advice. You think I give a rat's ass about being safe?" He looked at me. "When you get to be my age, you'll understand it's not about how much time you got. It's about how much life you get. Sitting on my ass in a rocking chair isn't a life, far as I'm concerned. Besides," he flicked on the cassette player and Rachmaninoff blasted through the speakers. "You need me."

***

We pulled into Oggie's place an hour later. The small, cinderblock house with a metal roof sat in the middle of the square dirt plot surrounded by a split rail fence. A lemon tree and two mesquites stood sentry at the back of the lot near the house, providing the only shade.

I glanced back down the driveway. My nerves screamed at me to get moving, now.

"What's going to stop Frank from finding your place?" Oggie didn't appear to be a person who flew under the radar. His home would probably be the first place Frank would check.

"Only two people know where I live. I pick up my messages in town, and if there's an emergency, the gal at the post office comes and gets me," he replied. "I like it that way. Less bother."

Something told me I wasn't the only person who didn't want to be found. "Who's the other one?"

He shrugged a bony shoulder. "A lady friend. We haven't spoken in a while, though." He unscrewed his flask to take another swig, raising his eyebrows as he offered it to me again. I shook my head.

"No thanks. I need my wits about me."

"Wits are highly overrated," he muttered.

The one room house had a small bathroom off to one side. The kitchen lined one wall and a bed and dresser stood in a far corner. A wooden table, piled high with old newspapers and stacks of books, took up half the living area. I didn't notice a television or a phone.

"This'll just take a minute," Oggie said over his shoulder. He opened the small refrigerator and took out a clear plastic bottle and a syringe. Then he walked around the side of the table. "Wild Bill needs his shot, don't you boy?"

I looked down and realized what I'd thought was a sweater on one of the dining room chairs was actually a large cat. Oggie gathered Wild Bill up in his arms and sat on the chair. He kissed the hairy feline on the head and murmured into his ear.

"We don't have time for this." I kept a nervous eye on the driveway.

"If I don't give the little feller his insulin, he'll lapse into a coma and probably die. Now, if you'll just quit your chit chat, I can give him the shot and we'll be on our way."

He injected the cat and set him on the floor. Wild Bill meowed at me, annoyance plain on his face. Then he shook his head and slowly trundled out the door.

Oggie and I heard it at the same time. A dark-colored SUV barreled down the dirt drive toward us.

"Oh, God. It's Frank." My voice matched the panic that constricted my chest.

He squinted at the car. "Quick—" He shoved me toward the back door. "There's a root cellar behind the mesquites."

I grabbed my pack and ran.

The cellar turned out to be a hole in the ground with a weathered wood door covering it. I heaved the door open and dropped the pack inside, then scrambled down the handmade ladder, slamming the door behind me.

Bad Spirits

Not the best hideout. The thought of disrupting a nest of snakes or scorpions crossed my mind. Scorpions I could live with. Snakes, not so much. Light streamed in through gaps in the door that allowed me to see, once my eyes adjusted. I pulled the gun out of the front pocket of the pack and crawled as far back as I could go, behind jars filled with some kind of preserves and boxes of dried vegetables.

I stuffed the pack in the rear of the space, underneath a couple of boxes, then turned back toward the door and held my breath, listening. A sickening feeling twisted my stomach, and visions of Frank beating Oggie to death for information played like a bad movie in my brain. Frank wouldn't care who he killed to get the money.

I had a gun. I could use it to help him. But, then again, so did Oggie. He knew how to take care of himself.

I closed my eyes and took a deep breath. I needed to be calm. If I tried to make a decision in panic mode, things could go to hell, fast.

The gun felt faintly reassuring. I opened my eyes and stared at the door, willing Oggie to appear and tell me everything was fine. The longer I sat there, the less certain I became.

I raised my gun at the sound of someone approaching, and aimed it at the door. The footsteps stopped and a shadow fell across the gaps in the wood.

The door opened and fell to the side with a bang. I blinked against the bright light, at first unable to make out the person who peered inside the cellar. Then, I recognized him.

And pulled the trigger.

A ROCK AND A HARD PLACE

Frank's guy dropped his gun and fell to the ground, groaning and clutching his knee.

I moved to the front of the cellar, next to the ladder under the door, body humming with tension.

"You're not going to make it, Kate." Frank's voice sounded like he was near the house. "I guarantee I've got more bullets than you do. And a hell of a lot more time."

I leaned back and pounded my head against the cold dirt wall.

"I don't have the money, Frank," I yelled back. I searched the darkness at the rear of the cellar to make sure the pack couldn't be seen from the doorway.

"Well, then we have a problem, don't we? Tell you what—" Frank paused.

I waited, but he didn't say anything. Then, "You tell me where the money is and I'll let the old guy live."

He sounded closer. Frank was using the conversation as a diversion so he could move in on my little hideaway. I turned and aimed the gun at the doorway, perspiration running down my back despite the chill of the cellar.

The ragged breathing from Frank's guy made me want to scream at him to shut the hell up. I was tempted to pull a Jack Bauer and climb out of the cellar shooting for all I was worth. But this wasn't a television show and that would get me killed. My mind raced for an alternative to winding up dead. At least Oggie had survived.

Unless Frank was lying.

"Come on out, Kate. It's over."

He was right on top of me, near the door. The bastard was smart. He stayed out of my line of sight so I didn't have a clear shot.

If I stayed below, he'd wait me out and eventually I'd either fall asleep or die of thirst. If I surrendered, he could kill me, which didn't seem likely since I knew where the money was. No, he'd torture me until I told him where I'd stashed it.

Then he'd kill me.

I could always try to wait them out, hope they fell asleep first. Maybe Frank's guy would bleed out and then it would be a more equitable standoff.

Not many choices.

"You know, Frank. I'm kind of caught between a rock and a hard place." I hoped that my voice so close to the door would make him show himself and I could get a shot off.

"That's true."

No such luck. He stayed where he was.

"See, giving myself up just doesn't seem to be a healthy alternative, if you know what I mean."

The sound of Frank's chuckle sent chills up my spine.

"Well, Kate, you probably should have thought that one through before you took the money."

I sighed. The gun weighed heavily in my hand.

DV Berkom

"Tell you what, Kate. I'll give you a break, for old time's sake, all right? You throw out whatever firearms you have down in there and come out real peaceful-like, and after you tell me where the money is, when I do kill you I'll make it quick."

"Gee, Frank. You're the man."

I had no choice. Killing myself wasn't an option. I'd figure out a way to escape before he killed me. I had to.

After I quieted the screaming in my head, I took a deep breath and tossed the gun through the door.

"You win, Frank. I'm coming out." I climbed the ladder and crawled onto my hands and knees. Frank picked up my gun and aimed his 40 caliber at me. I stood, hands behind my head, and glanced at the man I shot. He'd removed his shirt and was using it as a tourniquet around his leg. He looked pale and clammy and was shaking like a wet dog.

"You should probably get your guy to a doctor, Frank. Looks like he's going into shock."

"Shut up." Frank walked behind me and gave my arm a vicious twist. "You should be more worried about what I'm going to do to you." He shoved me forward and marched me toward the house, leaving the other man on the ground.

I stumbled through the front door, Frank's gun at my back. Oggie sat taped to a kitchen chair, his face a mess. Frank pushed me into another one alongside of him. He grabbed a roll of duct tape from the table and proceeded to wrap it around my wrists and ankles, and then to the chair.

Oggie's right eye had swollen shut. I gave him a look that I hoped said how sorry I was. He shrugged and shook his head. It broke my heart.

Bad Spirits

Frank dropped the roll of tape on the table and walked out the door without a word. I turned to Oggie.

"God, Oggie, I'm so sorry you had anything to do with this."

One-half of his mouth twitched up in a grimace. The other side was too bruised. It gave him a macabre look with the streaks of blood down his face.

"My choice, Kate. Not yours." Wild Bill meowed at him and rubbed against his leg. "Probably one of the worst ones I ever made, but it's mine."

I grew silent at the sound of crunching gravel. Frank walked back inside.

"I usually let Manny do the honors, but since you shot him, it's up to me. Now," he slid a chair over and sat down in front of me, leaning his arms on the back. "Are you going to tell me where the money is, or am I going to have to beat it out of you?"

"It's gone, Frank. I just wired the last thousand to a friend when you found me at the bank." If I could get them away from Oggie, maybe he'd forget about him. Let him live.

Frank sighed and shook his head. "Now I'm the one caught between a rock and a hard place, Kate, darlin'. If I don't bring the money back, my ass is in a sling. I already searched the house and that rat-infested cellar. It ain't here. Your old buddy here didn't know anything about it, either. Didja, killer?" He reached over and ruffled Oggie's hair. Oggie jerked his head away.

"I can't kill you until I get my hands on that money, so I think we're at what you call an impasse." He rose from his chair and moved it out of the way. Then he stepped closer and punched me, hard, in the stomach.

I hinged forward, gasping. Good thing I hadn't eaten recently.

"Stop!" Oggie strained against the duct tape.

"Why? Are you going to tell me where the money is? Hmm. Didn't think so." Frank cracked his knuckles and turned to me. "Salazar said not to mess you up too badly. I won't leave any marks."

So I'd be a blemish-free corpse? I sucked in a breath and sat up. Little spots appeared before my eyes.

"What do you mean, Salazar? I thought you worked for Anaya?" I wheezed.

"I do." He grinned and leaned over, next to my ear. The thick, oily scent of Aqua Velva drifted toward me. My gag reflex was working overtime.

"You stole Anaya's money." His hot breath skated across my cheek. Icy dread reached deep into my gut and twisted.

"What do you mean? The money was in Salazar's van, at Salazar's house."

"Yeah. Well, that van was on its way to Anaya's camp in the mountains. It was Salazar's payment to Anaya for a shipment." Frank shook his head. "You really fucked up, Kate. Not only did you steal from Salazar, but in reality, you actually ended up stealing from both of them."

The import of what he said hit me like another blow to the stomach. I was a dead woman. Vincent Anaya wasn't known for his temperate ways. With Salazar, I might have had a slim chance of staying alive. He loved me, once. Didn't he?

A cold-blooded bastard, Anaya's reputation had risen to mythic proportions in the Mexican and Central American drug running communities. No one messed with Anaya. Not unless they had a death wish. Or were incredibly stupid.

Apparently, I fell into the latter category.

Frank pulled his gun from its holster and stepped next to Oggie. He rammed the barrel against his temple. Oggie closed his eyes.

"Where's the money?"

"I told you, I—" He pulled the trigger and I screamed.

Click.

I stared at his hand. The gun hadn't fired.

Frank chuckled as he raised the gun, as if to inspect it. "Hmm. Must not have had a bullet in there. Fancy that." He pulled the slide, chambering a bullet, and held it back against Oggie's head.

"Don't give him the satisfaction, Kate." Oggie practically spat the words out.

Frank sighed and rolled his eyes. "Where's the money?"

"I told you, I don't have it anymore." My voice shook.

"Not the answer I'm looking for."

"Wait—" A sob escaped me. I squeezed my eyes shut. I had to tell him.

But then Frank would kill us both.

Out of nowhere the theme from the 1960s television show Hawaii 5-0 filled the small house.

"Shit," Frank swore under his breath. He pulled his gun away from Oggie's head, reached into his front pocket and took out his cell phone.

"Lanzarotti," he said, as he turned and walked away.

I tried deep breathing to calm myself, but the adrenaline proved too much to conquer. Oggie had his eyes closed. His thin chest rose and fell with his breath. Frank stopped talking and walked back to where we sat, holstering his gun.

"Seriously. Hawaii 5-0, Frank?"

"Why not? At one time I was quite the surfer. Nobody rode the tube like I did."

My shock must have shown. A strangely defensive expression crossed his face.

"Hey, I was a teenager once."

"Were you an asshole then too, or did you grow into it?"

"Fuck you." He produced a switch blade and stepped behind me. I winced, waiting for the pain. It never came. He cut my hands free, then bent down to do the same to my ankles.

"Hands in front," he barked.

I did as I was told. He wrapped duct tape around my wrists, and yanked me to my feet.

"What are you doing?"

"Time to go," he said in a clipped tone.

"Where?"

He didn't answer.

***

Frank parked the SUV in the expansive front drive, under the portico. Salazar's hacienda-style mansion hadn't changed in the short time I'd been gone.

But I had.

I'd known where we were headed as soon as Frank turned onto the familiar highway. The hammering in my chest made it hard to breathe.

Once Frank had secured me in the front seat of the SUV at Oggie's, he'd gone back inside the house. A single gunshot shattered the quiet. I hung my head in despair. The old man was right. Bad spirits surrounded me. I hoped Wild Bill would be all right.

Bad Spirits

Frank had laid Manny on his good side in the backseat. He'd slipped in and out of consciousness during the long drive. As soon as we arrived, two of Salazar's armed guards hustled out and carried him inside.

Frank came around to my side of the truck, threw open the passenger door and yanked me onto my feet. He dragged me up the tile steps to the huge copper doors leading into the courtyard. The beauty of the setting didn't register. I was Salazar's prisoner.

Again.

Frank shoved me through the door into the cool interior. Salazar's imported Italian gravel crunched under my feet. I used to love coming home to the splashing fountain in the beautiful courtyard. Now it grated on my nerves. The cheerful yellow walls and lush hanging plants had been my idea. How could something that once seemed so good turn so bad?

That's the last time I fall for the head of a drug cartel, I thought. Oddly, the gallows humor made me smile.

I was sick, sick, sick.

"Bring her here."

I looked up to see Salazar standing on the second floor balcony. His dark hair framed his tanned, handsome face, and I reluctantly remembered why I'd fallen for the bastard. Conflicting emotions fought their way to the surface. Revulsion, attraction, fear. I checked, but found no trace of tenderness. There might be hope for me yet.

"Move it," Frank muttered. He grabbed my elbow and pulled me toward the stairway.

My legs wouldn't budge. I'd seen Salazar's men take others up these stairs against their will, and my body froze. I was now one of them.

Frank half-dragged, half carried me up the steps. We reached the second floor. I dug in my heels and dropped to the floor. Frank wheeled around, his face twisted in anger.

"Get up." He reached for his gun.

"I'm not going in there, Frank. People don't come back out." I shook my head and squeezed my eyes shut to stop the tears. Salazar would view crying as a weakness, and he despised weakness.

"Let her go." Salazar stood at the end of the long hallway, smoking a cigarette. His eyes held the same flint-like coldness as when I saw him slit the throat of his friend. It seemed like such a long time ago, although I'd been gone only days. I tried to say something to him, but my mouth had run dry.

Frank released me and I struggled to my feet. I wiped my eyes with the back of my hands and stood tall. Damned if I'd be on my knees when he killed me.

Salazar walked slowly to where I stood. He ran his hand under my jacket, caressing my breast, and smiled. I shivered, though not from desire. I thought my head would explode from the searing hatred that coursed through my body. I fought to keep my expression neutral.

Salazar made a *tsking* sound as he circled me like a wolf with its prey.

"You disappoint me, *mi corazón.*" He leaned against the balcony railing, and shook his head. "I give you all this." He spread his arms wide. "And you repay me with betrayal. Not only that, but you have betrayed Vincent Anaya, and at the same time trampled my name in the dust." He stared into the distance. His jaw flexed.

I didn't say anything. He would not let me speak unless and until he gave his permission. I'd seen a similar game with those below him in the pecking order, although it was different with me. Not only had I betrayed him, but in his world, a woman would never leave him. His enemies would view this as a crack in his control of the organization.

Frank stood by at a discreet distance, hands clasped in front of him. The perfect soldier, I thought. Just in case the crazy American woman did something stupid, like hurl herself off the balcony into the courtyard below.

I had to admit, it occurred to me. If I could have guaranteed myself no broken bones, I'd have launched myself over the railing as soon as Frank let me go.

Salazar turned to Frank and muttered something about whether he had recovered the money, to which Frank replied that he hadn't. Salazar gave him a dark look. "Anaya's waiting by the pool. I will be there shortly." Frank nodded and left. To me he said, "Walk with me."

Salazar's voice was deceptively gentle. I mirrored his slow, deliberate steps down the long corridor.

"You know I have to make an example of you, yes?" He glanced at me, as if to gauge my reaction.

"Actually, Roberto, you could prove your great strength by letting me go free. Only the most confident of men would let his woman go in peace, with no need for revenge." It took a tremendous amount of effort to keep my voice steady.

Salazar erupted into laughter. Not the reaction I'd hoped for.

He wiped his eyes and draped his arm around my shoulders. "I have missed your unique way of thinking. It's so refreshing."

We stopped next to a closed, wooden door. He pushed it open and we entered the room. I tried to calm the voices inside my head, urging me to turn and run. I knew if I tried anything, things would turn out far worse.

The smell of fresh paint still permeated the air, and the tile floor looked like it had recently been scrubbed.

The desk and chair in the corner belied the room's true function.

There were no windows. Illumination came from a bank of track lighting along the ceiling. On the wall opposite the door hung various lengths of chain with leather cuffs attached to the ends. These chains were connected to a pulley that dropped from the ceiling. My former body guard, Eduardo, sat at a large console with rows of buttons in the middle of the room.

Eduardo stared straight ahead, avoiding my eyes. At the end, he'd been the one shining example of humanity in this madhouse of ego and greed. He always excused himself from Salazar's "meetings" and I'd never seen him raise a hand to anyone. If I ever needed a person to talk to, he was always there to listen.

And, he taught me to shoot.

He'd been the one who showed me how to handle every kind of weapon Salazar possessed, including a machete. The other guards called me *mujer Americana loca* because of my dedication to target practice. I liked being referred to as crazy. People left me alone.

I cherished my time with Eduardo.

The fact that Salazar chose him to perform whatever torture he'd devised for me spoke volumes. But of course, he would blame Eduardo for my escape. He was my body guard. He'd been assigned not only to protect me, but to watch me, too.

"Eduardo has been given the task to find out where you hid the money." Salazar walked to the wall of chains and lifted one, inspecting the cuff. "He has my permission to use any means necessary to extract your confession." He stared hard at Eduardo, then at me. "Any means. Although, I have ordered him to keep you alive. For now."

"I don't have the—"

"Silence!" Salazar's expression held a sharp warning. I swallowed my words.

As Salazar walked out, he paused for a moment to whisper something in Eduardo's ear, then moved past me and closed the door with unnerving finality. The room started to spin and I placed my hands against the wall to steady myself. I wondered briefly what would happen if I fainted.

Eduardo rose immediately and came to my side. He guided me to a chair and lowered me into it. Old habits, I thought. I leaned back and watched the only person I'd thought of as a friend during my time here. I'd been wrong about that, too.

"Eduardo, please—"

He held his finger to his lips, a warning in his eyes. Silently, he slipped over to listen at the door. After a few moments he came back and squatted in front of me.

"You know that Salazar or one of his guards is outside that door, listening for your screams," he whispered. I nodded, unsure what he was getting at.

"We have to make this look real, like you've been tortured in the extreme, or Salazar will replace me with someone who is not sympathetic to you. *¿Tu comprendes?*" Again, I nodded that I understood.

"I will have to use some electricity to shock you." He glanced at the console in the middle of the room. "I can make it so that you only feel a light jolt, but you must moan and carry on as if it's the most excruciating thing you've ever experienced." A vein throbbed in his neck. "But first you have to tell me what you did with the money."

My body tensed. So that's the way we were going to play it. Good body guard, pretending to be bad, but getting the information all the same. If I broke down and told Eduardo where I hid the money, there would be no reason to keep me alive. If I didn't tell him, I'd be alive, at least for a little while. Only then Salazar would replace Eduardo with some sadistic creep who'd be happy to draw out the pain.

Eduardo reached over and took my taped hands in his, looking deeply into my eyes.

"I am not going to let them kill you, if I can help it. You must trust me."

An idea began to formulate in my brain. Why hadn't I thought of it before?

In a low voice I said, "Frank stole the money."

Eduardo looked surprised for a moment, then a slight smile played at the edges of his mouth. "You're lying."

"What do you mean? He took the money."

Eduardo shook his head. "Your eyes move to the right when you lie. Remember that when Salazar questions you." He thought for a minute. "They'll confront Frank. They have to. Salazar and Anaya are already paranoid about each other. If you cast doubt on Frank, it will buy us time."

I didn't know why Eduardo thought more time would help my situation, but I would work with whatever he decided. At the moment, he was my only chance.

"We need to begin. Someone will come in to see why I haven't started yet."

Eduardo led me to the wall of chains. He cut through the duct tape that bound my wrists and then slid a cuff over each one, securing them. Little wires sprouted from each cuff, attached to a larger wire that had been threaded through the chain attached to the ceiling. The rest of the wiring ran to the console. He walked back to the controls and flicked a switch. The chain started to clank its way through the pulley, and as the slack decreased, it lifted my arms over my head, stretching me so that my toes barely touched the floor.

The first shock came as a complete surprise. I didn't have to pretend to scream. My muscles contracted and I jerked like a fish on a line. I glared at Eduardo.

"Where's the money?"

"I told you, Frank stole it." My voice came out shaky at first, but grew stronger.

Another shock wracked my body, this time less intense, but still nothing I wanted to repeat. It reminded me of the time I'd accidently grabbed onto an electric fence on a friend's farm. I screamed, hoping it matched what others had done before me. By the look on Eduardo's face, I was convincing.

"Where's the money?" Eduardo raised his voice.

"Frank has it," I said, through clenched teeth.

The shocks continued before finally he signaled to me that I needed to ratchet up the screams. The next bolt of electricity shot through me. My fingers curled in on themselves as my body contracted with the current. I broke out in a cold sweat as I threw my head back and screamed.

"Where's the money, Kate?" Eduardo's voice echoed off the walls of the small room.

"I—told you." The words came out in a ragged gasp. "Frank."

Eduardo nodded and rose from his chair. I heard the door slam as he walked out. My arms had no feeling left in them. My shoulders throbbed as though they'd been dislocated from their sockets. I hung my head, too weak to look up. I realized he had to do what he did, and shuddered to think what the real thing would be like.

Eduardo returned a few minutes later. Or maybe it had been a few hours. I'd drifted.

"Look at me." A hand grabbed my chin and yanked my head up. I opened my eyes and stared into Salazar's face. The anger in his eyes would have made me weak in the knees, if I wasn't there already.

"You told Eduardo that Frank stole the money?"

I nodded.

He dropped my chin and began to pace.

"Anaya will never believe it," Salazar muttered.

"Of course not." Eduardo replied. "Don't you see? It's the perfect alibi. Why take her word against his?"

"Yes, yes, I see. But we can't accuse him in front of Anaya. He would kill us both for the insult, even if it is true." He stopped pacing. "You're sure she's telling the truth?"

"She didn't change her story, even when I gave her the highest voltage I could without killing her."

Salazar's breathing was the only sound in the room.

"Take her down."

***

I struggled out of the dim fog that shrouded my brain. They'd left me lying on a bed in a dark room with the shades drawn. Disoriented, I sat up and slid backward on the mattress until the headboard stopped me.

Something thudded against the door. I froze, holding my breath as I strained to hear.

Silence.

With difficulty, I rose from the bed and groped my way to the door. I thought I heard movement in the hallway. I tried the light switch, but nothing happened.

Bad Spirits

I slid my hand along the wall, and backed away from the door. First a chair, then a dresser impeded my progress. Neither of them held anything I could use as a weapon. There wasn't even a telephone.

The sound of a key being inserted into the lock had the same effect on me as an electric shock; both my muscles and my breathing stopped. I recovered and backed against the wall, wanting desperately to hide, knowing I didn't have a chance. I slid to the floor and curled into a ball.

The door opened, followed by the thud of more than one set of footsteps. Several hands grabbed my arms and hauled me to my feet. A ripping sound preceded a piece of tape slapped over my mouth. I couldn't get a good look at anyone, even with the light from the hallway. Each of them wore dark clothing and a ski mask.

Then someone yanked a hood over my head.

My executioners had arrived.

LAST CHANCE

The hood over my head disoriented me and I stumbled, but my captors held me steady. Unable to do anything except try to stay on my feet, I didn't have time to think about what was happening. The group moved me through the hacienda with a silent swiftness that left me wondering why Salazar would want to keep my execution quiet.

We stopped, and someone threaded a strap of some sort underneath my arms and cinched it tight across my chest. Someone else stood behind me and wrapped their arms around my waist in an iron grip. We frog marched a short distance, then they lifted me off my feet and pulled me backward over what must have been the second floor railing. The falling sensation hit me hard, but a zipping sound told me we were connected to something that would break our landing.

We reached the ground, and the strap around my chest loosened. Other sets of feet hit the gravel in addition to the one who had a hold of my arm. We'd gone maybe ten steps when the first pop of gunfire echoed through the compound.

"*Merde*," my captor muttered under his breath, and dragged me forward. Someone returned fire and then a full gunfight erupted behind us, automatic weapons fire splitting the night. I ran, stumbling, trusting the man beside me to guide us to safety.

Safety? The idea confused me, but I couldn't sort it out. I could only run.

We veered to the left and I heard a car door open. He shoved me inside. I slid to the floor and attempted to climb onto the seat.

"Stay down," he said, in thickly accented English.

I ducked my head and pulled the hood off, gulping in air. I lay on the back floor of a large, idling SUV. The gunman that shoved me into the vehicle walked toward the front of the pickup. I peered over the seat back. He stopped and leaned across the hood, aiming his gun at a large gardening shed. Three dark figures rounded the corner, running straight toward us. It must have been his buddies, because he didn't shoot. One of the figures stopped alongside the building and waited while the other two made it to the truck and climbed inside.

An unmasked man raced around the corner, but then checked and fell back behind the structure. The figure alongside the building melted into the shadows around the back. Two gunshots followed. The masked gunman reappeared and resumed his position next to the garden shed.

The man standing at the front of the truck sprinted back, got in next to me, and slammed the door closed. The SUV spit gravel as it rocketed forward. When he realized I'd taken the hood off, he grabbed it and yanked it over my head. At the same time he pushed me back down behind the seat.

"Keep the hood on and stay down."

We skidded to a stop next to the shed. The back door opened and closed, and a pair of legs shoved me to the middle. Then we started moving again. The sporadic gunfire faded in the distance. It wouldn't be long before Salazar's men followed.

"Milo?" one of them asked.

"Dead," came the reply. No one spoke after that.

We sped through the night. I fought to keep my legs from cramping and shifted in the small space.

After a while, the man to my left nudged my shoulder. "You can get up now, but keep the hood on." I crawled onto the seat and stretched my legs, careful not to disturb either gunman.

Who were these men? Did they rescue me only to kill me? They weren't Salazar's thugs, obviously, or I'd be dead by now. Would they hold me for ransom? I doubted Salazar would pay to get me back. He'd probably tell them to go ahead and kill me— the only bright spot being that they might not know that.

The SUV rounded a curve and the road became rugged. We seemed to hit every pothole in existence. One of the men in the front seat lit a cigarette. The rancid smoke seeped under the hood, and I had to swallow to keep from choking.

Sometime later, we jolted to a stop. The guy to my left got out and pulled me from the truck. I tensed, uncertain if they meant to kill me here. My heart pounded in my chest. I took a deep breath, hoping to relax. It didn't work so well with the hood.

"Take it off."

Bad Spirits

Someone yanked the hood off my head and the sweet, fresh night air filled my lungs. The others had taken off their masks and stood next to the truck. I'd counted correctly- there were four of them. Five, if I included the unlucky Milo back at the hacienda. I didn't recognize any of them.

"Who are you? What do you want?" I asked.

One of the men stepped forward, a glint of metal flashed in the headlights.

A knife. Not a pretty way to die.

He lifted my hands and sliced through the ties that bound my wrists.

"We will wait, now," he replied.

The rest of the men leaned against the SUV, talking in low voices. I rubbed my wrists where the ties had dug into them. We were parked somewhere out in the middle of the Sonoran desert, the stars the only light visible for miles. A lonely yip of a coyote echoed in the distance.

The men broke off their conversation and everyone turned to watch as a pair of headlights danced along the dirt road toward the group. I didn't know if I should be relieved or afraid. Was it Salazar's men, or the person they were waiting for?

The four of them reached for their weapons, and one motioned for me to get into the back of the SUV and duck down.

"Uh, guys, can a girl get a gun around here? I mean, if it's someone you don't want to see, I know how to shoot. I'd be able to help." I'd also feel a hell of a lot better with a gun in my hand. At least I'd have a fighting chance.

One of them started for the back of the SUV, apparently to retrieve a gun.

"I don't think that's a good idea," said a big guy with a goatee. The one heading toward the truck looked at me and shrugged. At least now I knew there were more weapons. I gave the big guy a dark look and climbed into the SUV.

The headlights drew closer and the tension rose in the group. All four of them stood on alert, weapons raised, using the truck for cover. Careful not to draw attention to myself, I glanced over the back of the seat to the cargo area to see if I could get a look at what they had for extra fire power. It was too dark to be sure, but I thought I saw the shadowy shapes of several large automatics.

A dark-colored four-wheel drive pickup pulled alongside the SUV and stopped. The gunmen lowered their weapons, and I let out a breath. The driver opened the door and got out. I didn't know him. He stood half a head taller than the rest of the men there, although dressed in similar clothing. He walked toward me as the passenger door opened and the other occupant exited the truck.

Eduardo.

So he'd been the one behind this midnight invasion. I'd wondered how they'd broken through Salazar's security without raising the alarm until the end. Now I knew.

The taller man's lips pressed together in a grim line. He shook his head.

"You did this for her?" He frowned as he looked me over.

Confused, I looked from him to Eduardo as he approached. "Did what?"

The taller man turned to Eduardo. "She damn well better be worth it, Ed. There ain't no going back, amigo."

Eduardo nodded, his expression unreadable.

"They were going to kill her, whether she gave them what they wanted or not. She lived with Salazar for over three years. She knows him." He looked at me and said, "She'll cooperate."

"Well?" The taller man crossed his arms and cocked his head to one side.

"Uh, Eduardo, can I have a word, please?" I didn't like this guy, whoever he was. I grabbed Eduardo's arm and pulled him out of earshot.

"What the hell am I supposed to tell him? And who the hell is he, anyway? How do I know I can trust him?"

"He's DEA. And these men," Eduardo indicated the others standing nearby, "work for a special arm of Mexican drug enforcement."

"And you're involved, how?"

"I give them information on Salazar's operation. I knew when Frank brought you back that I would have to do something or they would kill you, like the others, so I told them you had important information."

"But if you go back now, they'll kill you." The look on Eduardo's face confirmed my suspicions. "You're not, are you?"

Eduardo shook his head. "No, they will kill me, if only for letting you escape again. I made a deal with Chance—" He glanced back at the DEA guy. "—to place me in the US federal witness security program, in exchange for my help." He shrugged. "I will just have to go sooner than I expected."

"I'm in enough trouble as it is. If I give them information and Salazar finds out, it's going to get a lot worse- you know how far he'll go to find me."

"Talk to Chance. Maybe he'll make a deal with you, too."

Great choice. Make a deal with the DEA, and go into hiding for the rest of my life, never contacting my family or friends again. Or, don't make a deal and look over my shoulder for the rest of my life, wondering when Salazar, or worse, Anaya, would find me. I had no doubt that one of them would.

It didn't take long to make a decision.

"You put your life on the line for me, Eduardo. For that I am grateful. I will give them whatever information I have, as long as they promise protection for us both."

Eduardo smiled, relief evident on his face. He wrapped his arm around me as we walked back to the group.

Chance leaned against the SUV, talking with one of the government guys. He looked up as I approached.

"I'll tell you everything I know, on one condition. You have to guarantee that you'll put me in the witness protection program in the states, the same as Eduardo."

"I can arrange it, if what you tell me has any value."

"Fine. Where do I start?"

***

The interview with Chance took over three hours. He was thorough with his questioning, prying out bits of information I'd forgotten and didn't think were worth remembering. He was particularly interested in John Sterling's role in Salazar's organization. When I got to the part about my first escape, I conveniently left out stealing Anaya's drug money. It would be nice to think that the men who now surrounded me had altruistic tendencies, but Sterling had been DEA. Money did strange things to people.

The safe house sat nestled in a tidy neighborhood in an innocent-looking town near the Sea of Cortez. The sea-salt air and briny humidity reminded me of happier times. Chance had determined it would be best if I remained in Mexico for now, and he'd assured me I'd be as safe there as anywhere. I assumed it was because once I was stateside there'd be more of a temptation for me to walk away. It wouldn't matter where they hid me—if Salazar or his people got wind of my location, they'd stop at nothing to kill me.

I found it ironic and not a little annoying that I was so close to my original destination, yet now unable to go through with my plan to obtain a forged passport and leave the country under an assumed name. The only thing stopping me, other than the armed guards, was the belief that sending Salazar to prison would give me a slight reprieve from the fear that now ruled my life.

Monotonous days fluctuated between sleeping, reading, watching Mexican soap operas, and jumping at every sound. I was allowed an hour or so of outdoor recreation each day, and even that was monitored closely. The back yard had a high cement wall and for all intents and purposes I felt like a prisoner, not an asset. Meals consisted of tortillas and beans, with alternating chicken, pork and beef. I craved vegetables. Definitely a first for me.

The day Chance visited, I'd just beaten three of the guards at poker. I was feeling flush what with all the toothpicks I'd won.

We walked to the far end of the enclosed backyard and sat in a couple of lawn chairs in the shade of a large palm tree. The intensity of the midday heat created a death-like stillness. Even the cockroaches decided to take a siesta.

"So when do I get to leave?"

"An arrest warrant has been issued with an extradition order. All we have to do now is pop Salazar."

"What about Sterling?" I sure as hell didn't want John Sterling free to move about the country, not when he knew about the money. And me.

Chance took out a pack of cigarettes and shook one out. He held them up, and I shook my head.

"He's already in custody in the states, waiting for his trial date." He lit the cigarette, leaned back and crossed his legs. "How're things going here? The boys treating you all right?"

"Except for some of their taste in television, it's been fine. But I have to be honest, Chance. The longer I'm here, the more nervous I get. I'm a sitting duck. You can't tell me Salazar doesn't have government informants. Eventually, somebody's going to get lucky and figure out my location."

"I've taken extra precautions and set up a bogus safe house down the street. All transmissions regarding you refer to that address. Only a select group of people from either agency know your actual location. If we think this house has been compromised in any way, we move you." His serious gray eyes made me want to believe him.

"What's the word on Witness Security?"

"Good news there. You've been cleared to enter the program as soon as you give your testimony at trial. New identity, relocation, a job, the works."

"Can I ask you a personal question?"

"Sure."

"What percentage of takers end up dead?"

Chance shifted in his chair. "I'm not sure I understand your question."

"Let me clarify. How many people who go into the program have their locations or identities compromised and wind up taking the big dirt nap? I mean, there must have been a few, right?"

A flash of something I couldn't quite read flickered across his face. Then his expression hardened back to the competent DEA façade.

"Very few, Kate. And those were anomalies. Most were traced to the wit contacting a family member or friend."

"How many is most, Chance? And can you tell me about the ones who did everything right, but still ended up dead?" I'd started to re-think this whole stupid testifying thing, mainly because I couldn't shake a growing sense of dread. Granted, I didn't have a lot to keep my mind occupied at the moment, but I tended to trust my gut instincts. I had a pretty good average.

Except with men. I had a long way to go before I could trust my feelings there.

"I can't give you numbers. We don't handle the program. U.S. Marshals do and they're damned good at it as long as you follow the security guidelines." He took a drag off his cigarette and leaned forward in his chair. "Listen. Nothing is fail-safe. Life isn't that kind. It's the best we can do at the moment. And it's worked for countless people who did the right thing and testified against the big, bad criminals of the world. Without wits, a lot of scum would go free. I can tell you the program works for ninety-nine-point-nine percent of the people who go that route."

"You don't know Salazar." Or Vincent Anaya, I thought.

Chance raised his hands, palms up.

"Your choice, Kate. Everybody has second thoughts about the program, and I mean everybody. It's not easy to leave everyone and everything you know and start over. But what else are you going to do? Very few people know how to disappear. The ones that think they do end up dead or worse. You're on Salazar's list now, so anything that can help you stay alive is going to be better than going it on your own."

***

After Chance left for the field office, I tried to occupy my mind by re-reading every book in the house. One of the security guys, Luis, shared my love of American thriller writers, so at least I had a way to get interesting reading material. It didn't take long before I developed insomnia, and early mornings found me wandering from room to room, usually ending up in the kitchen for a pre-dawn snack or a shot of tequila to calm my nerves. The guys left me to my own devices for the most part, and didn't insist on my adherence to house rules. Except for one—I couldn't leave the premises.

It drove me bat shit crazy.

Late one night, I talked Luis into going with me for a walk. Not far, I assured him. Just so I could forget the bland yellow paint on the walls, and smell anything but enchiladas, if only for a little while. He caved when I promised to buy him the newest thriller by his favorite author in hardback.

Since we had to steer clear of the neighborhood streets, we hiked through the darkness in the dry arroyo behind the safe house, Luis with his AK-47, and me with nothing but my fear. Luis spoke of his family, whom he'd sent to live in the states.

"My father has said that Mexico reminds him of Colombia in the 1970s. The drug gang violence is escalating, and I can see it spreading to non-gang members. It's very sad. Mexico is filled with good, honest people. It is only the brutal few that crave power and stop at nothing." He glanced at me. "How did you get involved with a man like Salazar?"

"It's not a good excuse, but I had no idea what he did for a living when I met him. By the time I figured it out, I knew too much about his family and friends. If I said anything about leaving or even wanting to visit my family, he threatened me. The more I learned about him, the more afraid I became. I knew then I'd never be free unless I escaped."

Luis nodded, as though something connected for him.

"I won," he said.

"Won?"

He looked a little sheepish. "The other guys and I took bets on why you were with Salazar."

I crossed my arms. "And what was the consensus?"

"The majority agreed with Chance. That you were interested in the money and power, but that something happened to make you run—either a death threat or he wanted to use you as a mule, something like that."

"And what did you think?"

"That you were naïve and got caught in his web. The other guys all dismissed it like I was romanticizing you, that no one would be that stupid..."

Luis had the decency to look embarrassed.

"I'm sorry. I didn't mean to—"

"No apologies needed, Luis. I'm the first one to admit to being an idiot."

We continued to walk in silence. The night sky glittered with brilliant stars. Insects sang to each other, reminding me of a time when I wasn't constantly looking over my shoulder. What would my life look like in a month? A year? Once Salazar was locked up and I went into witness protection, maybe then I could relax, start a new life without the debilitating fear I'd been living with for so long.

The old man had said that only when I lost everything would I be safe. Not being able to contact my friends and family again sure felt like losing everything.

We started back toward the house. The inky black sky had lightened to a deep blue, signaling the approaching dawn. As we crested a small rise, a deafening explosion ripped through the still night. I fell to the ground, covering my head with my hands, and curled into a ball. Luis dropped to a crouch next to me and scanned the area.

"Get up. They blew the house." Luis' words came out hard and flat. I sat up and turned to watch as the house that once had the word *safe* attached to it was consumed in flames.

The rooms where I'd been less than an hour before were now a scorched, blistering scar on the once peaceful neighborhood. Blackened outlines where windows should have been gaped like toothless mouths open in a perpetual scream. Flames shot out from the second floor bedroom windows, the blinds and drapes feeding the fire like so much kindling.

No other houses on the block had been firebombed. What happened to the other safe house, the one Chance said he'd set up as a decoy? Confused, I looked at Luis. His jaw set, he grabbed my arm and pulled me to my feet.

"Come with me."

We cut across the arroyo and up the bank, keeping to the shadows. Thankful that he apparently had a plan, I followed him past the hulking, dark shapes of trees and bushes, jumping at every little sound. My rapid breathing and galloping heart were byproducts of the adrenalin shooting through me. I wondered briefly if a stroke was in my future.

"They knew which house to target."

Luis grunted. "Yes."

"This means that Salazar has someone high up in either your agency or Chance's."

"Yes."

"Could you please answer me in complete fucking sentences? Because I'm a little freaked out right now and really need you to talk me down here."

Luis stopped and wiped his hand across his face. "Or it was someone at the safe house."

I hadn't thought of that. Had anyone survived the blast? Luis was in the clear, since he'd been with the target. I ran through the different guards in my head, and couldn't recall any of them acting out of the ordinary. My gut told me it was somebody within one of the agencies.

That was a problem.

Hyperventilation seemed much more imminent than a stroke, and just my luck, no paper bag to breathe in. I bent over, hands on my knees, and sucked in air, trying to control the anxiety that threatened to take over.

Luis rested his hand on my back. The small gesture helped to calm me enough that my thoughts became semi-coherent. I straightened and inhaled deeply into my lungs.

"All right?"

I nodded. I wasn't, but that couldn't matter. The distant glow of the burning house lit up the early morning sky. I turned to Luis.

"I want to see Chance. Now."

***

Luis called Chance and told him what happened. He sent a car and driver to pick us up near a vacant lot several streets away from the safe house. Twenty minutes later, we pulled up next to a dark sedan with blacked out windows idling behind an abandoned building outside of town. The passenger side window slid down and Chance's face appeared. Luis and I transferred to the back seat of the sedan.

Chance twisted around in the front seat and focused on Luis.

"From the reports, the house is toast. No one survived the explosion."

"Diego and Raphael were inside-" Luis cleared his throat. Once he'd composed himself, he said, "Raphael's wife just had their second child. A boy." He stared out the car window.

Chance shook his head. "My guys have been with me for four years. They were the best team I've ever worked with. Survived Afghanistan." He shook a cigarette from a pack on the dash and lit it, inhaling deeply. "Who would have thought an IED in Sonora would get them?"

My eyes started to water from the smoke. Chance hit the button on the door and the window slid down.

"Where were you two?" he asked.

Luis looked at me and then turned to Chance. "We—ah, well, we were outside."

"Outside? You mean the backyard, right?"

Luis shook his head. "No sir, we—" He shifted in his seat. "I accompanied her off the premises."

Chance glanced at me and frowned. "So you broke protocol." The statement landed flat between them.

"Sir, I—"

"She survived. If you hadn't done what you did, she'd be dead." He narrowed his eyes and looked directly at

Luis. "Do it again and you're off the assignment." Chance leaned back with a disgusted sigh. "How did he get the info? If anything, the decoy should've been blown."

"Simple. He's got someone in one of your organizations." I'd been living with Salazar's reach for the past three years. It didn't surprise me. "And, unless you have a better idea, I think I'll take my chances on my own." I made to open the door, but Chance put a hand on my arm.

"You can't walk away from this. Our case against Salazar can't go forward without you."

"What about Eduardo? He's got more than enough information to put him away for years."

Chance bowed his head, then looked at me, weariness evident in his eyes.

"Eduardo's dead."

I sank back against the seat, too stunned to speak. My stomach twisted into knots as fear's icy fingers wound their way up my spine.

"How?" I asked, not sure I wanted to know.

"They found his head in a plastic garbage bag at the border. We haven't recovered his body."

Anger boiled deep in my chest, and it was hard to breathe. "He trusted you. You were going to get him into the program." My hands clenched so hard the fingernails cut into my skin.

Chance sighed. He looked twenty years older.

"That's just it. The Marshals had him in protective custody, on his way to the states. They were ambushed just before they got to the border. We have no idea how they found him so fast."

"Then Salazar's got someone there, too." My calm, steady voice belied the fact that I wanted to reach over the seat back and strangle the man sitting in front of me."Remember the question I asked you that day in the back yard? About the ones that didn't make it?" Chance nodded. "How many were involved with Salazar in some way?"

"None."

"How many?" I leaned forward, inches from his face. He looked past me at Luis, then back at me.

"Three."

I recoiled as if he'd hit me. "Three? You put Eduardo in knowing that three of Salazar's people died? And you think I'm going to cooperate? How fucking stupid do you think I am?"

Chance leaned forward, his face deadly serious.

"It won't happen again. Yes, there's a leak, but nothing is one hundred percent secure. Travel with armed agents is a hell of a lot safer than going solo. I put in the request to move you to the states. Once there, we'll record your statement. After that, you choose what you want to do."

I opened the door and got out before either of them could stop me. I turned and looked at Chance through the open window.

"You got it all wrong, Chance. I'm choosing what to do right now."

BAD CHOICES

K ate—" Luis called as I walked away from the car. I turned and watched him make his way across the weed covered lot.

"Here." He handed me a wad of bills. "It should be enough to get to wherever you're going."

I gave him a half smile and tucked the money in my pocket.

"Thanks. Luis, I'm sorry I—"

He shrugged. "Don't be." He nodded his head at Chance waiting in the idling sedan. "I think even he understands." He pulled out a pen and a scrap of paper, wrote on it and handed it to me. "My cell. In case you change your mind."

I folded it and put it in my pocket. "Goodbye, Luis. Take care of yourself and your family."

I started to walk away when the car rolled up next to me. Chance leaned his head out the window.

"At least let me get you to a bus stop, for Christ's sake."

***

Luis handed me a canteen of water and they watched me board the bus to Mazatlán before speeding off into the early morning. Chance had continued to try to persuade me to stay, to trust him to keep me safe, but my mind was made up. Eventually, he conceded defeat and promised he would keep my surviving the explosion quiet for at least the next few hours. Grateful for that small window of time, I made it look as though I was heading to the large seaside city, knowing I'd have to delay the actual trip until I made a phone call.

As the desert scenery raced by, I felt a pang of guilt for not sticking around to testify. But then I remembered Eduardo and the thought of his execution hardened my resolve. I needed to take things into my own hands, stop trusting strangers. My life tended to work out better when I relied on myself. The times that I got into trouble directly corresponded to my bad choices in men.

All I had to do was avoid falling for anyone.

Simple.

I got off at the next stop—a small, dusty town several miles from the safe house—and found a phone. I dialed the familiar number and had to stifle a sob when my sister Lisa's voice came on the line and accepted the charges.

"Lisa—"

"Kate? Is that you? Where are you?"

"I—I'm still in Mexico. Did you get the money I wired?"

There was a pause. I thought the connection cut out. Then I heard a sigh.

"Kate—I, yes, I did get the money."

Relief flooded through me. "Oh, thank God. Lisa, I need you to wire it back to me-"

Another pause.

"I can't. I promised not to." The anguish in her voice spoke of indelible pressure from my older siblings. The ones who thought they knew best, always judging my life choices. Granted, they had a point this time, but I would never forgive them their lack of support. To me, family meant acceptance, love. I hadn't hurt anyone but myself.

And Oggie.

"Lisa, you have to listen to me. It's the only way I can get out of the country. I wired the money to you because I knew you'd do the right thing and keep it safe until I needed it."

"I. Can't." I heard her take a deep breath, then slowly let it out. "They told me you'd just get into more trouble if I did. Kate, I'm so sorry I-"

I switched tactics and tried a harder line. "The money's mine, Lisa. You need to wire it to me, now." Lisa was the youngest of all of us and she caved whenever someone exerted authority. I hated doing that to my sweet, sensitive sister, but damn, my life was at stake.

She cried softly on the other end.

"I—I can't, Kate. I'm so sorry-"

"Lisa, wait—"

The line went dead.

I stared at the phone. The overwhelming sense of abandonment surprised me. I'd always just assumed I could count on Lisa for anything. Anger soon replaced the loss I felt. I took deep breaths to calm myself and extinguish the dark thoughts I was having of my other sisters. Anger wouldn't help me now. I needed to formulate another plan.

I hung up the phone and walked to a nearby bench to sit down and think. A scruffy, battle-scarred tabby slid past my leg and rubbed its head on my shoes, purring loudly. I reached down and scratched it behind its ears, glad for the company. Unscrewing the cap from my canteen, I poured some of the water onto the sidewalk. The cat lapped up the liquid, raised its head and meowed. Once it realized I had nothing else to give, it flicked its tail and disappeared behind a concrete building.

The way I saw it, I had two options, and neither one was exactly risk-free. I could go back to Lana's in Los Otros and dig up the money I'd buried in her yard. Or, I could go back to Oggie's. My stomach twisted at the idea.

The Lana option appeared to be the biggest risk. Her place was a long way from where I currently found myself, and much too deep into Salazar Country. The thought of having to retrace so many steps in such dangerous territory scared the hell out of me. I relegated the idea to Plan C.

But Oggie's presented serious risks, too. When Salazar and Anaya got wind that I'd survived the explosion, they could conceivably post lookouts near his place in the event that I really had stashed the money somewhere nearby. I'd have to do a little surveillance of my own, make sure no one was watching the place before digging the backpack out of the cellar. But that used up precious time I didn't have.

After agonizing over the pros and cons of each option I made my decision and purchased a ticket for the next bus to the small town near Oggie's.

***

The bus rocked me into a kind of stupor and I fell into an exhausted sleep, waking sometime later when we lurched to a stop. The bus driver glanced at me in the rearview mirror and indicated that we were where I'd told him I wanted to get off.

As I walked past him, I thanked him and handed him a tip. He smiled and nodded.

"Muchas gracias, Señora."

I watched as the back of the bus disappeared in a cloud of dust. The late afternoon sun inked the terrain with dense shadows. Careful to stay off the road in case another vehicle happened along, I began the long walk to Oggie's house. I couldn't take the risk of being seen. The only people who knew my current location were the bus driver and two older women passengers. I wasn't too concerned about the women, and the bus driver had many miles to go before he'd mention the *juarita* he dropped off earlier that afternoon.

The temperature difference soared between the coast and the interior. Thankful for the canteen of water, I drank deeply to replace what I lost in perspiration. I could refill it once I made it to Oggie's.

A few kilometers later, the small concrete house came into view. I stopped and scanned the area, searching for the telltale sign of someone waiting, watching. A fly buzzed next to my ear and I swatted it away from my sweaty face. Not seeing anything out of the ordinary, I settled down in the shade underneath a *palo verde* to wait for night fall.

As soon as the shadows had melted together in the deep twilight, I stood and stretched, then checked the main road. Nothing moved. I crossed the road to Oggie's, stepping over the split-rail fence into his yard.

No sound greeted me—not even the chirp of a cricket. The place felt abandoned. I don't know what I expected as I crossed the dirt lot and stopped in front of the broken cellar door. A dark discoloration stained the ground in front of me. Dried blood from Frank's guy. I cast a nervous glance behind me, half expecting Frank to be there with a gun pointed at my back.

I shook off the fear and lifted the door. The gaping maw of the dark cellar yawned open, mocking me with visions of snakes coiled and waiting to strike. With clammy hands, I took hold of the ladder and climbed the few rungs to the dirt floor. I waited for my eyes to adjust to what sliver of light the moon gave me. The back of the cellar rested in total darkness.

Careful not to knock anything over, I groped my way toward the rear wall. A chill settled in my bones as cobwebs clung to my face and hair. Shuddering, I took a deep breath and wiped away the sticky filaments.

Finally, I reached the stack of boxes I'd stashed the backpack under and began to lift them out of the way, digging down to the bottom.

The pack was still there. I realized I'd been holding my breath and let it out with a sigh. My heart in my throat, I unzipped the main compartment and reached inside. Relief washed through me as my fingers closed around a fat stack of bills. I zipped the bag closed, got up and made my way back to the entrance.

I climbed out of the cellar and closed the door behind me. The falling darkness cast odd shadows across the abandoned homestead. Oggie's house crouched in front of me in silent condemnation. I wondered if anyone had checked on the old man and his sick cat. What if no one had bothered to rescue Wild Bill? Too much time had passed since Oggie gave him his last insulin shot.

Without thinking, I skirted the side of the house and slipped around to the front door. I had no idea what the local authorities would do once they found the body.

Murder probably wasn't unheard of in these parts, but I doubted it was a common occurrence.

Oggie's VW sat parked in the same place. I walked over to it and looked inside. No keys in the ignition. I reached in and checked under the seat.

Nothing.

A sense of dread traveled upward from my stomach as I walked toward the house, not knowing what I'd find when I opened the front door. What if no one had found him yet?

My mind rejected the thought. I'd read somewhere that a rotting body had a unique odor that was hard to forget. I doubted I'd be able to get this close without smelling something.

The door handle turned easily. I nudged it open, staying to the side in case I'd been wrong and someone waited for me. There'd been no activity during the time I watched the place, so I felt relatively safe in entering.

I edged in and closed the door behind me. Relieved the place smelled of stale kitty litter, and not a decomposing body, I crossed the floor to the kitchen sink and filled my canteen from the faucet. Then I searched the drawers and cabinets for car keys. In the third drawer I checked, I found a small wind up flashlight. I spun the handle until I got a thin beam of light and swept it around the room.

The chair Frank had tied me to still sat upright, but the one Oggie'd been sitting on lay on its side, pieces of tape still attached where his wrists and ankles had been. Dried blood stained the floor surrounding the chair. The scene blurred as tears welled in my eyes.

Oggie died because of me.

I angrily wiped the tears away and took a deep breath to clamp down on my emotions and continue my search.

The fridge light blinked on when I opened the door. The only items inside were a few bottles of Pacifico sitting next to a moldy *bolio* and an empty box of insulin. I closed the door and walked over to the small night stand next to the bed. The top drawer held a torrid romance and pair of reading glasses, along with a bottle of sleeping pills, but no keys. I looked under the bed, wondering what happened to Wild Bill. I quickly checked everywhere in the house a cat might hide, even though I knew Wild Bill would have come out to greet me if he was still around. Part of me wanted to stop looking, in case I did find him. The tiny bathroom held only the dirty litter box, and it didn't look like it had been used recently.

I gave up the search and walked back into the living room, ready to leave.

A car door slammed.

Voices.

Cold fear arced up my spine. Gravel crunched outside the door.

I sprinted to the back door and slipped through just as the front door opened.

"If Frank is right and she does come back, I've got a little present for her." The man spoke gutter Spanish. The other man mumbled something I didn't catch. Probably because of the blood pounding in my ears.

"Who's going to know? He wants her dead. What we do before we kill her will be our little secret, eh?" The men's laughter ricocheted off the walls of the small house.

I backed away from the window, careful not to make any noise. Once I'd gone a few feet, I spun around and slammed into an old bicycle, connecting to it with a thud. I grabbed it before it toppled, and froze, waiting for the two men to come running out after me. I started to breathe again when the laughter resumed inside the house. I skirted the mesquites and slipped behind the cellar, hopped the low fence and started running.

***

I didn't stop until the lights of the house had long disappeared behind me. Grateful for the shadows and the soft, blue moonlight, I continued to walk, working out how to hotwire Oggie's car without being caught. No matter how I looked at it, it was a fool's errand, and I'd end up dead. With no gun, I didn't have a chance against those men. The weight of the money against my back assured me that I'd be fine without the car.

There was just one thing.

Salazar obviously knew I was alive, and by extension, so did Anaya. I had to get to Mazatlán. I needed the anonymity of a big city, both for dropping off their radar as well as securing a passport. There was no way I could go to San Bruno now. Salazar or Anaya would have someone searching for me in every town between here and Nogales, and I had history in San Bruno that Salazar knew about. Besides, I'd be able to fly anywhere from Mazatlán's international airport. Salazar may have an extensive reach, but if he didn't know my name, he wouldn't be able to find me in a sea of tourists.

***

I woke to lush, tropical terrain flowing past me outside the bus window. I hugged my coat tighter against the bus' frigid air conditioning. Outside, the air would be humid and warm. Memories of shrimp dinners and late night walks on the beach from a less complicated time crowded my mind, temporarily pushing away the fear that had become my constant companion.

The bus pulled into the brightly lit station in central Mazatlán. I grabbed the backpack from the overhead compartment and got off, orienting myself before negotiating with a cab driver for a ride to the hotel strip along the beach.

Mazatlán hadn't changed much since the last time I'd visited. It was like remembering another person's trip; a friend and I had just graduated from college and spent a week at one of the luxury hotels on the strip, dancing and eating and flirting with sexy Mexican guys, all the while believing this was our last hurrah before going back to the states and throwing ourselves into climbing the corporate ladder. She had an internship at her father's law firm waiting for her, and I was going to be on the fast track at a prestigious investment company in downtown Minneapolis.

Then I met Roberto Salazar.

It's funny how your life can change with one fateful choice.

I shook off the memories and had the cabbie drop me at a big luxury hotel midway down the strip. I paid cash for the room and ignored the front desk clerk when she looked questioningly at my attire. Good job being inconspicuous, I thought.

When I got to my room, I stuffed the backpack in the closet safe, stripped to nothing and threw my clothes on the king sized bed. Immediately, I went into the bathroom and filled the large tub with hot water and the hotel's lavender bath salts. A phone call and half an hour later, room service delivered two margaritas and a perfectly grilled steak. I tipped the waiter with the last of the money from Luis, handed him my dirty clothes for valet service, sat down and inhaled the meal.

Margarita in hand, I wandered out to the balcony in my fluffy white robe to watch the orange and purple sunset over the Sea of Cortez. Tourists frolicked in the gentle surf several floors below. The joyful sounds of a large, seaside resort floated up toward me. It all felt so normal and safe. I sank into the comfortable chair and put my feet up on the low table. I was nothing if not good at denial.

The first margarita took the edge off. The second one helped me forget.

***

The next morning, I woke early and headed for the nearest drug store. I bought a pair of scissors, some hair dye and three pairs of sunglasses. On my way back to my hotel, I stopped in a trendy boutique and bought myself a little black dress with matching shoes and handbag, and another pair of jeans. An hour or so later when I looked in the bathroom mirror, I barely recognized myself. Goodbye, California blonde with long, sun streaked hair and no mascara; hello, serious looking woman with short, brown hair and exotic makeup.

I kind of liked the change. The shorter hair felt freer, and made washing it simple and fast.

After a late lunch of grilled prawns, I slid on a pair of faux tortoise-shell sunglasses and the stretchy black dress and shoes, and took the elevator to the lobby. I got in the first cab I came to and gave the driver directions. He glanced in the rear view mirror with a frown, as if to make sure I knew where I was headed. I nodded. He shrugged and drove away from the curb.

A short time later, we pulled up to the *Mapas y Más* storefront in the old section of Mazatlán. I paid the driver and asked him to wait for me, and then went inside.

The long, narrow shop held dozens of neatly stacked maps and books of maps, along with globes, magnifying glasses and intricate ships-in-a-bottle. A man dressed in board shorts and a Baja hoodie with hipster glasses and hair the color of wet sand stood on one side, paging through a large, leather bound book. I walked past him to the back and rang the bell on the counter.

Behind the register, the dusty velvet curtain parted and a short, muscular man with a neck as wide as his head and the expression of an angry pit bull appeared. Dressed in black jeans, a white golf shirt and worn huaraches, he drew his shoulders back and lifted his chin when he saw me. I removed my sunglasses and smiled at him. His answering smile softened his hardened demeanor, but only a little.

"*Hola, Señor.* Are you the owner?"

"*Sí.* May I help you, Señora?"

I'd overheard Salazar mention the map store where I now stood as the best place to obtain forged documents in Mexico. The owner was well-known in the drug cartel world, and gladly acquired any kind of documentation requested. He worked fast, and asked no questions, preferring to remain silent about his clients, as many were members of rival cartels.

I cleared my throat and replied, "Please. I have heard that not only are you the purveyor of the finest, most comprehensive collection of maps in all of Mexico, but deal in procuring other items, as well."

His eyes narrowed as he considered the gringa standing before him. He clasped his hands on the counter in front of him, his eyes shifting to my chest, emphasized by the low-cut, clingy black dress.

"It depends on what you need, Señora. I have many items for sale." He continued his perusal, his gaze trailing up my neck to my eyes. My heart skipped a beat. I'd seen that look before. I could only describe it as deadly, and this man had it in spades. I tried to swallow.

Tentatively, I reached forward and touched his sleeve, wearing what I hoped looked like a flirtatious smile. "I've mislaid my passport. I am to leave your beautiful country soon, but can't wait for my replacement, as I would forfeit the large sum of money I've paid for the remainder of my trip." I leaned over the counter to give him a better view. "An old friend told me on good authority that you may be able to expedite the process- for a price."

The man grinned, his neck muscles bulging even more. We both knew this was a bullshit story, but protocol dictated the false reasoning. That way, no one expressly acknowledged the true nature of the transaction. At least, that's what I assumed.

I was wrong.

"I'm sorry, Señora, I wish I could help you with your dilemma." He shook his head and lifted his hands, palms up. "Life would be very good indeed, if I would be able to do such a thing. I'd be a rich man."

My cheeks burned as I realized my mistake. Of course. He didn't know me from Adam. He probably thought I was going to turn him in- that I was part of a sting operation or worse. Why did I think he'd respond to a complete stranger? A woman, no less. I could have kicked myself for my stupidity.

"You should visit the American consulate. I'm sure they will be happy to help you."

"I—I'm so sorry. My friend must have been mistaken." I turned to leave and noticed the sandy-haired man staring at me. Still embarrassed, I ignored him as I passed, heading for the door. It looked like I needed a Plan B.

"Let me—" the sandy-haired guy said, and reached around me to open the door.

Australian accent. Looked like a surfer.

"Thanks," I said, and walked through the door onto the street. My taxi was where I'd left it, the cabbie's head laid back against the headrest, apparently taking a siesta.

"Is this yours?" he asked, indicating the cab. His brown eyes had an earnestness that made me smile. I was tempted to brush his tousled hair away from his face. He wasn't bad looking, for a surfer.

I nodded and reached for the cab's door handle.

"I can help you," he said.

I turned to face him, sizing him up.

"What do you mean?"

"What you asked Juan for in there—a passport." He looked around, casually. No one was within hearing distance.

"You know him?"

"Sure. Everybody knows Juan. But only a few know what he does on the side."

Well, then. Maybe there was hope for this idea yet.

"Can I buy you a drink?"

He grinned, and his face lit up. "I thought you'd never ask."

***

His name was Tristan. He was in his mid-thirties and I'd guessed right—he was from Australia and loved to surf. He landed in Mazatlán a month before and decided to take an extended break from his year-long surf odyssey.

"I wasn't getting any younger, you know? I knew if I didn't do it this time, I'd probably never get the chance."

We sat at an open-air bar under a palapa, sipping margaritas. The ocean breeze felt like a caress on my face. If I closed my eyes, I could almost believe I was on vacation.

Almost.

"So what's your story, Ava?"

I'd given him the name I picked out for my fake passport. The less people who knew me as Kate, the better.

"I'm a little embarrassed," I began, sliding my finger around the rim of my drink to remove some of the salt. "My boyfriend and I had a fight and I left in a huff, forgetting my passport. Now he won't give it back, and my flight leaves the end of the week. I met a guy who told me about Juan, but he didn't mention I had to have an introduction in order to deal with him." I shrugged and took a sip. "I didn't get a number."

Tristan leaned closer, his shoulder touching mine. He smelled faintly of salt water and spicy aftershave. I found myself relaxing for the first time in weeks. The margarita helped, and Tristan had a personal magnetism that reminded me of much better days.

Not to mention he had a great ass.

"If you don't mind being from a different country than the U.S., I think it would only take a couple of days to get one made. Although, I'm warning you now, it will be exy."

"Expensive?"

"Yeah. I think the last time it was ten grand, easy." He finished his margarita and ordered a beer from the bartender.

"You want another?" he asked.

I nodded. What the hell. I hadn't felt this good in a long time. An execution didn't appear to be in my immediate future. And ten grand for a fake passport didn't sound so bad.

Not if it meant getting as far away from Salazar and Anaya as possible.

We left the bar an hour later, headed for a nearby taco stand, giggling like fools from his outrageous surfer stories. He finished off a humungous burrito in the time it took me to eat a taco.

"Why don't you come with me?" The invitation was delivered with nonchalance, but I detected intense interest in the answer.

I reached over and wiped a drop of salsa off his chin.

"You mean to Fiji?"

"Yeah. What do ya think?" He grinned and nudged me with his elbow. "There's no better place to learn how to surf, guaranteed."

He'd mentioned earlier that his next and last stop would be Fiji before returning home to Australia.

"Get me a passport, darlin' and we'll talk about it."

"Too right!" He grabbed me around the waist and started to Samba in the street. I laughed and followed his lead.

He talked me into continuing our dancing at a club, but first, he'd parked his rented van along a side street and wanted to move it closer to the strip so it would be easier to find later. Once we'd accomplished that, we headed for a Latin dance club and more drinks.

Bad Spirits

By the time two o'clock rolled around, I was seriously ready to get back to my hotel room, and I wanted Tristan to join me. I felt a small measure of safety with him around, even though I knew I was deceiving myself.

As he walked me up the steps to my hotel, I leaned into him and nuzzled his neck. He tightened his arm around me and kissed the top of my head.

"Stay with me?" I asked.

He nodded, and we took the elevator to my room.

***

The echo of laughter followed by a door slamming shut in the hallway jolted me awake. I lay still for a minute, trying to remember where I was. The memory of Tristan naked brought a languid smile to my face and I rolled onto my side to snuggle up next to him.

The bed was empty.

I sat up and ran my fingers through my hair.

"Tristan?" No answer. I wrapped the sheet around me and slid off the bed, padding over to the open door to the balcony, half-expecting to see him reading the paper and drinking coffee.

Two empty glasses and a napkin from the night before sat on the low table. No Tristan. I mentally shrugged. Maybe he'd gone for coffee. I turned and walked back into the room, heading for the bathroom.

I stopped. Something wasn't right.

I back tracked a couple of steps and looked again.

My breath caught in my throat. I sank onto the bed and stared at the closet.

At the open, empty safe.

No.

The events of the night before clicked into place, as though a lock had just tumbled to the right combination.

The sinking feeling in my gut told me the memory that I'd opened the safe and given him the ten thousand dollars for the passport after we'd made love wasn't a dream.

But I also remembered resetting the safe and closing the door.

How long had he been gone? I flung myself off the bed and rushed to the closet where I threw on my freshly laundered jeans and tee shirt, slid into my shoes and ran out the door to the elevator. The lift took too long, so I raced to the stairwell and flew down the six flights to the lobby.

When I reached the huge front door, I stopped to orient myself.

Left. We'd parked the van down the street to the left. Almost knocking the doorman over, I sprinted down the sidewalk, past the few early morning tourists sipping cups of steaming coffee, toward where we'd parked the night before.

Halfway down the next block, I spotted the van. Relief surged through me. At the same time hurt and anger at Tristan's betrayal boiled to the surface.

I spotted him as he crossed the street, carrying my backpack. I was still too far from the van.

"Tristan!"

Startled, he looked up. Our eyes met. Without breaking stride, he opened the door, tossed the backpack into the van, got in and shut the door. He bowed his head for a moment, and then glanced up and watched me through the windshield as the engine turned over.

The force of the blast threw me backward onto the sidewalk. The explosion rocked the boulevard, shattering plate glass windows and setting off car alarms up and down the street. I rolled to my side and lifted myself onto my elbow. A still burning door from the van landed in the street with a crash, narrowly missing a red car driving past. Pieces of what looked like singed hundred dollar bills fluttered to the ground. A child's wail split through the chaos.

I struggled to stand, and held onto the granite storefront next to me for support. Enveloped in flames, the van was a hulking, charred chassis, reminding me of pictures I'd seen on the news of roadside bombings in Iraq. I staggered closer, bracing myself in case some part of Tristan remained, but it seemed improbable that any of him survived.

The wail of sirens broke through the shock. I had to leave, now.

In a panic, I turned away from the scene, and realized I had nowhere to go, no one to turn to. I couldn't go back to my hotel room. Obviously, someone knew exactly where I was, who I was with and where I was going. I leaned forward and tried to catch my breath.

People ran in all directions. I scanned the crowd that had started to gather around the burning van, afraid I might recognize someone from Salazar's army of gunmen.

That's when I realized it could be anyone. Male, female, it wouldn't matter. If they could get to me this fast, I didn't have a chance. Fear rooted my feet to the spot. My brain screamed at me to run.

I forced myself to walk away.

Luis. I had to call Luis. It may not be the most secure option, but it was the best. They'd be careful. They knew Salazar had an informant in one of the agencies. Or, maybe it was Anaya. I had enough information on both to put them away for years. And, I knew how to find Anaya's camp in the northern mountains.

I reached into my pocket, praying that the piece of paper with Luis' cell phone number was still there. It was. I sighed with relief. The valet must have removed it prior to laundering the jeans, and then replaced it before delivering them to my room. With knees shaking, I walked into the next hotel and found a phone.

***

Twenty-four hours later, I was onboard a helicopter, headed for the states. The game had changed after Luis transferred my phone call to Chance, and I told him that I had information on Vincent Anaya as well as Salazar. After his arrest, Salazar had made a deal with the Mexican government to betray Anaya in return for a lesser sentence. Ultimately, the DEA agreed to the terms, as Anaya headed an organization that reached well beyond Mexico. In return, they anticipated Anaya's extradition to the U.S.

That didn't happen.

With my recorded testimony, and that of two other witnesses, Anaya was sentenced to twelve years—in a Mexican prison. The Mexican judge was well known for being open to bribes, and the prison he chose for Anaya was well known for taking good care of its prisoners, for a price. He'd be able to run his empire easily from his cell, all with the protection of armed guards. Infuriated by what he viewed as the betrayal of the agents who lost their lives during the operation, Chance vowed to find a way to bring both Anaya's and Salazar's operations down, whatever the cost.

As for John Sterling, he received ten years in a federal penitentiary outside of Tucson. I'd be a distant memory by the time he got out.

The sentencing didn't give me much peace of mind. I knew Anaya would be able to contract someone to kill me from prison. Salazar could, too, but paying someone to kill me would be more an expensive nuisance, especially if Anaya was trying to do the same thing. Why duplicate the effort? Anaya would certainly have Salazar killed in prison for his betrayal. Salazar could pay for protection, as well, but Anaya was more feared than Salazar, so I assumed it was just a matter of time.

Chance offered to place me in Witness Protection, but again, I refused. One of the agencies still had a leak, and supplying either Anaya or Salazar with my contact information would paint a big red bull's eye on my back. I opted to get identification on my own, with a little help from an informant Chance knew. Both Luis and Chance pooled their resources and came up with a few thousand to get me started, for which I was grateful.

The only problem being I had no idea where to go.

I couldn't go home to Minnesota and put my family at risk, and I didn't want to be anywhere near Mexico, at least for a while. The money I'd buried at Lana's could wait. Things had to cool down before I could even think about planning a trip back there.

What I needed now was another plan. A plan to get me as far away from Mexico and Salazar as possible.

Luis walked me out to the field office parking lot and handed me a set of keys.

I glanced at them. "What are these for?"

He smiled and turned me around.

"It's yours."

Parked in front of us was a slightly beat-up, tan colored Jeep. The two-door, sporty kind. I looked at Luis.

"Really?" I'd always loved Jeeps.

"Really. It's got a full tank."

"Thanks." It was all I could say. Luis turned to go, but stopped.

"Be safe, Kate. And remember—you can call me, anytime."

I nodded, already making plans. I walked over to the Jeep. The asphalt radiated a furnace-like heat from the hot Arizona sun, but it didn't bother me. The Jeep's doors had been taken off and lay in the back. I'd have to buy a canvas top, if I was staying in this part of the country.

That was a big if.

I was now Kate Jones, unemployed, unencumbered, and completely on my own.

Time to go.

THE END

Dead of Winter

ONE

It never had a chance.

The burnt red of the fox's fur stood out against the white background. Blood saturated the snow. I wanted to look away, but found myself morbidly fascinated by the rabbit's death throes. The fox lifted its head from the rabbit's neck and watched, almost bemused, as the small paws kicked at empty space.

Finally, it stilled. The fox bent its head and began to rip off bits of fur. I turned and walked past the gory scene.

It fit my state of mind.

Daylight was scarce this time of year, and I quickened my pace to make it back to my rig before dark. I needed this hike today. Normally, I'd be leading a group of guests on a hike from the local hotel, but business was soft this time of year, and I wanted to keep my guiding abilities sharp. Hiking alone always honed my awareness of my surroundings and allowed me to forget my past.

For a while.

I fell into a rhythmic stride, comforted by the crunch of the snow under my feet. As I rounded the corner that marked the lonely stretch of wilderness that lay between me and the roughed in trailhead, I noticed movement to my right. Thinking it was probably more wildlife trying to break through some ice in a nearby pond, I stopped.

A series of odd grunts punctuated the silence. It was still early in the season, so the possibility it might be a late-to-hibernate bear was real, but not necessarily the only explanation. Silently, I moved in the direction of the noise, peering at the frozen pond through winter-stripped alders.

There were three men; two standing and one on his knees on a gray tarp. It took me a minute to realize what was happening. The sharp report of the gun flushed a small murder of ravens from a nearby tree. The man on his knees crumpled forward.

Unable to breathe, I dropped to a squat behind the trees, scanning the area for better cover. The barren white landscape held no place to hide.

Just sit tight, Kate. If I moved now, I'd be dead. The low murmur of voices drifted past me, accompanied by the occasional scrape of a tarp-wrapped body being dragged over the crusty snow.

They were speaking Spanish. And it wasn't Castilian, but the Mexican dialect spoken by the men who worked for my ex-lover and drug dealer, Roberto Salazar.

Shit. Shit. Shit. I didn't recognize them, but that didn't mean anything. The poor schmuck who bought it could've been someone paid to track me. They wouldn't need him anymore, once my location had been confirmed. I'd hoped getting lost in Alaska would lessen the fear that continually stalked me. True, I'd changed my last name a couple of times in order to confuse anyone who might try to find me, and I never got close enough to people to let my guard down, but the constant fear of discovery settled warily into the recesses of my brain, like a feral cat with sharp claws.

My Jeep was in the shop and I was driving the hotel manager's rig—a big, hulking twenty-year-old Chevy Blazer. This was a good thing. If the two thugs were looking for me, they probably didn't know I'd stopped at this trailhead.

I crouched by the trees a while longer, waiting until the men had moved completely out of sight. Not hearing anything, I stood, keeping trees and shrubs between me and the trail, in case they came back.

Satisfied I was alone, I moved back onto the trail and followed the two men's tracks. They veered to the left at a fork that led to the official parking area. The path to the right was one the locals used for overflow parking in the summer. I turned right.

My heart had slowed to a semi-thud by the time I made it to the Blazer and started the engine. I slid the semi-automatic I always carried out of my waistband and put it on the seat beside me. I hadn't needed a gun recently, and I didn't look forward to the possibility of having to use it for more than target practice. An old, familiar fear crawled up the back of my neck. I did some deep breathing to keep from hyperventilating.

I turned the heater on full blast and stared out through the windshield at the slowly darkening afternoon. The word bleak came to mind. Would I always have to run, to look over my shoulder? My life had become an endless series of evasive maneuvers designed to keep me detached from people, places. My hand shaking, I picked up my cell phone and hit speed dial.

"Luis Gonzales."

"Luis. It's Kate." Luis was one of the DEA agents who helped me get out of Mexico.

"Kate—? Is everything all right?"

"I—I'm not sure. I just saw a guy get killed, execution-style and I'm a little freaked out right now." I shifted into reverse and backed up, then threw the Blazer into gear and nosed onto the highway, checking both directions for any sign of the killers. "They were speaking Spanish."

"So? There are millions of Hispanics in the U.S."

"Not in Quilete. None, that I know of. These guys were using Mexican Spanish. Not Cuban, not Puerto Rican. Mexican. Salazar and Anaya are still locked up, right?"

"Far as I know. But you know they both have reach." He paused, then, "This might be a good time to think about leaving. Go somewhere warm. Ever been to Hawaii?"

"Hawaii's a bunch of islands, Luis. How the hell am I supposed to run if they follow me there?"

"Hey—Alaska's not much different. Where you gonna run? Into the wilderness? Ever see the movie? It didn't end well." Luis paused to let the implication sink in. "And, there are way more places to hide a body."

"Thanks for that."

Hawaii sounded good. This snow and ice shit was getting old. Maybe spending a little time on the North Shore wasn't such a bad idea. I had good memories from a few years back. "I'll give it some thought. For the time being, can you put me in contact with someone up here? I'm not too far from Anchorage."

"Hold on a minute-"

The staccato click of typing was followed by silence.

"Got a pen? There's a field agent up near you by the name of Brad Pickering. He's a twenty-five year veteran. Used to work busting importers and such, but now he's strictly narcotics. I'll give him a call and brief him, tell him you'll be getting in touch. Have you contacted anybody about the murder yet?"

"No, I just left the trailhead." I took a deep breath, glad that for once I had someone on my side. "I was going to call it in as soon as I got off the phone with you. There won't be much evidence, though. They had him on a tarp. Very efficient."

"Jesus, Kate." There was a pause on the other end. "You still have a gun, right?"

I glanced at the Glock. "Yeah. Though it doesn't do me a lot of good if they know where I live. As I recall, they prefer explosives." The brief silence that followed told me Luis was remembering the night they blew the safe house.

"Let me know what you decide, okay? And tell the chief to give me a call if they have questions."

"Thanks, Luis." I ended the call and put the phone in my pocket. Part of me wished I lived in Arizona, so I could be near Luis, have some semblance of protection from people who understood. The other part wanted to stay far, far away from anywhere near Mexico.

My survival instinct had led me to Alaska. Apparently, it needed to be recalibrated.

.

TWO

Chief Miller immediately sent a unit to investigate the scene, although it was almost dark and he doubted they'd be able to find anything until the next day. I was told to come down to the office and give a report. As I sipped a cup of watered down tundra coffee, I described the men as best as I could, and gave them Luis' cell phone number, recounting a shortened version of my role in testifying against the two drug lords and DEA agent. Miller whistled softly when I told him I thought that the men might be contract killers hired by either Vincent Anaya or Roberto Salazar.

"That's a little out of our depth here, Kate. Hell, there hasn't been a killing in this community since the 1920s, when one of the Hokstrands mistakenly ran over a transient out at the old train yard." He tapped the piece of paper I gave him with Luis' number. "I'll be getting in touch with your friend here. Looks like we'll need all the help we can get."

"I'm sorry to be the cause of all this, Chief. I can't guarantee it's got anything to do with the events that happened in Mexico, but I thought it best to tell you, in case it does."

"Well, I appreciate that." He looked over the top of his reading glasses. Despite his weathered face, he had a youthful quality; a sparkle in the eyes, something. "Have you got somewhere to stay? If these men are who you say they are your place isn't safe. Since you haven't been directly threatened, I can't spare the resources to park one of my deputies outside your house twenty-four-seven, and I'd feel a whole lot better if you weren't there."

"I'm staying at the Dew Drop Inn in Yarnell tonight. Here's my cell phone number in case you need to reach me." I wrote it out on the same piece of paper as Luis'.

"Good. I'd like you to stick around a couple of days in case we get lucky and find something. A positive I.D. would expedite the case."

"As long as I feel safe. The minute I think things are going sideways, I'm on the next plane."

Miller leaned over and punched a button on his desk phone. "Sam, come on in here for a minute, will you?"

A couple of minutes later a man I assumed to be Sam walked in wearing an officer's uniform. His straight black hair was pulled back in a ponytail, and he had the lean look and carriage of a long distance runner.

"Sam, this is Kate. Kate, Sam. I want you to drive her over to her house out on Blake Road so she can pack up a few things. She's going to be staying somewhere else for a while. Seems she's got some unresolved issues that might've caught up with her." He held my eyes for a moment, then looked at Sam. "Be careful. If this is related, these assholes already killed one guy."

Sam gave him half a nod. His dark eyes radiated a stillness that somehow transferred to me, calming my agitated state. I'd only encountered one other person who made me feel that way, an old man I'd met briefly in Mexico. I figured I felt safe around him because he'd carried a large gun.

Miller tossed him a set of keys. "Take the four-by. Let 'em know we know they're around."

"Sure thing." Sam stood quietly, watching me, apparently waiting. I got up from my chair and started for the door.

"And Kate?"

I turned.

"Stay safe."

***

Sam drove to my place in silence. That was fine by me. The realization I would have to leave again had hit me, hard, and I didn't feel like making small talk. I had just begun to carve out a kind of a life for myself here, some tiny piece of the world I could call mine. The locals had begun to accept me as one of their own, and I knew the shop keepers and restaurant owners by name. Greg, the hotel manager, set me up with clients throughout the year, and let me supplement my living tending bar in the hotel's lounge. But now, none of it mattered.

Not if they found me.

My mind kept flashing back to the gunmen and the man who'd been executed. None of them looked familiar, but I'd been running long enough to know that Salazar and Anaya didn't use their own people to track. Running drugs tended to be more economically rewarding, and they made sure they had plenty of folks to handle that end of the business. Murders could be outsourced to a professional. Besides, with an outside pro, there was more recourse if things went sideways.

"Stay here until I tell you it's safe." Sam got out of the marked SUV and walked up to the back of the one-story wood-slat house. I'd left the porch light on. I never used the front, preferring to park in the small detached garage near the rear entrance.

Out of habit, I always locked the door. I'd given Sam the key. He checked the perimeter with his flashlight before he came back to the porch and unlocked the door. He disappeared into the one bedroom rental, reappearing in the doorway a few minutes later to motion me inside.

"Find anything?" I asked as I walked past him. He shook his head.

"No sign of forced entry."

"That's a relief."

"There are footprints leading to the front door." He glanced at my boots. "But I can't determine the tread, or how recent they are."

I stopped. Our eyes met. "I never use the front door." Adrenaline spiked through me.

"Have you had any deliveries? Fed Ex? DHL?"

"None."

"Where do you get mail?"

I nodded toward the road. "Mailbox on the driveway."

"Neighbors?"

"I guess it's possible someone stopped by, but I don't get too many visitors out this way."

"I didn't see a basement or attic ingress."

"There's an old root cellar out back, but I don't use it for anything." I crossed my arms. Someone had been here. But when? And who?

Sam wrote something in a notebook, then flipped it closed.

"I'm going to check the garage and the cellar. You okay in here?"

I nodded. "Yeah. Sure. It shouldn't take long. I'll meet you outside."

I retrieved my backpack from behind the couch and started to fill it with the stuff I figured I'd need. I didn't know when I'd be able to come back, so I grabbed what I could.

Clothes and my laptop were next. I moved into my bedroom and started to disconnect the router. I'd bundled up the cords and had just tucked my computer in my pack when I noticed it. The odor was faint and reminded me of cheap aftershave. Not even close to the masculine cedar scent Sam wore.

I scanned the room. Things looked fine at first glance, but something wasn't right. The feel of the place was different. I stood quietly near the bed, trying to understand what had changed.

All the dresser drawers were shut, and my bed looked like how I'd left it that morning. I turned around and immediately realized the problem.

My closet door was closed.

I never close my closet. It's a phobia I've had since I was three. I always made my parents leave the door open. I was convinced that if they ever shut it, a huge, snarling, hairy something would materialize and when I opened it in the morning it would grab onto me and rip me to shreds.

Sam has already checked. You're safe. There's nobody behind that door. He probably shut it by accident.

I ran through the living room and kitchen and was out the door and onto the porch steps in record time, almost colliding with Sam.

"What?" He grabbed my arm and turned me so he could look into my face.

"Was the closet door in the bedroom shut?" I asked, out of breath.

"Yes."

"I never shut my closet door. Childhood thing. Did you notice the cologne?"

He shook his head. "Are you sure it wasn't mine?"

"Yes." I leaned forward and sniffed, my hair falling onto his chest. "I'm absolutely positive. I smelled yours in the truck. It has a clean scent. This was cloying."

His eyes narrowed and he nodded toward the SUV. I moved to the far side of the truck and watched as he walked back to the house and disappeared inside.

A few minutes later, Sam reappeared. He walked around the yard, dropping to a squat at intervals, shining his flashlight on the ground as he went. There wasn't much snow left, and the frozen dirt was rock hard, so I doubted he'd pick up any tracks, but I'd learned never to underestimate Alaskans. People in this part of the country continually surprised me with their resourcefulness. With such a harsh climate, death claimed the unwary and impractical with little remorse.

He jogged back to the truck, holstering his gun.

"I caught a whiff of the odor in the bedroom. Whoever was wearing it hasn't been gone long." Sam opened the door to the truck and slid into the driver's seat. "Get in."

I hopped in and slammed the door shut. He threw the truck into gear, spitting gravel as we shot down the driveway. We slid to a stop at the highway. I scanned either direction, but this section of rural road didn't have streetlights, so my distance was limited.

Sam shined his door-mounted spotlight first left, then right. Seeing nothing, he turned onto the highway, strafing the bushes on either side with the light. They could have been hiding in a ditch or behind a tree. We'd never know.

My scalp tingled as a chill danced up my back.

They've been in my house.

***

Sam radioed the incident in to the office. Chief Miller's brusque voice over the speaker telegraphed his concern.

"Watch to see that no one's following you. Pick up her car and then follow her to Yarnell. Make sure she's safe. Stay there if you have to."

"You paying?" Sam shot back.

"The taxpayers, Sam. The taxpayers."

***

I unlocked the door and threw the keys on the side table. I'd opted for the room with two queen beds, hoping for more space. There's nothing worse than having to stay in one place for an extended period of time and not have enough room to change your mind. Sam took the room next door after making sure there was a door connecting the two.

"You hungry?" I asked.

Sam nodded. "I could eat."

"My treat. I'd hate for the taxpayers to pay for that, too."

We found a decent pizza place within walking distance, and ordered a pie with the works to bring back to the motel. At my request, we stopped and picked up a bottle of red wine. Sam opted for bottled water with lemon.

"How long have you been in law enforcement?" We'd decided to eat in his room, since it had a larger table.

"Eight years."

"You like it?"

Sam shrugged. "It's interesting."

I asked him a couple more questions and got more one—and two-word answers. After the third try, I gave up and we ate in silence. It wasn't uncomfortable, though. Neither of us felt the need to fill in the gaps.

With my blessing, Sam ate the last piece of pizza while I sipped my second glass of wine. I liked to watch him eat. He had an economy of movement I found fascinating.

"You run, right?" I asked.

He nodded, swallowing his last bite before he replied. "Yes. Long-distance."

Wow. More than two words. I pressed my luck. "How far do you usually go?"

He shrugged. Silence.

I sighed and took another drink, writing Sam off as a closed book.

"What are *you* running from?" His eyes locked onto mine. I shifted in the chair.

"What makes you think I'm running?"

"You're living in Quilete, Alaska. Not much of a place for a woman in her prime." He took a drink of his sparkling water, watching me. I stared back at him.

"Well?" he asked, apparently expecting an answer.

"Death."

"Why?"

"Because I don't want to die." It's possible I meant to be that sarcastic.

"Do you think you won't?"

"Die? No, of course I know I'm going to die. I'd like to delay it as long as possible."

Sam rose from the table, wadded his napkin and tossed it on his plate. "You can spend a lifetime avoiding death," he replied. "If I were you, I'd spend it living."

"Easy for you to say. You don't have contract killers trying to use you for target practice."

"I suspect the killers aren't your biggest problem."

"Really? And what *would* be, oh wise and omniscient one?"

"Trust."

"You're kidding, right? Why the hell should I trust anyone? Trust kills."

Sam looked at me with an expression that could only be construed as pity. Pissed, I tossed my fork and paper plate into the pizza box and brushed past him, headed for the door.

.

THREE

I found a movie on cable and watched it, alone. Around ten o'clock, Sam opened the door between our rooms and said goodnight, then retired for the evening next door.

I can't lie. It made me feel safer.

Later, as I lay in bed and stared at the ceiling, I sorted out my next move. Life on the run was not something I would ever consciously choose. The consequences were too great. Every time I started to feel some kind of normalcy somewhere, things would change and I'd have to rip my new life to shreds, uproot everything and move on to the next place. It left me in a vacuum filled with only myself. I had no friends to speak of. I'd learned the hard way that getting close to someone could be lethal.

For them.

If I contacted my family, they'd use them to get to me. I hadn't spoken to my parents or any of my sisters in years. As far as I knew, they still lived in the suburbs in Minneapolis, still had the husbands and one-point-five kids. My sisters had never understood my need for adventure, expecting me to eventually settle down, buy a house down the street, have a family, yadda-yadda.

Not that my present circumstances were better. Sam had me pegged—I did have trust issues. With good reason. But he was also right about another thing. I could spend my life avoiding death. I needed to live.

I needed to leave.

***

The next morning, I called my mechanic to find out when the Jeep would be ready. Two days. Then I called Greg, the hotel manager, and asked him if I could keep the Blazer for a couple more days. He said it would be fine, since he had another vehicle. I thanked him, and Sam and I headed for Anchorage, calling Agent Pickering on the way to set up an appointment.

The DEA field office was on the third floor of a five story building in downtown Anchorage overlooking a parking garage. The agent at the front ushered us into a nondescript office. Brad Pickering sat at his desk reading, a Styrofoam cup filled with black coffee at his elbow. In his late fifties, his graying hair fell in a bushy wave across his forehead. He smelled like Old Spice and cigarettes.

He stood and everybody shook hands. "Have a seat." He indicated the two chairs near the desk. "Luis Gonzales called me with the details of the case. Sounds like the shit's hit the fan."

I put my pack on the floor and sat down. Sam remained standing.

"You could say that. I thought I should check in with you in case I can give you any information that might help you track these guys." I crossed my legs, trying to get comfortable. "Since, apparently I brought them here."

"I remember the case, followed it closely. Everybody in the DEA did. John Sterling was one of our own, gone to shit." He shook his head. "Not the best P.R." He looked directly at me. "If I learned one thing through the years, it would be to never trust anybody. Sterling was one of the best. He was smart, too smart, and he got greedy. Roberto Salazar and Vincent Anaya were already there. These people don't mess around."

"They blew the safe house where I'd been staying. Luis and I were the only survivors."

"Yeah. Luis mentioned that. Kate, I'm not going to lie to you." Pickering leaned forward, forearms on the desk. "You need to think about getting out of Alaska. They tracked you here, and yes, they could track you again, but you're better off leaving. Alaska's big, but essentially it's a small town. Word gets around. It won't be hard for them to find you."

I'd come for confirmation, and here it was, my stark reality. "So you're saying there's not much you can do."

Pickering looked from me to Sam, back to me. "I'm sorry. Leaving's your best option. These assholes don't care if there's collateral damage. Anyone gets in their way, they'll kill them. You think your life stinks now? You don't want that on your conscience."

Oggie's memory came flooding back. Too late, I thought.

He leaned back, his lips a thin line. "I know you don't want to hear this, but nobody can spare resources to try to track down a couple of suspected contract killers who you say murdered someone. As of this morning, there's no case—no body and no missing persons report. The DEA's indebted to you for your testimony, but you chose not to go into Witness Protection." He raised his hands and shrugged. "No one will touch this, Kate. I'm sorry."

I grabbed my pack and stood, feeling the anger starting to rise. "I figured so. But it's always best to get it straight from the horse's—" I paused, "—mouth."

Pickering narrowed his eyes, trying to figure out if I'd just insulted him. I wasn't about to confirm his suspicions. And really, it wasn't his fault. My mood had tanked and I felt like taking it out on the closest person.

"I appreciate your time, Agent Pickering. Have a nice day."

Throughout the whole exchange, Sam had remained silent. He nodded at Pickering and left with me. We walked out of the building into the steel gray day, back to the SUV. I was in a dark mood. Sam stayed close, but gave me space. He started the engine, switched the heater to high and pulled into traffic. I brought up an airfare app on my phone and bought a plane ticket to Honolulu, scheduled to leave on Friday. I figured I'd be able to tie up loose ends by then. If Miller hadn't caught the shooters by then, he probably never would.

The thought of seeing my friend Gabby again brought a smile to my face. It had been a long time since I'd been on the North Shore. Thinking about the warm, tropical breezes drifting across my skin and the heady scent of pineapple saved me from having a full-on anxiety attack.

If I kept my mind off of what was actually happening, I'd be fine.

The Jeep would probably be an easy sell, since it was a four-wheel drive, but I knew Greg would take care of things if someone didn't buy it right away. I'd already paid my rent for the month. My landlady would more than likely keep the deposit, but there wasn't a lot I could do about that. The furniture came with the house, so no worries there. Other than those two things, I didn't have much else I needed to do.

It paid to travel light.

***

An hour later, we were back at the Dew Drop Inn. After a brief nap, I showered and changed, and knocked on the door between our rooms to see if Sam wanted to join me for an early dinner. There was no answer. Worried that I didn't get a response, I stepped outside. The curtains on his window were partially open, and I glanced inside. Sam sat cross legged on the bed, his eyes closed, still as stone. I tapped on the glass. He didn't twitch.

The temperature was beginning to drop, and I hadn't worn my jacket, so I went back to my room and turned on the television for company. I checked the clock: four-thirty. If I didn't hear movement in the other room by five, I'd try knocking again. Half an hour should be enough quiet time for anybody.

When five o'clock rolled around and I still hadn't heard anything, I put on my coat and shoes and walked next door. This time, Sam stood in the middle of the room with his back to me, bare to the waist. He'd moved the bed against the far wall, leaving space between him and the door. His dark hair hung loose to the middle of his back. Before I could blink, he'd executed a perfect reverse roundhouse kick, followed by several other moves. Fascinated, I watched him as he continued practicing.

"Honey, what are you doin', stalkin' somebody?"

I jerked back at the sound of the woman's voice, and came face to face with a statuesque redhead dressed in a full-length, lime green coat and a pair of furry mukluks, carrying a hot-pink Hawaiian print makeup case. A thin black cigar dangled between her lips and her green eyes danced with amusement. She lifted her hand and tapped a blood-red acrylic nail to her temple.

"I—it's not what you think—" I stammered.

Her laughter echoed off the brick wall.

"Of course it is, darlin'—in all my years in this god-forsaken frozen tundra, *everything* is *always* what it looks like."

I smiled, embarrassed, and nodded toward the window. Sam hadn't paid any attention to the voices outside his room and continued practicing. Red leaned over and let out a low whistle.

"My, my, he *is* worth stalkin', isn't he?" She made a smacking sound with her lips and shook her head as she turned to me. "Is he yours?"

"No," I said, surprised at the disappointment in my voice.

Red grinned as she sneaked another peek in the window. "Not yet, you mean." She pulled the slim cigar out of her mouth and exhaled a cloud of smoke. Then she turned and gave me a once-over.

"Honey, if I were you, I'd get that man between my thighs and ride him hard until the sun comes up." She glanced at the ever-present darkness and sighed. "Lord knows, that'll give you both plenty of time."

Red patted my cheek, and then strode past me, taking the steps down to the parking lot. She reached the bottom, then stopped and looked back to where I stood on the second floor. With a hand cupped to her mouth, she stage whispered, "Remember, Life is short, darlin'. You gotta live."

Now where had I heard that before? I turned back to the window as the door opened and Sam walked out.

"Who were you talking to?" he asked, looking over the metal railing. Red had already disappeared.

"Some motel guest."

He watched the parking lot for a few more seconds, and then turned and motioned for me to follow him into his room. He shut the door and grabbed a navy blue t-shirt off the bed, shrugging it on.

"We're getting takeout. The less you're seen, the better."

"Fine." My reply held more heat than I'd intended. I still felt foolish for watching him.

We ordered Thai and found a movie on cable that we both could agree on. The only comfortable place to sit and watch it was the bed, so we each took a side, using the headboard for a backrest.

My attention drifted and I found myself watching him out of the corner of my eye, intrigued by his ability to remain motionless for long stretches of time. I let my mind wander and had to pull back when I realized my thoughts tended toward the erotic and included him.

I sat up straight and crossed my ankles, folding my hands in my lap. Sam glanced at me.

"You don't like the movie?"

"No, it's fine. I'm just restless." And horny, I thought. I hadn't let my libido out to play in a long time, and here I sat next to a sexy, available man who was supposed to protect me, on a bed, in a motel. How the hell else was I supposed to respond? Red's comments didn't help, either.

I started to slide across the bed, intending to go back to my room, when he placed a hand on my arm.

"Don't go. I'll turn off the movie." He aimed the remote and clicked the television off. I slid back onto the bed, wondering what was on his mind, half-hoping I knew.

"You can't stop the dialogue in your head, can you?" His dark eyes searched mine.

"Only when I sleep." My libido had now left the building. I started for the door.

"What if I could teach you how?"

I stopped, halfway off the bed and turned to look at him, intrigued. "Yeah? Good luck with that."

"Get comfortable and close your eyes. I'm going to bring my hands up like this—" I slid against the headboard, and he cupped his hands over my temples. I felt a gentle buzzing flow through my head. I opened one eye.

"Close."

I did as I was told and a feeling of incredible peace enveloped me, relaxing every muscle in my body. The idea that my life was in danger floated in the background, as though it wasn't important.

"Damn. If you could bottle this, you'd make billions."

"Shh. Just enjoy it. I'll show you how when I'm done."

FOUR

My eyes flew open. At first I didn't remember where I was. Sam's deep, even breathing told me he was asleep next to me on the bed in his room. I rolled onto my side to watch him.

He was even sexier asleep. He lay on his back, one hand across his stomach, the other tucked under his head. The smooth skin of his face and lips begged for my touch. At least, that was my story. I trailed my finger along his jaw, tracing a delicate line under his ear.

His hand shot up and captured mine in an iron grip. At the same time he spun me onto my back and straddled my hips, pinning my arms over my head. He paused for a moment, his eyes burning through me, searching. Then he lowered himself until his lips barely brushed mine. I arched my back and parted my lips in invitation, lifting my chin and closing my eyes. He let out a low growl and nuzzled my neck. I strained against him, trying to loosen his hold, but he wouldn't budge. Raising my head, I nipped at his neck. He returned the effort with a penetrating kiss.

He backed off the foot of the bed and tore his t-shirt off. I met him there and grabbed his belt, unbuckling it and unbuttoning his jeans as fast as humanly possible. As I pushed them past his hips, his erection sprang to life.

Now it was my turn to growl.

He took hold of my sweater and tugged it over my head, unhooked my bra and threw me backward onto the bed. I slipped out of my panties and pulled him down on top of me, relishing the feel of him, wanting him to do things to me I didn't have the words to describe.

Luckily, I didn't have to say a thing.

Later, when I recovered my ability for speech, I told him what had happened in Mexico. The words poured out of me, and to his credit, he listened with no judgment. I didn't stop until I came to the murder at the trail. We sat in silence, both of us absorbing the moment. I'd never told anyone everything, always holding important details back that I thought could get me, or them, killed. I was both relieved and afraid. Afraid he'd turn away, unsure what to make of me.

Relieved to finally have the whole thing out in the open.

As a sort of *quid pro quo*, he told me about his childhood. He'd been chosen by the village shaman as an apprentice. There was only one response allowed a child in that situation, and he embarked upon a rigorous, sometimes mind-blowing education. At sixteen, he rebelled and ran away from his village and the shaman, eventually finding work as a long-haul trucker.

"Didn't take long to realize life on the road wasn't for me, although it gave me plenty of time to think. I studied for my high school diploma, and went to college on a scholarship from the Nation. The police department recruited me in my second year."

"Did you learn that calming stuff from the shaman?"

Sam smiled. "Sort of. He liked to keep information close in order to control things, so I had to find out the rest of the steps from another spiritual teacher I met later. I also studied martial arts, which helped."

"I was watching you practice last night through the window. You're good."

"I've still got a long way to go." He smiled and shifted his weight to stretch out behind me. "Time to rest. I'm going to want more of you the next time we wake up."

I let out a contented sigh as he wrapped his arms around me. It wasn't long before we fell asleep.

***

"No!" Sam lurched to a sitting position, reaching into the darkness to stop some unknown phantom. "Fifty-eight—"

I was instantly awake.

"What?"

Sam shook his head. "I—it's nothing. Go back to sleep." He slid off the bed and walked over to the window.

Like I could go back to sleep after that.

"Bad dream?"

Sam nodded. "Something like that."

"Want to tell me about it?"

"No."

I sighed and lay back on the bed, a familiar knot of fear forming in the pit of my stomach. *Trust, Kate.* An image of the fox tearing the hare apart on the trail slid unbidden into my mind.

Sleep took the rest of the night off.

***

The next thirty-six hours would have veered between nerve-racking and monotonous if it wasn't for getting to know Sam better. His calm demeanor and subtle sense of humor kept the mood light between us, and helped me ignore the twisted lump that had formed in my stomach. Making love like a pair of teenagers helped, too. Madge, the woman that worked the front desk, commented that we acted like a couple of honeymooners, hardly coming out of our rooms to eat. The comparison made me laugh. If she only knew.

Thursday night and Friday morning slid past in a blur and then it was time to head for the airport. My mood was bittersweet as I started to pack, using only a carry-on and my backpack. Part of me was relieved to be leaving with so little; I'd already donated all my sweaters, sweatshirts, jeans and coats to the local thrift store. Shorts and t-shirts would be all I'd need once I arrived in Hawaii.

The other part of me hated to say goodbye to Sam. We both knew I had to go, but it had been such an intense couple of days that it was hard to break free from each other. We promised we'd keep in touch, but we both knew how difficult a long distance relationship would be.

"Better go. Your flight leaves in a few hours." He buttoned the last button of his shirt over his bullet-proof vest. There hadn't been any contact from either of the two gunmen, and it looked like there wouldn't be any, but he followed protocol, nonetheless.

I'd begun to feel safer and more foolish, thinking that maybe the aftershave I smelled and the closed closet door were all figments of my imagination. I'd probably shut the door that morning without thinking. It was possible that the murder I'd seen at the trailhead had nothing to do with me. Maybe it had been a meth deal gone bad.

Sam grabbed my carry-on bag and I shrugged the laptop case strap over my shoulder. We checked the rooms one last time, and walked down the stairs to the parking lot. Sam's SUV was parked near the office. He opened the passenger door for me and threw my bag on the floor.

He slid in the driver's side and closed the door, starting the engine. Before he put the car into gear, he picked up the radio and called the office. Miller's assistant, Angela, answered.

"Hi Sam."

"Hey, Angela. I'm getting ready to transport Kate to the airport."

"Okay. I'll tell the chief if he ever calls in."

"How long has it been this time?"

Angela sighed. "Since yesterday. There's no answer when I try his cell. He's probably ice fishing again and lost track of time. I'll try calling Edna. She'll know how to get a hold of him."

"Tell him to call me when he gets in."

"Roger that. Have a good trip."

Sam replaced the hand set, frowning.

"What?" I asked.

Sam shrugged. "Nothing. It's just a little strange, is all. Joe doesn't usually get off track when we're working a case. He makes sure someone can contact him." Sam threw the truck in reverse and backed out of the parking space.

Madge grinned and waved at us through the window as we drove past.

FIVE

It had snowed the night before, and everything looked
fresh. A dusky orange sun hung midway over the
horizon, threatening to disappear in the afternoon
twilight. Traffic was light. By the time we reached the
half-way mark to Anchorage, there was no one left on the
road to keep us company.

I always marveled at how in-your-face, extreme
Alaska wilderness existed in relation to the man-made
attempts to tame this rough country. The huge ruts in the
road indicated deep winter freezes followed by great
thaws, and made driving akin to riding a mini roller
coaster. Less than a quarter mile off road and you were
knee-deep into raw nature. Most Alaskans I'd met
wouldn't go hiking without a firearm.

Not that it would do you much good against a grizzly,
unless you were packing large.

"Are you ever going to tell me what your bad dream
entailed?" I asked. "I mean, seems to me after the last few
days I'm entitled."

"Why is that?"

"I told you my deepest secrets, and you told me some pretty intense stuff, so why not? It might even help to talk about it."

Sam's expression hardened. "It was nothing. Forget it."

I was about to argue when Angela's voice came over the radio.

"Three-thirty-four, come in."

Sam picked up the mic. "Three-thirty-four. What's up, Angela?"

"Sam, I just got off the phone with Edna. She hasn't heard from Joe, either. She thought he was working the murder and forgot to call her. I'm worried."

Sam opened his mouth to respond when the sound of a revving engine interrupted him. As I turned to look, a black truck broadsided us, shoving our SUV toward the ditch. Slammed against the passenger door, the groan of crumpling metal and rupture of bullets smashing through glass drowned out my screams. Pain radiated across and down my shoulder.

Sam hit the brakes and turned into the other vehicle, slowing the slide, forcing both trucks perpendicular to the road. The stench of burning rubber filled the cab as the screeching sound of locked brakes screamed in protest. I braced myself against the door and engraved my feet on the dash.

Sam floored the accelerator and at the same time yanked the steering wheel to the right, breaking the two trucks apart for an instant. We edged ahead of the other vehicle and gained a few yards.

The other truck recovered and came at us, this time from behind. My head snapped against the headrest on impact. Sam struggled to keep the SUV on the road, but they rammed us again, knocking the truck onto the shoulder. Bullets shattered the rear windows.

"Get down!" Sam grabbed the back of my head and forced me over as we headed for the ditch and he fought to keep from rolling.

We hurtled through brush, flattening saplings before we smashed against something and lurched to a stop. Sam reached across me, yanked my seatbelt open and yelled, "Out. Now!"

I wrenched the door open and fell onto the snow. More glass shattered as rounds strafed the truck. Sam launched himself across the console computer and out the door, rolling to the side as bullets tore through metal. My pack fell out with him. He shoved me toward the rear wheel well, hard, and took a position behind the front passenger wheel using the engine block for cover. There'd be a bruise where he'd pushed me.

If I made it through alive.

"Three-thirty-four, shots fired. Get me backup. We're at mile marker fifty-eight on Chiknuk Road," Sam yelled into his portable's mic as he returned fire.

Panicked, I ransacked my bag, searching for my nine. I'd left it in the bottom zipper compartment, still loaded, intending to give it to Sam as a gift. I pulled it out and crouched beside the back bumper. Slowly, I peered around the side of the truck to get a good look at who we were up against.

At first, I saw one man next to the front of the black pickup, but knew he couldn't be the only shooter. Movement to my left confirmed my suspicions. The second gunman crouched near the back bumper. They were the killers that I saw on the trailhead. The one in front popped up from behind the hood and started shooting. Sam returned fire. The guy's head snapped backward from the bullet's impact. He wavered for a moment, then fell to the ground. Sam dropped his spent magazine and reloaded.

The other gunman disappeared behind the truck. I could see his feet moving under the chassis and took aim, firing just before he reached the front wheel.

The loud grunt and clatter of the gun on asphalt told me I'd found my mark. Sam flashed a thumb's up.

"Three-thirty-four, two males down, one Hispanic, one white. Driving a black, late model Dodge pickup," Sam radioed. He turned to me. "Stay here. I'm going for his gun. Cover me, in case there's more."

I nodded and took his position. Gun drawn, Sam started up the embankment. Too late, I saw a flash of red, followed by several pops. Sam grabbed his side and staggered as he returned fire. Alarmed, I searched for the source of the shots.

Sam stumbled the last few feet to the SUV and collapsed against the tire.

"Is it bad?"

He pulled his hand away. Blood soaked his shirt, just under his vest.

"Did you get a look at who shot you?" I reached into my pack and pulled out a t-shirt, wadding it into a ball. Sam took it from me and pressed it against the wound.

"Female. Redhead." Sam's breath came in short gasps.

Spots swam before my eyes. *A redheaded female?* My stomach felt as though it dropped to my ankles.

"Tall?"

Sam nodded.

"Sam, remember the woman I was talking to outside your room at the motel?" Our eyes met. He nodded, slowly.

"Kate, Give it up, honey." Red's Southern drawl sliced through the air. "You're only prolonging the inevitable. The sooner you die, the sooner he can get to the hospital. I've got no quarrel with him. In fact," her low chuckle drifted the distance between the two trucks, "if he doesn't die right there, I'd surely like to give him the old college try myself."

Sam's breathing sounded ragged. The blood had soaked through the t-shirt and was spreading. He keyed the mic, but I could tell he was losing strength, fast.

"Three-thirty-four. Officer down—"He drew in a shallow breath.

I leaned closer. "Sam's hit bad. The shooter's a white female, red hair, and still alive. Not sure about the other two." I risked a look around the bumper at the first man Sam shot. He lay on the ground. "I think one's dead."

"Roger." There was a brief pause, then Angela's voice crackled over the radio. "Medic ETA is twenty minutes. Backup in fifteen. Hang in there, Sam."

Gunfire erupted from both sides. The second gunman was mobile and they'd split up. Sam propped himself on one elbow and aimed toward the front of the vehicle. I scrambled to the rear, gun drawn.

"I really don't want to have to kill you both," Red called, "but I will. Give it *up*, Kate." She sounded annoyed. "We've got plenty of time before anyone shows up, and old Mario here is up and running. That makes it a rather unfair advantage, being that your lovely deputy's been shot."

I turned to Sam. His complexion had turned a pasty white. Beads of perspiration dotted his forehead. Damn it, he was not going to die. Not because of me. They wanted me dead, not Sam.

I scanned the terrain, looking for the nearest route with some kind of cover. It looked like there was a faint animal trail through the trees to my left. Except for a short section at the end, most of the path would be hidden from view by the SUV. I chanced a quick look at Sam. He glared at me and shook his head. I put my finger to my lips.

And then I ran.

SIX

I plowed through the foot-deep snow in a crouch. As soon as I broke cover, gunfire erupted behind me. The bullets hit the snowy ground with a thud and a slight hiss. I pushed on, zigzagging through salmonberry and hemlock saplings, before making cover in the woods. Red's shouts followed me in, but then grew faint.

I continued running, my focus on clearing whatever got in my way, whether jumping over old nurse logs or dodging devil's club. I kept an eye out for some place to hide, but short of digging a snow cave there wasn't a lot to choose from.

The lack of direct sunlight created confusing shadows, and I slowed to keep from stumbling, but also to remember the terrain. Even with the waning light, my tracks would be easy enough to follow. I needed to obscure my footprints.

Further in, I spotted a downed hemlock and headed the other direction, toward a deep ravine filled with snow covered bunchberry and red alder. A dead tree branch allowed me to scrape a path further down the ravine, making it look like I'd continued into the brush. Then I retraced my steps to the hemlock. I skirted its circumference and climbed onto the dead tree from the back.

The trunk was wide enough for me to comfortably walk along its length a few yards. About two-thirds to the end, I climbed back down. Then I picked up a cedar bough resting on the ground and dragged it behind me, stopping every few feet to obliterate my footprints. It might not fool anybody during daylight, but it would slow them down for now. I just hoped it would be enough.

For cover, I ducked under the branches of a good sized cedar.

It didn't take long before I was no longer alone. What at first glance appeared to be deep shadow soon became a moving, amorphous shape lacking features. The shape drew nearer, coalescing into Red's tall silhouette, gun drawn, slowly following my trail.

I waited for the other gunman to show; apparently he hadn't come along for the ride. I hadn't heard gunshots. My stomach twisted. Was Sam dead? Had the loss of blood been too much? Or did one of them sneak up behind him and finish the job with their bare hands? Sam wouldn't be able to fight anyone off—not in his weakened condition. I should have stayed by his side.

The thought paralyzed me.

A twig snapped.

She walked within a yard of me and approached the ravine, dropping to a crouch to inspect the trail I'd left. I stepped from beneath the cedar and slipped up behind her. Her head and back snapped upright, aware of my presence. I stopped, knowing I'd have to shoot her, wondering if there was some way out of it.

"Drop your gun."

She relaxed her shoulders and shook her head as she tossed her gun to the side, her laughter barely audible.

I stiffened. That was too easy.

"Your boy's dead, Kate. Died alone." She made a *tsking* sound. "That makes three dead, all because of you, sweetheart. That make you feel special?"

I closed my eyes as pain and despair threatened to engulf me. Sam was dead. I hadn't done anything to help him. Then what she said registered.

Three?

"What do you mean, three?" Dread burned its way into my gut. *Who else?*

"Well," she said, as she slowly rose to her feet and pivoted to face me, "first Lester, then Joe, and now Sam."

Lester must have been the man I saw murdered at the trailhead, but I had no idea who Joe was.

Red smiled, her white teeth clearly visible in the rapidly waning daylight. "Aw, honey, you look confused. Maybe I can clarify things. You see, Les was the private investigator I hired to find you. My guys hit him on the trailhead. I certainly didn't mean for you to see that happen. If you hadn't, we could've been done with this little ordeal days ago." She sighed and stretched her neck from side to side.

How the hell did she know I'd seen the hit on the trail? She was playing for time. I wondered if the other gunman was trying to find his way back here. Probably would take him a while, since he was wounded. I moved to one side and turned slightly so I could get a better look in the direction of the highway. Red did the same, matching me.

"Who's Joe?" I aimed the gun at her head. She flinched, recovered.

"Chief Miller, of course."

I must have looked as shocked as I felt, because she grinned, a calculating gleam in her eye.

"He was a hard one to break, I must say. Good thing Mario had some training in enhanced interrogation techniques." She paused, a look of distaste on her face. "I had to leave. It got pretty messy. That ol' boy had some *cajones*, let me tell you. Even Mario mentioned it." She watched me closely, reminding me of the fox I'd seen on the trail. Then she reached inside her coat.

Fuck it.

I shot her. Twice.

Once in the shoulder, once in the foot. I wasn't about to play rabbit.

She dropped to the ground, her screams echoing through the still forest. I stood quietly and watched her rock back and forth, hunched over, gripping her shoulder with her good hand.

"Twice?" she growled, tears streaming down her face. "You had to shoot me twice?"

"You're lucky I didn't know Lester." I held out my hand. "Give me the gun- butt first."

Red shook her head, incoherent from the pain. Swatting her hand away, I reached inside her coat, found what I was looking for and stepped back, her second gun in my hand. It should have bothered me that I felt no emotion after shooting someone. A numbing mindlessness had taken over.

I slid her second gun into my waistband, picked her other one up off the ground, and started to walk away.

"You can't just leave me here—" Her voice held a note of panic.

"Don't worry. I'll let them know where to find you. It's the least I can do," I replied, trying to smile, not quite able to pull it off.

My feet felt as though encased in cement as I made my way back to the road. About half way there, the sound of a helicopter beat time through the forest, echoing off the nearby mountain. Had it only been twenty minutes since I ran? It seemed like a year.

I reached the edge of the forest and stopped, taking in the chaotic scene: sirens, lights, the *thwap* of helicopter blades, uniformed personnel everywhere. Medics had already lifted Sam's body onto a stretcher, and had yet to pull the sheet over his face. I wanted, needed to see him once more. The force of the emotion rising in my throat threatened to overwhelm me, but I stopped myself before the tears came.

I threw Red's guns on the ground and, hands raised, stepped into the open. A trooper near Sam was the first to notice. He yelled to an officer closer to me, pointing my direction. They both turned and drew their weapons, followed by every single law enforcement officer on the scene. I braced for the bullet that would come if I couldn't convince them I was surrendering.

"Hands on top of your head. Lace your fingers," the first officer shouted. I did as I was told.

"There's a gun in my waistband. I threw two other weapons on the ground, over there. The other shooter's about a hundred yards in, shot twice." I nodded behind me toward where I'd left Red. "I'm Kate Jones. The officer on the stretcher—" my breath caught, "was transporting me to the airport when we came under fire."

The officer pulled the gun from my waistband, gripped me by the arm and roughly turned me around. Then he patted me down. Although, I'd have to say 'patted' would be too gentle of a description.

"You have I.D.?"

"It's in my backpack next to the truck."

"Hey, Gordy." The young officer yelled to the first guy who'd seen me, and waved him over.

Gordy said something to the medic who was in the process of strapping Sam's body into the stretcher, and then strode down the ditch toward us, a frown etched across his face.

"Her ID's in the pack by the truck. She says the other shooter's in the woods, shot twice."

Gordy turned and whistled at a group of three officers hovering around the dead gunman next to the black pickup. He met them halfway, had a conversation, and then came back to where I was standing. Two of them took off into the woods while the other moved toward the SUV, apparently to check my I.D.

"Can I put my arms down?" I asked.

"Not until we hear back from Quilete with a positive description."

"The officer—" I started, but stopped, choking back the tears. "Sam killed the guy on the ground. There was another one. I wounded him, but he was mobile."

"Yeah, we got him. He lost a lot of blood, but he'll be able to stand trial." Gordy looked at the younger guy. "She have a gun?"

"Here." He showed Gordy. "The other shooter's weapons are over there, in the snow."

"Can I see Sam before you—you know, before you take him?"

"Like I said, not until we have word from—" He stopped mid-sentence as a young trooper ran up to where we were standing.

"It's her. Quilete I.D.'d her, says she was on her way to the airport."

Gordy glanced at me. "You can put your arms down now."

Relieved, I lowered my hands. "Can I?" I asked, nodding in Sam's direction.

"Make it quick. We need to get him loaded as soon as possible."

"Why?" Sam was dead. It's not like time was of the essence. I doubted even Alaska State Police were that efficient.

Gordy looked at me like I was seriously dense.

"They have to get him to the hospital, like, now, or he's not gonna make it."

"He's still alive?" My heart leapt in my chest.

"He won't be if he has to wait much longer."

I didn't hear what he said next. I was halfway up the other side of the ditch before he finished. I reached Sam and took hold of his fingers. His hand was cold and his eyes were closed. He opened them at my touch.

"Hey."

"Sam. You're still here." My eyes filled with tears.

"Barely."

"Ma'am, we have to go." A medic tapped me on the shoulder.

"I know. Hold on, please? Just for a second?" I turned to Sam. Happiness coursed through me. Sam was still alive. A brief smile appeared on his face, then was gone. It looked like he'd been given a shot of something.

"Kate—the dream—" He tried to swallow, but couldn't. "I dreamed I was shot. That's why I didn't tell you. Didn't want you to worry."

"Was it the redhead?"

He shook his head. "The only thing else I remember is a red fox and the number fifty-eight."

"Time to go, Ma'am."

With difficulty, I stepped away from the gurney as the medic wheeled Sam to the waiting helicopter.

"Excuse me, Kate?"

I turned at the sound of my name. It was the younger state patrol officer.

"I'm going to need to get a statement from you."

"Sure. No problem." Distracted, I watched the medics load Sam onto the chopper and close the door. I wiped at the tears in my eyes and brought my attention back to the trooper.

He shivered, once, as he pulled out a form and a pen.

"Sure gets cold when the sun goes down, doesn't it?"

"Yeah," I said. The helicopter rose, hung suspended for a moment, then headed toward Anchorage. "Dead of winter's like that."

THE END

Death Rites

ONE

North Shore, Hawaii

The walkway between the vendor stalls was packed with tourists and locals. Fresh pineapple, bread, organic meats and cheeses, soap, lawn ornaments, t-shirts; you name it, it was offered here. Being around people was like handing a lifeline to a drowning woman. I hadn't realized how starved for conversation I'd been. I suppose talking back to the television the night before should have given me an idea.

I filled my bag with fresh greens, a couple of bars of soap and some banana bread. The dark clouds building in the distance and uptick in humidity signaled one of the North Shore's infamous winter squalls was about to unleash its fury, so I reluctantly headed for my scooter. I had just locked my purchases in one of the side compartments when I felt the skin on the back of my neck crawl. I turned, but saw no one.

Shaking it off, I straddled the scooter and started the engine. As I began to ease out of my spot, I glanced behind me toward the crowded market. A dark haired man stared back at me, his arms covered in what looked like prison art. At least, I thought that's what he was doing. He wore a pair of dark sunglasses and might have been looking at something else. He took out his cell phone, punched in some numbers and turned his back. Despite the eighty-plus degrees I felt a cold chill skitter down my back.

Stop it, Kate. You don't know he was looking at you. Have you ever seen him before? Besides, you don't look like Kate anymore. He couldn't possibly know it's you. As for recognizing him, it was hard enough to identify someone in sunglasses. I didn't get a decent look at the tats so positive identification wasn't possible. Salazar's people used very specific designs. They'd be easy to recognize.

Unless he was an outside pro.

I kept an eye on the rear view during the ride home.

***

"So then what happened?" Gabby leaned forward, absorbed, and took a drink of his Mai Tai, complete with a tiny yellow umbrella.

"They airlifted Sam to Anchorage, took my statement and brought me to the airport in time for my flight." Touching down in Honolulu felt like a death sentence reprieve in paradise.

"Did Sam survive?"

"He's on life support." I stared into space, despair being the only emotion I allowed myself to feel these days. True, Sam had lived, but not long after I left Alaska, they found Chief Miller's naked body in a shallow grave near an abandoned cannery. He'd had several digits severed and other things done to him I didn't want to think about.

Gabby patted my arm and signaled the waitress to bring us two more. I looked at my almost empty Piña Colada. Maybe getting drunk would help.

Then again, maybe not. I needed my wits about me. Stumbling back to my rental didn't sound like the smartest thing to do at this point.

Not with a price on my head.

The outdoor patio at Panama Bob's glowed with lit tiki torches that ringed the perimeter and candles flickering in hurricane lamps on the tables. The soothing waves of the Pacific Ocean crashed nearby, and the temperature hovered around a balmy seventy-eight degrees. I was dressed in less clothing than I'd ever had to wear in Alaska, and the geckos had taken care of the mosquitos.

Any other time, this would be a perfect evening. Tonight's meal was marred because it would be the only time I could allow the two of us to be together. Gabby was a breath of fresh air, even though I vowed to never get in touch with him. I told him it wasn't safe, but safety never mattered to Gabby.

I did.

For five years in Alaska I'd been able to live a somewhat normal life, but eventually my luck ran out. Salazar's killers found me, and Sam and I had barely escaped with our lives. I didn't want to tempt fate.

"And why aren't you staying at my place? You know I cook a mean pineapple chicken." Gabby's wiry gray hair surrounded his tan, unlined face like the mane of an old lion. Apparently he'd had a little work done since I'd been gone. His diametrically opposed love of the sun and endearing vanity required some serious upkeep.

"Legendary. I know, and I'm heartbroken I won't be graced with your culinary excellence." I pushed my drink to the side and leaned forward, resting my hand on his forearm. "Gabby. I want you to listen to me. It's too dangerous. You will die. This isn't a joke. If you're in the way when they try to kill me the next time, they will kill you."

Gabby waved my warning away. "Oh, pish. I'm not worried. My home is protected by ancient Hawaiian gods and one big motherfucking Samoan named Henry. I don't think there'll be a problem." His eyes locked onto mine. "How many times have you been out since you got here?"

"A couple of times. Mainly at night."

Gabby raised his bushy eyebrows, reminding me of a middle-aged Einstein.

"No wonder you look so pale. How about I have Henry meet you in the morning with a couple of surfboards? He loves being on the beach at dawn and he can look out for you at the same time." He leaned back in his chair. "Not going out in daylight's a tad vampiric, if you ask me."

"Cautious, Gabs, cautious. I've got a fenced backyard, so I can get out and play. I just want to limit my exposure to old friends."

Gabby smirked. "Tell me. I had a hell of a time finding you. If it wasn't for Jimmie, I probably wouldn't have known you were in town."

"Jimmie?"

"You remember, the guy who owns Smiley's? His delivery kid mentioned a good looking brunette had rented McCallum's old place. One who had a tat of Honu on the back of her shoulder. Said it was some of the best ink he'd seen. He also liked the saying underneath it.

Reminded him of Star Wars. That's when I knew it was you, brunette or not."

So that was how he'd found me.

I really needed to get the thing removed. I'd gotten the tattoo the last time I'd been on the North Shore. The sea turtle was small, but unusual. The most distinctive part was the intricate Maori design along its shell with the words 'There is no try' written below. I'd never run across another one like it. Not a good thing when you're trying to hide from contract killers.

Gabby swatted at a fly buzzing near his drink. "Come and stay with Henry and me. I know he'd love to take care of you, not to mention I'd have somebody to talk to about something other than surfing."

"Sorry. Much as I'd love to, I won't chance putting either of you in danger. It's risky enough being here with you."

Gabby sighed. "Fine. But I'm going to dog you anyway. That way, it's all on me. You can't feel responsible if anything happens."

I couldn't tell if it was heartburn from the drink or anxiety that lanced through my stomach.

Maybe coming to Hawaii hadn't been such a good idea.

TWO

The next day I woke up early and headed for the water. I'd rented a two bedroom house in the middle of several other rentals a couple of blocks off the beach, and getting to the ocean was easy.

Gabby was right. I couldn't live my life in fear. Besides, this time of day was probably safer than most.

Not that killers slept in.

The way I figured it, the less crowds, the more I'd notice anything unusual. Of course it cut both ways—it would be harder for me to blend.

The pink light of dawn still painted the sky even though two days earlier the Kona winds had changed direction and the fog from Kilauea, or vog, cast a thick, gray haze over most of Oahu.

The beach was all but deserted. I counted two surfers bobbing in the waves forty or fifty yards out. I dropped my towel on the sand and left my t-shirt on to cover my tattoo. The gentle breeze and soothing sound of the waves reached deep, melting the layers of cold steel I'd had to create inside of myself in order to function. The numbing grief of these past weeks slid away, my tears mixing with the ocean as I dove beneath the surface.

North Shore waves were known to be challenging for swimmers during the winter, but this morning they lifted and dropped me in gently rolling swells. I swam from one end of the beach to the other, enjoying the sun as it crested the palms, sending golden beams to dance on my skin through the salty water. I floated further from shore and was rewarded with the company of a playful pod of spinner dolphins. I stopped to watch them, treading water, wishing the moment would go on forever.

Too soon, their fins sliced past me as they swam toward open ocean and I was once again alone. I stayed out a while longer, hoping they'd make another appearance, but they were long gone.

My arms started to tire, and I swam for shore. As I walked back to my towel I passed a good looking surfer with his board, headed for the water. He smiled and tipped his head my direction. I returned the gesture, noticing the carved necklace he wore; mother of pearl glinted from inside intricately carved bone. A complex tattoo decorated his bicep, running along his shoulder onto his chest. It had the hallmarks of Hawaiian, rather than Maori or Samoan, art.

I turned to watch as he launched himself into the surf. Like most in the sport, he had a powerful stroke. Unlike many except the best, his movements had an elegance that made it seem effortless.

The beach had started to fill with people. I made it back to my towel and shook off the sand, ready to leave. A large shadow near a bench by the tree line caught my attention. I smiled to myself as I sauntered over to say hello.

Henry's brilliant white teeth glowed in his koa-colored face as he enveloped me in a fierce, Henry-style bear hug, lifting me off my feet. I hugged him back, laughing as he lowered me gently to the ground.

"Aloha, Sistah. Good to see you."

"Thanks, Henry. You too."

He picked up a strand of my hair and inspected it. "How long you been a brunette?"

"A while." His comment reminded me of the reason I'd changed my look. Salazar's people would be looking for a blonde. Henry lowered his large, sequoia-sized body onto the bench. I hesitated, then took a seat next to him.

"You can't be seen with me, Henry. I told Gabby it was too dangerous."

Henry snorted. "You think I'm afraid of a bunch of gun-toting *cholos*?" He shook his head as though the idea was ludicrous. "Besides, Gabby told me you and your police bruddah took care of the three they sent after you. Ain't that easy to find good killers."

"I don't think it'll be too hard for the guys that are after me. Their business is like an incubator for murderers." That was a sobering thought. "How'd you know where to find me?"

Henry laid his massive arm across the back of the bench and squeezed my shoulder. "Gabby told me to watch you. I been hanging outside your place every morning. Got your board in the back of the truck." He nodded behind us, toward the parking lot. "You sure took your sweet time, woman. I knew you'd go crazy if you didn't get to play in the water."

I smiled, remembering the times I pestered Henry to teach me to surf. He finally relented and I learned the basics, but only because he had the patience of a saint. After that, you couldn't keep me out of the water.

Henry's attention had drifted to the dozen or so surfers waiting for the next set. A large swell rose behind them, and several kicked out to catch it, riding its face as it curled in on itself. Two dropped out right away, followed by all but one, who rode it to the end. It was the surfer I'd seen earlier.

"Who's that?"

"Local dude. Name's Alek."

"He's good."

Henry turned and gave me an appraising look. "You thinkin' about maybe gettin' some?" He made a lewd gesture and wiggled his eyebrows.

I laughed. "Yeah. Maybe I should sleep with every good looking guy I see? Get a little reputation going?" I shook my head. "What is it about you islanders? All you think about is sex, surfing, food and sex."

"Don't forget sex." Henry's dimples deepened with his grin.

I leaned over and kissed him on the cheek. "God, Henry. It's good to see you." I stood and pointed my finger at him for emphasis. "But stop shadowing me. It's not safe. I don't know what I'd do if anything ever happened to you or Gabby." I reached over and ruffled his hair, then turned and left him sitting on the bench.

***

After a couple of days and a heavy dose of cabin fever, I stopped worrying about my imminent death and reacquainted myself with Oahu by taking a drive around the island. On my way home, I stopped at Ted's Bakery to pick up lunch and a chocolate haupia cream pie. Addiction would be too tame a word to explain my deep, burning need for the coconut-chocolate cream slice of paradise. That, warm water and hot sand, and I'm done.

As I stood in line waiting my turn, I had the peculiar feeling of being watched again. I scanned the other customers, but no one maintained eye contact. My turn came and I stepped up to the register to pay for my order. A few minutes later, my sandwich in hand, I stopped at the refrigerated case to pick out a pie. As I reached for the container, I realized someone was standing directly behind me. Thinking it was someone who wanted the pie as much as I did, I slid one out and backed away to give them room.

"Is that all for you?"

It was the surfer from that morning. Alek. His disarming smile caught me off guard and I felt myself getting flustered.

"No. Yes. Yeah. I guess you could say that." I smiled, regaining my composure.

He raised his eyebrows as he looked me over. "Seriously? You can eat a whole pie and still look that good? Damn." He grinned. I couldn't help but grin back.

"Weren't you on the beach the other morning?" he asked.

"Yep, that was me." My attention shifted to the carving he wore around his neck. "That's quite a piece."

"Thanks. It's my talisman." He held it up and pointed to a graceful curve, punctuated by the mother of pearl. "This signifies water."

I leaned in closer to get a better look. He smelled good, like coconut and citrus.

"And this," he indicated the other side of the carving, which resembled a gecko, "represents the earth. The bird figure is a symbol for air."

"It's well done." I'd seen the cheaper, machine-carved pieces, and this was definitely not one of those.

"I've been doing it since I was a kid."

"You carved this?" I'd met several carvers, and most of them were well into their forties before they'd made it to this level. Not to mention the best ones tended to be islanders, backed up by centuries of tradition. Alek couldn't have been more than early thirties, and had light brown hair and blue eyes. Not exactly native. He looked down at both of our sandwiches.

"You need company? It so happens I'm free for the next hour."

We got lucky and scored a table outside. A party of four left as we walked out the door. I took it as a good sign.

"I'm Alek," he said, extending his hand.

I shook it and replied, "Evelyn." I'd been reading a book with a character named Evelyn. It sounded good.

"Well, Evelyn, do you live around here?"

I shook my head and took a bite of my sandwich. "Nope. Just visiting." No sense giving him any ideas. It was nice to have an actual conversation with someone, though. And, having lunch was innocent enough. I doubted he'd end up dead because of one meal.

The conversation acquired a kind of patina it might not have, had I been willing to see him again. One habit I'd developed in response to living life on the run was a profound appreciation for simple, everyday events. Like a friendly conversation with someone interesting.

And, not being dead.

After we finished our sandwiches, I offered him a slice of pie. He squinted at me, tilting his head.

"Are you sure? I wouldn't want to deprive you."

I rolled my eyes and pushed the piece toward him. "Like I need the entire calorie-laden goodness. Take it."

He laughed and dug in.

"How long have you lived around here?"

Alek shrugged and took a sip of his soda. "Most of my life. I lived in California until my folks died. A family friend took me in until I could make it on my own. I've been here ever since."

"What made you get into carving?"

"My uncle. Actually, he's the family friend, but he's like my uncle. He's one of the best. Comes from a long line of carvers."

That explained a lot. "I noticed your tattoo this morning. It's Hawaiian, right?"

He nodded and sat up straighter. "Yeah. The design belongs to my uncle's family."

As we continued our conversation, I deflected most of his questions about me with generic answers. He seemed to accept my reticence to talk about myself.

When we finished our slices of pie, he picked up the paper plates and napkins and threw them in the trash. Then he walked back to the table and sat down next to me. Close. He exuded a raw sexuality that almost took my breath away. I moved a few inches away from him, trying to get some distance. After what happened with Sam, I wasn't in a rush to get involved with someone new. The pain that came with leaving him in Alaska was too fresh, too raw. I'd have to wall myself off from those kinds of emotions for now.

Or maybe forever?

"When can I see you again?" he asked.

"I'm sure we'll see each other at the beach."

"No, I mean something more. Give me a time, a date, your phone number. Whatever."

"Sorry," I replied, shaking my head. "I'm not staying long. I'd like to keep things as uncomplicated as possible. Let's just leave it at this. I enjoyed talking with you. A lot. Okay?"

The surprised expression on his face morphed into what appeared to be anger. Then, like an afternoon squall it passed, replaced by a crooked grin. He shrugged.

"Hey, no problem." He rose and flashed the Hawaiian *shaka* sign. "See you around, Sistah."

"Sure."

He walked away, nonchalant and gorgeous. I'd bet women rarely turned him down. It was probably a shock to his system. I decided I'd be better off avoiding him.

He didn't appear to take rejection well.

***

As I walked back to my scooter, a melancholy feeling drifted over me. It wasn't until I'd stashed the rest of the pie in the side compartment that I realized how much I needed to hear Sam's voice. I pulled out my phone and called information for the hospital's number.

"Hello?"

He sounded far away, weak. I hadn't expected him to answer so quickly and I didn't say anything, too surprised to speak.

"Hello?"

"Sam?" I forced his name out before he hung up.

"Kate—is that you?" He coughed away from the phone. It sounded like he was in a tunnel.

"You're out of ICU."

"They put me here yesterday."

Silence. There was so much to say, but how could I say it? I needed to be there, to touch him, see him, make him know how much he meant to me. How the hell do you do that over a phone?

"Sam, I-" I stopped, unable to form the right words. Tears welled in my eyes and I blinked them away. "I—"

"Are you all right? Nothing's happened?" He coughed again and I heard the bed squeak in the background.

"No, no. I'm fine." I needed something safe to talk about, but this wasn't anywhere close to safe. "How are you feeling?"

"A little messed up from the drugs, but so far, so good."

"I'm so sorry, Sam." I stifled a sob, hoping he didn't hear it.

"Kate—" He sighed. "It's not your fault. It was just bad timing."

"No, it wasn't bad timing. It's my past and I have to take responsibility for it. If I hadn't moved to Alaska and stayed so long in Quilete, this never would have happened to you."

"It happened. Don't look at the past. Always look forward. If it wasn't you, it would have been something else. My job carries risks. You were worth the risk."

I closed my eyes and tried to imagine myself there, next to his bed. I'd never wanted to be anywhere so desperately.

"Kate."

"What?" It was becoming difficult to hold back my emotions. I'd need to hang up soon.

"We'll see each other again."

He stated it so plainly, as if it were fact. I opened my eyes as a glimmer of hope emerged.

"I have to go." I wiped at my eyes with the back of my hand. "Take care of yourself."

"You too. Be safe."

Death Rites

I disconnected and stared at the phone in my hand.
I could never let anyone get that close to me again.

THREE

Later that afternoon, I sat in the shade of a palm tree in the backyard with a cold beer and the local newspaper. The headline caught my attention. "*Rare Tiki Statue Missing from Royal Hawaiian Museum— Grisly Murder Scene.*" I was halfway through the article when my phone rang. I checked Caller I.D. It was Gabby.

"Did you see it?" His breathless voice practically vibrated.

"You mean the article about the murder? I'm just now reading it."

"Oh. The murder. Yeah, that was a terrible tragedy, wasn't it? No, I'm talking about the statue. The *tiki* statue."

Gabby had a collection of rare Polynesian artifacts, many of them tiki related. He'd been invited to lecture around the world about the intricacies and meaning of the ancient carvings. I didn't understand much about tiki spirits, but didn't want to get on their bad side. I'd learned that inexplicable things happened when someone angered the gods of Hawaii. To a person who wasn't immersed in the culture from an early age, it was downright spooky.

The Hawaiians I met shrugged and couldn't exactly explain it. Not that they were inclined, anyway. They just chalked it up to the way of the gods.

"This is huge. The statue is one of the most important artifacts ever discovered in the area. It's been linked to the earliest days of Hawaiian settlement."

"Did you know the woman who was killed? I'm thinking that was an incredible loss for her family, as well as the museum."

"Sonya Farnsworth. I didn't know her well. She was a volunteer." Gabby's voice dropped an octave. "This stays between you and me, but the security guard who discovered the body showed up at my door late last night, completely freaked out."

"Yeah, seeing a dead body can do that to a person. You knew him?"

"We've known each other for years. But it was more than seeing a corpse. From what he told me, ritual torture was used."

The thought brought back unpleasant memories of Roberto Salazar. I shoved them deep, refusing to relive it. "Like satanic stuff, you mean?"

"Not exactly. That's the intriguing part. It has all the hallmarks of a secretive Hawaiian sect active centuries ago, Kate. The group was shunned by the Kahunas for their unrelenting use of torture. Ritual killings of innocents were used to test the loyalty of new members. Much like violent street gangs do today."

"Couldn't it have been the work of a street gang?"

"Why would common thugs steal an artifact? It can't be fenced. There's no monetary value, at least not to someone without the right connections. Plus, they would have taken more than just the statue. My radar says it was someone itching to revive the old ways."

"Unless someone with those connections hired a thug to steal the statue and suggested the torture might throw law enforcement off their trail."

"Possibly. I still think it has something to do with the sect. When George told me what he'd found, I got chills. His description parallels what little information I've come across."

"Isn't there a huge black market for artifacts? What would that piece be worth?"

"Priceless. I couldn't begin to put a value on it."

"They'd have a hard time unloading it with all the media attention."

"Exactly. Even more reason to assume it was the work of that type of organization."

"How did they make it through security? I would think they'd at least have been caught on camera."

"Nothing showed up on the monitors. Several statues were being restored away from the main building. No one knew except the restoration team and museum staff."

Gabby cleared his throat. "On another, more delicate subject, Henry mentioned you asked him to back off."

"I told you, that's non-negotiable."

Gabby sighed. "I only want to protect you. Henry's good at protecting. Use him."

"No."

"You're a stubborn woman, you know that?"

"So I've been told."

***

The next morning I drove to a different beach, hoping to elude Henry. When I swam back to shore and walked to my things, he was standing next to them, his surfboard by his side.

"You really have to stop, Henry." Working to control my frustration, I stuffed my towel into my beach bag without shaking it off, giving my camera and clothing a sand bath. Good thing I'd stashed my gun in an outer pocket.

"Hey now, easy, Kate." Henry patted me on the shoulder. "No worry 'bout me. I be fine. Can you think of anyone better to take on a contract killer?" He rolled his hips and flexed his biceps, reminding me of a comical Mr. Universe.

I had to laugh.

"I appreciate you looking out for me, but I'm going to have to leave Hawaii if you keep it up. And damn it." A heavy sigh escaped me. "I'm tired of running."

Henry watched me for a moment. Then he said, "Okay. I promise you won't see me again." He nudged me in the arm. "We okay?"

I looked up from wrestling with my bag. "We'll always be okay." I gave him a quick hug. "And it will be a long time of okay if you stop hanging out near me. At least for now."

"Gabby's not gonna like this."

"You don't have to tell him that you're not watching me. How's he going to know?"

"Yeah, I guess so."

His expression told me he was wrestling with the whole idea of going against Gabby's wishes, and I knew he'd probably end up telling him, anyway. I'd done everything I could to protect them, short of leaving Hawaii.

We said goodbye and I walked back to my scooter and stowed my things, feeling terrible for having to keep Henry at arm's length. Claustrophobia threatened to take over, and I felt like a rat in a box with no way out. First

153

Gabby, then Henry, Jimmie and Alek. There were too many people who knew I was here. Maybe it was already time to move on, before Salazar's or Anaya's goons caught up with me.

But where?

My mood grew dark at the prospect of always running, never feeling safe. Was there anywhere I could go that they wouldn't find me? Both Anaya's and Salazar's pride ran deep. Neither one would rest until they killed the gringa who stole their money. No matter that I did it to escape Roberto Salazar and his bloodthirsty world. I would have stolen the money anyway, even if I had known it was scheduled to be delivered to his cartel boss, Vincent Anaya.

I'd been that afraid.

In hindsight, it wasn't the best idea I'd ever had. Desperation-based decision making rarely worked for me, but I'd seen no other option. The day Salazar slit the throat of a friend over what was actually nothing, I knew it wouldn't be long before his paranoia seduced him to mistrust even me.

I removed my helmet from the back of the scooter and was about to put it on when I noticed a group of men staring at me from across the parking lot. Alek separated himself from them and strolled over.

"Hey, Evelyn."

My grip tightened on the helmet. How did he know I'd be here? This meeting seemed a tad too coincidental.

"What are you doing here?"

He shrugged, smiled. "I saw your scooter."

My scooter resembled a hundred other ones on the island. No odd identifying marks. "Who are your friends?" The four men stood near the concrete block restrooms, watching us talk.

He glanced at them. "The three on the left are my brothers, and the older dude's my uncle." He leaned in close and said, "They wanted to meet you."

"Why?" Was he serious? This sounded way too much like going home to meet the parents.

Alek's smile froze. "I told them about you. That you were new in town."

I strapped on my helmet and straddled the scooter. I was going to have to nip this non-romance in the bud. Before I could say anything, he grabbed the handlebars and stood in front of me, barring my way.

"Who's the big dude you were talking to?"

I shrugged, unwilling to get Henry mixed up in anything having to do with me. "No one."

"You hugged him. He must be more than that."

"Alek, who he is to me is none of your business. I told you, I wanted to keep things simple."

He frowned, the look of anger I'd seen at the restaurant rising to the surface. I laid my hand on his arm, hoping to calm him.

"I'd be happy to meet your family any other time, but I'm already late for an appointment."

He yanked his arm out from under my hand, his face contorted with anger. Alarmed, I started the scooter.

Then, as if I imagined it, his features relaxed and he smiled. Just like before.

"That's okay, I understand. I'll catch you later, Ev." He turned and swaggered back to his group, attitude dripping with every step.

I didn't wait to see his family's reaction.

***

On my way home, I stopped off at one of the shrimp trucks that dotted the Kam Highway along the North Shore, the incident with Alek replaying in my mind. How did he know where I was going to be that morning? And why did he want me to meet his family? The answers had the words "unstable" and "stalker" attached to them, and I wondered if I should move to another rental. The claustrophobia deepened the more I thought about his behavior.

I sat down at one of the picnic tables to wait for my order when I noticed an older Asian man dressed in a green Hawaiian shirt and cargo shorts staring at me from across the patio. His flip flops had seen better days and his wild gray hair stuck out in tufts. Gray-green eyes burned with intensity in a weathered face. I gave him a tentative smile, uncomfortable under his scrutiny. He continued to watch me until they called my order.

I grabbed a can of soda from the guy at the window and walked back to my table with a plate of garlic shrimp and two scoops of rice. Before I had a chance to peel the first one, the wild man crossed the concrete floor and sat down across from me. Not knowing what else to do, I held up a shrimp.

"Want some?"

He shook his head and smiled, revealing a gap where a couple of his teeth should have been.

"No? Mind if I eat?" I asked.

He remained silent, losing the smile and frowning as though concentrating. I ate a few of the shrimp, sucking the garlic sauce from the shells, wondering what the hell he was all about, when his eyes rolled back in his head and he let loose with a low moan—similar to a wolf howl, only not as on key. I glanced at the other customers, but no one seemed to care.

Then he started to pant. Like a dog.

I didn't want to stick around for the encore, and stood to leave when his head snapped forward.

"You the one," he hissed, spittle flying from his mouth onto the table between us.

I sat down and tried to remain calm, not wanting to aggravate him. I caught the eye of a woman sitting three tables down. She shrugged and turned back to her lunch. *What the hell?*

He closed his eyes for a moment and started to mumble to himself. His eyes opened to slits as he shivered from head to toe and began to make a clicking sound with his tongue. Then he leaned forward. I waited, not sure how to respond but ready to run if things got dangerous.

"No worry, Turtle Woman. I no harm." He cocked his head as though listening to something no one else could hear. Then he looked at me, his focus laser-like.

"Gods say you must accept Kamohoali'i. Do this, balance will return." He began to shake and put his head down on the table and moaned. I was ready to dial 9-1-1 when he looked up and pointed a gnarly finger at the sky.

"The headless Honu will show way. No be afraid."

Crazy boy leaned back, all smiles, apparently finished. Stunned, I wondered if it was safe to leave.

"Don't mind him. It's just his way." One of the cooks from the shrimp truck had come out onto the patio area and was bussing a nearby table. "The regulars are used to him. He means no harm. Do you, Ray?"

Ray nodded and smiled, then stood and shuffled off to sit at another table.

"Good to know." My knees turned to gel as I walked to the counter to grab a container to take my meal home. I'd seen some strange rangers in my life, but I didn't expect to encounter it in rural Hawaii. Central Park, yes. The North Shore of Oahu, not so much.

"Hey, Evelyn."

Startled, I turned.

And found myself looking directly into Alek's face. I almost lost my grip on the plate.

"Alek."

Clearly, this dude was stalking me. Anger fueled by fear rose in my chest. I didn't need this right now.

"I was hoping I'd run into you."

"You do know what you're doing could be construed as stalking, right?" I jerked open the container and dumped in the uneaten shrimp and rice, struggling to maintain control of my emotions. Closing the box, I strode past him toward the parking lot and my scooter. He put his arm out to block me.

I glared at him.

"I wanted to give you something." He reached into his pocket and brought out a small bone carving with a wrapped cord. He held it out, letting it dangle.

"It's for you. For protection."

I glanced at it and shook my head.

"I can't accept."

"Yes you can. It's nothing, really." His face fell and he looked down, avoiding my eyes.

Jesus, Kate. Just accept the damned necklace. He made it for you. And you sure as hell don't want to piss off this guy. You don't know what he's capable of. I forced a smile and took the necklace from him, holding it up to get a better look.

"Thank you." The carving was part-man, part-fish, with a divot removed from the figure's back and replaced with a red stone. It was well done, but not my choice of subject matter.

"I'm glad you like it. Would you like me to put it on you?"

"No, Alek. I'm going to leave now. And you need to stop following me. Let it go, okay?"

I searched his face, expecting to see a hint of the anger I'd seen earlier, but his expression betrayed only friendly interest. He moved aside with a sweeping hand gesture.

"Please, go. You looked like you were on your way somewhere."

I walked to my scooter and slid the box of shrimp into the saddle compartment. When I turned to see where he'd gone, I noticed the man Alek said was his uncle watching me from behind an old camper van. Alek walked up to him and said something, and they both turned to stare.

The uncle was the first to break visual contact as he opened the door and climbed into the van.

FOUR

Kate—" Gabby's voice cracked.

"What's wrong?" I clutched the phone, instantly awake and alarmed by the emotion in his voice. I glanced at the clock on my dresser—three a.m.

"Henry's—been hurt." Gabby choked out the words through gut-wrenching sobs.

"How? Where is he?" I pushed myself off the bed, pulled on a pair of shorts and t-shirt, and started hunting for a pair of flip flops. Dread filled my mind.

Not Henry.

"They're taking him to emergency. God, Kate. There was so much blood…"

"Where are you?"

"I—I'm just now leaving."

"Come and get me. I'll drive."

I drove Gabby's Jaguar like a mad woman to the hospital, ignoring stoplights and little things like traffic. Gabby didn't notice. He stared out the window, watching the car's headlights lick at the edges of the pineapple fields.

"What happened?"

160

Gabby looked dazed, the shock still fresh.

"I found him on the floor by the window. He'd been stabbed multiple times." A tear rolled down his cheek, breaking my heart. "Why would anyone hurt Henry?"

"It can't be anyone who knew him. We all love Henry." An idea I didn't want to acknowledge started to wind its way through my mind. "How did they get in? Isn't your house protected like a bunker?" Gabby had the best security on the market. Apparently, even that wasn't failsafe.

"As soon as the paramedics arrived, I checked the digital feeds before the police showed up. They'd been disabled. The police didn't find any signs of forced entry. One of us must have left something open."

Or Henry knew his attacker.

"Did they take anything?" His answer would tell me if the theory taking root in my mind had any validity.

Gabby nodded. "One of my rarest pieces—a tiki carving from the early fourth century."

That told me it wasn't any of Salazar's thugs. What would they want with a Hawaiian statue? Besides why warn me when they wanted me dead? It would give me a chance to escape. It took them five years to find me in Alaska. I doubted they'd risk losing track again.

The other possibility could be that Alek wanted to hurt Henry, that he thought we were together. Stealing the carving might have been an afterthought, maybe a ploy to throw off law enforcement. Stalkers could be seriously unhinged, especially when it came to jealousy. I'd had a girlfriend in college who'd been a victim. Her stalker didn't let little things like reality or the word 'no' get in his way. Alek's behavior didn't give me any reason to think he was stable.

But was he capable of trying to kill someone?

The hospital had the same death-and-detergent smell I remembered from my childhood. The nurse at the desk told us Henry was in emergency surgery, had been stabilized and would be moved to the ICU soon. Gabby and I found seats in the waiting room, prepared for a long wait.

An hour later, a doctor wearing scrubs and a weary expression approached. His nametag read Dr. Kamaka. He told us Henry was unconscious, but resting in the ICU.

"Unconscious? That's not good, is it?" Gabby looked stricken.

"He had a reaction to the anesthesia. We're monitoring him closely. We'll know more soon."

"Can we see him?" I asked.

Dr. Kamaka frowned. "You family?"

"Eh, bruddah, we closer than family," Gabby replied.

Minutes later Gabby was sitting by Henry's side, holding his hand like he alone could make him live, his face a mask of grief.

Henry lay on the bed, connected to an IV, monitors blipping steadily. His usual robust demeanor had been replaced by a shrunken copy of the big-hearted man. The skin around Gabby's eyes sagged, adding a century to his age. I walked behind him and started to rub his shoulders.

"He's going to be okay."

Gabby nodded as a ragged sigh escaped him.

After a while I talked him into walking down to the cafeteria to get a cup of coffee. The doctor had said he might remain unconscious for several hours, possibly days. We brought the coffee back to the waiting room and sat, mindlessly watching some God-awful reality show about people with big hair and even bigger egos.

"You don't need to stay. Take the car." Gabby held out the keys to his Jag.

"How will you get back?"

His eyes were filled with bleak determination. "I'm not leaving without Henry."

Before I left, I made a reservation for Gabby at a hotel nearby and asked him to call me if Henry's status changed.

On the drive home, I called my rental company to find out what else they had available. Since it was Hawaii's high season, they didn't have a vacancy until later in the week. I asked to be put at the top of their list for another place that wasn't on the North Shore. Running into Alek was getting old. Not to mention possibly putting old friends in danger.

Granted, I was just delaying the inevitable, but I didn't have a clue where to run next. The old Mexican shaman's prediction came back to me with a force I hadn't felt in years.

Apparently, the bad spirits weren't done yet.

***

Within days Henry rallied, gaining consciousness and improving to the point of being able to give a statement to the police. He hadn't seen his attacker, having been stabbed from behind. The police opened an investigation of the robbery-home invasion in connection with the theft at the museum. Now that Henry was going to be fine, Gabby was inconsolable about the loss of the tiki carving.

"That piece was my most exquisite, a representation of Kamohoali'i. It's irreplaceable." Gabby sat with his shoulders slumped on a bench outside the hospital.

"Did you say Kamohoali'i?"

"Yeah. It's the Hawaiian name for the Shark God. Why?"

"It's probably nothing, but the other day someone told me I should 'accept Kamohoali'i so balance will return.'"

Gabby straightened, his interest piqued.

"Was this person Hawaiian?"

"More Asian. He was older, wild-looking hair, ancient flip-flops."

"He doesn't sound like any of the seers I've met. What else did he say?"

"You mean there are others?"

"Seers frequently choose to live here. In the old days, you'd probably have called them priests or medicine men. Nowadays most people think they're mentally impaired." Gabby shook his head. "It's unfortunate. In the past, these individuals were given great respect within society. Now they're shunted off to the fringes."

"It was pretty bizarre, Gabs, although most of the folks didn't react—apparently, they were used to him. The cook told me he was a regular."

"Locals tend to be more accepting of unusual behavior. Live and let live." Gabby took out a pack of cigarettes, shook one free and lit it with a match.

"When did you take up smoking?"

He shrugged, exhaling an acrid blue cloud. "I've been stressed." He narrowed his eyes. "What else did this guy say to you?"

"That I was 'the one' and to trust a headless sea turtle." I probably remembered that wrong, but it was close enough.

Gabby sighed. "Well, that was cryptic, wasn't it?" He patted my knee. "I wouldn't worry about it."

"There is something I am worried about, though. A local guy, Alek, saw me with Henry the other day. He's definitely stalker material—follows me everywhere. I don't know if he's capable of stabbing anyone, but thought I should mention it. And, he's a carver. A good one."

Gabby took another drag of his cigarette and leaned back. "Have you told anyone?"

"I thought I'd let you know and you could do what you wanted with the information. I'm waiting to hear from my rental company so I can move to somewhere other than the North Shore for the rest of my time here."

"You mean you have an end date?" Gabby sat up straight. "You can't leave, Kate. I don't know what I would have done without you during this."

"If I don't, more bad shit will happen, I guarantee it." I tried to ignore Gabby's puppy dog eyes. "That's the way it is right now. I don't have a choice."

"There's always a choice, Kate."

"Not for me."

After he went back inside to check on Henry, I walked through the parking lot to the Jag, mulling over what he'd said. I wouldn't have noticed the dark-haired man sitting in a black, four-door sedan across the parking lot if he hadn't flicked a cigarette out the window, drawing my attention. A knot formed in my stomach. It looked like he had the same tattoos on his forearm as the guy I'd seen at the farmer's market. I squinted, trying to get a better look at him through the car's windshield. The engine started and he slowly drove out of the lot.

Same sunglasses. Same guy.

FIVE

I opened my eyes to the dark and froze, every nerve alert.

Someone's in my room.

Barely breathing, I strained to listen, calculating how to get to the gun under the mattress. Before I could make a move, a gloved hand clamped down on my mouth and a hooded figure straddled me, pinning my arms to the bed. I struggled to push him off, but he outweighed me by a good fifty pounds. Another set of hands slapped tape over my mouth, muffling my screams. They flipped me over and the one straddling me taped my wrists together behind me, then my ankles.

Fear taunted me for letting my guard down, not taking enough precautions.

They hoisted me off the bed and carried me out the bedroom door and down the hallway. I writhed and squirmed, using my body like a bad slinky, but their grip on me was too secure. They hiked me through the front door and down the two cement steps, then dumped me into the back of a SUV. One of them pulled a pillow case over my head and slammed the door shut.

Shit. The idea of praying to some Hawaiian gods for protection crossed my mind, not to mention the Hindu, Muslim, Christian and Buddhist deities.

Who were these guys? Salazar's thugs favored SUVs. Though they hadn't spoken yet, I wasn't convinced it had anything to do with Mexico. If it did then I'd be dead, not in the back of a truck, still breathing.

I was pretty sure hyperventilating was considered a form of breathing.

They got in the front and closed the doors, starting the engine. I tried to place the familiar scent of coconut and citrus, but couldn't remember where I'd noticed it before. Suntan lotion?

The driver made a left out of my driveway and then turned right onto the Kam. I paid attention to the turns to get an idea of where they were taking me.

Alert for any indication of who my captors were, I strained to hear them, but they didn't engage in conversation. Obviously, they weren't after money; they'd left cash on the dresser and my jewelry in the drawer. The thought of rape crossed my mind, but I pushed it away, preferring to believe they would have done it back at the house.

Did they think they could hold me for ransom? Only a few people had any idea I was friends with Gabby. The one person I knew on the island with any net worth, not many people realized how wealthy he really was. Most believed he lived on a professor's retirement, supplementing that with speaking engagements.

Death was the only other option. But why?

I curled into myself and leaned against the side of the compartment, not knowing what to do next.

About fifteen minutes later, the driver hooked a left toward the water. That narrowed it down. There wasn't a lot of room between the highway and the Pacific Ocean. The briny sea air drifted in through the open windows, replacing the coconut/citrus scent as we bumped along a rutted track. Neither of my abductors uttered a word.

We came to a stop a short time later. They killed the engine and I heard both doors open and close. I tensed as the rear door of the truck screeched open and one of them grabbed my legs. He slid me forward until my feet rested on the ground. Then he bent down and cut the tape from around my ankles.

"Walk."

The word had no discernible accent. They kept a grip on my arms and directed me where they wanted me to go, holding me steady when I stumbled.

We covered a few yards and stopped.

"Eight steps up." The voice was gruff, unfamiliar.

We climbed the stairs to the top and paused again. One of them pushed me forward.

"Six steps down."

I counted six stairs and stopped, waiting for direction. He grabbed hold of my arm and led me forward until my legs bumped against something covered in fabric.

"Turn around and sit."

I did as I was told. The pillow case came off.

Lit by a single lamp, I sat on an old chenille-covered sofa in a large room evidently being used as storage. Boxes, tarps, and miscellaneous tools littered the floor. Dampness permeated the air. There were three doors leading off of the main room. One had a padlock attached to it, while the other two were closed with no visible locks.

The man standing in front of me had dark hair and the beginnings of a mustache. He appeared to be in his twenties, was heavy set and wore board shorts and a t-shirt. We both turned at the sound of footsteps coming down the stairs. My second captor emerged from the shadow of the stairwell.

Alek.

SIX

My face must have registered the shock I felt. He walked over and pulled the tape from my mouth.

"Welcome to my home, Evelyn." He acted as though he just now noticed the other guy standing next to him. "This is my friend, Calvin. Calvin, this is Ev."

Calvin nodded in acknowledgement. I half-expected someone to walk in with a couple of beers or a tray of lemonade, make it a party.

"Alek. What are you doing? You've just committed a kidnapping. I'm pretty sure that's considered a felony in Hawaii. And," I focused on Calvin, "Calvin here would be considered an accessory. Also a felony."

Calvin shifted from one foot to the other and glanced nervously at Alek. Alek smiled and shook his head.

"You won't consider it kidnapping when I show you why you're here." He turned to Calvin and said something to him in a low voice. Calvin nodded and left the room, heading upstairs. Alek turned back to me.

"You're not wearing the necklace I gave you."

"I was in bed, Alek. I don't usually wear jewelry when I sleep."

170

His gaze lingered on my bare legs and swept upward, finally coming to rest on my face. Then he reached in his front pocket and pulled out the necklace. He must have taken it off my dresser.

"Well, you're not asleep now. Here—" He bent down and fastened the necklace around my neck.

Citrus and coconut.

"What's this about? Why am I here?"

Alek sat on the couch next to me. I moved away. He slid closer and stroked my thigh, watching my reaction. I stared back at him, not about to give him the satisfaction of seeing me flinch.

"You'll see. Just wait."

Alek stood and walked over to an older stereo stacked on top of a footstool. He turned it on and the velvety voice of John Legend flowed through the speakers, filling the room. Alek executed a smooth turn followed by a couple of exaggerated dance steps. He held out his hand, as if asking me to dance. I shook my head.

"Did you forget?" I leaned to the side to show him my bound hands. If I could get him to cut my hands free, I'd have a better chance of getting the hell out of there.

He danced over, his hips and shoulders taking on a life of their own. Was the guy completely detached from reality? Did he think I'd be won over by a couple of dance steps? My fear factor ratcheted up a notch. He was skirting delusional.

And dangerous.

He leaned down and I caught the glint of metal in his hand. My body tensed, hoping he'd go for the tape and not my skin.

"Lean forward," he said in a low voice.

He sawed through the tape on my wrists. I brought them around to the front and rubbed at where the tape had cut off my circulation. Then he grabbed my left wrist and pulled me to my feet. I slammed the heel of my right hand against his face.

Alek recoiled, holding his nose as blood gushed through his fingers.

"You BITCH."

His voice was behind me now as I raced up the stairs, headed for the door. I collided with Calvin coming up the outside steps. We both tumbled to the ground. Alek's voice reverberated from the basement.

"Stop her," he screamed.

Calvin shook off the collision and grabbed at me as I scrambled to my feet. I'd almost made it clear when his hand clamped around my ankle and he jerked me back. Landing on my hands and knees, the fall knocked the breath from my lungs. I dug my fingers into the ground, trying to stop him from dragging me toward the house.

Footsteps pounded down the steps as Alek ran out the door. I flipped onto my back only to have the wind knocked out of me again as he jumped on top of me.

"Get the tape," he ordered. Calvin climbed to his feet and ran back inside the house. Alek held his head back, breathing heavily. It didn't look like it was doing a lot of good. Blood still flowed down his face.

Calvin returned a couple of minutes later with an old t-shirt and a roll of duct tape. Alek tore the shirt from his hands and held it to his nose, trying to stanch the blood as he slid off me. Calvin took his place and proceeded to tape my wrists.

"Want me to do her feet?" Calvin asked.

"Wait until we get the bitch inside." Alek removed the t-shirt. "How does it look?"

Calvin frowned. "Broken."

"Fuck." Alek glared at me as he held the shirt against his face again.

Calvin stood and I struggled to a sitting position.

"You might want to get some ice on that. And a doctor wouldn't be a bad idea—"

"Shut up, or you'll be the one who needs a doctor."

"Listen, Alek. This has gone way too far. You need to let me go. Now."

He turned to Calvin. "Let's get her inside. I need a beer."

They lifted me to my feet and dragged me up to the front door and back down to the lower level, shoving me onto the couch. With Calvin left to guard me, Alek disappeared into one of the rooms for a moment, returning with two beers. He handed one to Calvin and took a drink from his.

"We'd better tie her up if you're going to keep her here." Worried wouldn't begin to describe the look on Calvin's face.

Maybe I could use that to my advantage.

"If you do, it'll just compound the crime, guys." I looked pointedly at Calvin. "This will mean years, buddy. Think about that. Handsome man like you, I bet you'd be pretty popular in prison."

"I said shut it. Don't listen to her, Cal." Alek took another drink of his beer and wiped his mouth with the back of his hand. Cal began to pace. Alek stared hard at him, and he stopped.

A few moments ticked by before Alek's expression softened.

"We got off on the wrong foot, Ev. I'm sorry. I only wanted to show you something I've been working on." He reached for my hands and pulled me to my feet. "Come with me."

"What do you want me to do?" Cal played the heavy well, next to Alek's sleek persona.

"Stay out here, in case she runs." He glanced at a baseball bat standing in the corner. "Use that, if you need to."

Quite the romantic.

Alek led me across the room to the padlocked door and unlocked it with a key from his front pocket. He pushed the door open, flipped a light switch and stood aside.

Spots illuminated three large wooden statues in various stages of completion in the middle of the room. A layer of saw dust covered the floor. Off to the side was a table with several smaller pieces. He walked to the table, motioning for me to follow him.

"This is the one I want you to see. They chose me for the honor."

Alek held up a carved statue about eight inches tall, made of what looked like bone. It resembled the photograph I'd seen in the newspaper story about the museum theft.

Alek stole the statue?

Did he kill, too?

"Is that what I think it is?"

Alek beamed, his smile of pride tracing a cold path down my spine.

"I'm supposed to recreate it, exactly."

"What will you do with the original?"

"They're going to give it back, as soon as I'm finished."

They. Maybe Alek hadn't killed the volunteer.

"Who are 'they'? Did you steal the statue?"

He scoffed at the question. "No. They didn't want to chance my getting caught. They used somebody else, someone with more experience."

Relief swept through me, although it was short-lived. Alek placed the statue back on the table.

"Pretty cool, huh?"

"Are you serious? Alek, someone died because of this."

"They lost their life, true, but they should be proud of their contribution. The ancient rites were followed. It's the only way to restore the balance."

Restore the balance? Hadn't Crazy Ray at the shrimp truck said something about that?

"Who thinks balance needs to be restored? What does that mean?"

Alek sighed as though speaking to a child.

"So much development on the aina—the land—has ruined things. The old ways need to be honored, or the spirits will do it for us." He shook his head, concern evident in his face. "It won't matter who you are, then. Everyone will die. The gods have much power. You've seen what Kilauea can do. It will be much worse, unless we fix things." He bowed his head. "It's a deep honor to be a part of righting old wrongs."

He replaced the tiki carving on the table and took me by the arm to stand in front of one of the large statues.

"This is a statue of Kamohoali'i, the Shark God. He is the father of Nanaue, the figure on your necklace, and one of the most powerful gods in the islands. My uncle says he will finish this one soon, and we'll be able to hold the sacred ceremony. " He pointed at the other two statues. "That is Kane, Bringer of Light, and the other is Ku the Hawaiian God of War." Alek reached up to stroke my hair. "His wife was named Hina. She was a goddess, like you."

I jerked my head away.

"This has gone far enough, Alek. Let me go. I'm not your Hina, not by a long shot." My anger got the better of me and I continued, my voice dripping sarcasm. "And you're certainly no Ku."

At first, Alek looked surprised, but that was quickly replaced by a tightening of the skin around his mouth. His eyes darkened, the anger I'd seen before beginning to build in intensity.

He grabbed me by the arm and threw me against the wall. I struggled to maintain my balance as he advanced, fists curled, ready to strike. I widened my stance, went into a crouch and charged him head on, taking him by surprise. He fell backward and slammed into one of the large statues, knocking it over with a crash. I turned and ran.

I'd almost made the stairs when Cal grabbed me. He held me in a grip so tight I could barely breathe.

"That's it. We pau." Alek had picked himself up from the floor and was in the process of righting the statue. "I've done everything I could."

"What are you going to do with her?" Cal's grip tightened as I struggled to break his hold.

"Lock her up. We'll wait until my uncle gets home. He'll know what to do."

***

The moonlight against the statues cast eerie shadows across the sawdust covered floor. At least the shapes were discernible. Cal had re-taped my ankles and left me sitting propped against the far wall, in the dark.

Death Rites

No water. They must have figured I wouldn't be there long. I wasn't sure that was such a good thing. Alek's uncle was an unknown quantity. Best case scenario, he'd be horrified at what Alek had done and release me.

Yeah, and I had a knack for attracting the right people.

Who was I kidding? Alek screwed me the minute he showed me the statue from the museum, and compounded that by locking me in the same room. No way to deny knowledge of its existence. Not to mention admitting he knew who killed the volunteer.

I was dead.

A heavy hip hop beat from upstairs reverberated through the ceiling, punctuated by the occasional sound of laughter. Apparently, Alek and Cal had continued the party.

Knees up, I pushed at the floor and slid up the wall to a standing position. I stopped short as the hot sting of something sharp pierced through the thin material of my t-shirt. Alek had checked the area for tools before he left, but apparently he'd missed something else. I arched my back and elbowed my upper body away from the wall. On closer inspection, it turned out to be the point of a nail protruding from the paneling.

Maneuvering into position, first I worked on poking through the tape covering my wrists. Once the nail went through, I pulled up, trying to rip through it. One thing about duct tape: it's elastic. It took several attempts before I'd achieved a small tear near the edge.

Focused on freeing myself, I failed to hear the door open. When I realized someone had entered the room, I looked toward the door and froze.

Alek stumbled across the room and stopped directly in front of me, the smell of alcohol thick.

"You don' un'erstan' anything." he slurred.

I turned my face so I wouldn't have to breathe the fumes.

"You're Hina. You an' I will rule the islands after the ceremony." He caressed my face with clumsy fingers all the while swaying on unsteady feet. I kept my head turned away.

He lost his balance and staggered against me. Too late, I tried to sidestep him, but he'd grabbed onto my t-shirt. He lurched past me, ripping the material, only to catch himself with a hand on the wall. Alek turned and stared at the rip in my shirt, now barely covering my shoulder.

He stepped closer, hooked a palm behind my neck and pulled me toward him, whispering, "My Hina."

The smell of stale booze turned my stomach. Saliva dribbled from the corner of his mouth. I arched away from him, but he was too strong.

Then Alek's eyes drifted past me, his expression replaced by one of surprise. He let go of my neck.

"Dude, you're here." He stepped toward the door. "I told her—"

"Go to bed, Alek."

The quiet, steel-edged voice gave me goose bumps, and not the good kind. I turned my head to see who had walked in.

Alek's uncle.

SEVEN

Aw, man, no way. She'll come 'round, I know she will."

"Why is she here?" His fierce expression made my throat dry. This wasn't somebody's happy Uncle Bob.

"I just wanted her to see..."

"Go to bed, Alek," his uncle said, again. This time there was no mistaking the intent.

Alek mumbled something unintelligible and stumbled out the door. His uncle gave the room a cursory glance. Then he turned his attention on me.

I didn't like the look in his eyes.

His hand closed around my upper arm like a steel band. He lowered his head, pulled me toward him and threw me over his shoulder. I screamed and kicked, but the man was built like a bull. He handled me as though I weighed nothing.

He carried me outside and into a garage a few yards from the house, and dumped me hard onto the floor. I remained quiet, trying to conserve energy. Then he disappeared behind a bulky, tarp-covered shape in the middle of the structure. I knew I wouldn't have much of a chance if I stayed where he left me. With some difficulty, I wriggled onto my forearms and knees. Stretching forward with my arms, I dragged my knees up to meet my elbows. Stretch the arms. Slide the knees forward. Stretch the arms. Slide the knees...

A pair of feet wearing leather flip flops came into view. I sighed in resignation as he lifted me by the armpits and dragged me across the dirt floor without saying a word. This time, he deposited me on a wooden chair on the far side of the garage. I tried to stand up, but he shoved me back.

He held a long white rope in both hands. I was sure he was going to use it to strangle me. Instead, he wrapped it around my torso, securing me to the chair.

Next, he walked over to the tarp and began to pull it off. Underneath was a gleaming wooden outrigger canoe resting on a trailer. Intricately rendered Hawaiian designs decorated its hull and spars. The outrigger itself was attached by complex knots of interlocking rope.

"It's beautiful. Did you use Koa?" Couldn't hurt to try flattery.

He registered surprise at my question.

"You know traditional style?" He rolled the canvas and stowed it on a shelf next to the wall. "Yeah, wood is Koa. Everything follows ancient ways." His eyes glittered in the harsh light from the lone bulb hanging from the ceiling.

It has all the hallmarks of a secretive Hawaiian sect active centuries ago, Kate. The group was shunned by the Kahunas for their unrelenting use of torture. Gabby's words came back to me like a blow to the gut. A cold sweat began to form on my skin despite the humidity.

Alek's uncle walked outside, swallowed by the dark, leaving me alone. I tested the ropes holding me to the chair, but he'd done a good job with the knots. I needed to get out of there, now, or I wouldn't see morning. I heaved myself forward, onto my feet, but found the chair too heavy for me to move anywhere. With a frustrated sigh, I leaned back and the chair fell into place with a thud.

Not seeing any other options, I worked at the tape around my wrists, pulling and stretching, trying to get it to split further. I was rewarded with a slight ripping sound, but still had a long way to go.

A few minutes later, the large SUV Alex had used to transport me backed into the garage to the trailer and stopped. The taillights went out and the driver's side door opened with a metallic screech. I peered around the end of the canoe to get a better view of the driver. Alek's uncle climbed out and shut the door. He carried a full-length, opaque dry cleaning bag much thicker at the top than the bottom.

I'd thought shoulder pads had died with the eighties. He opened the back door and carefully laid the bag across the seat. Straightening, he backed away from the vehicle, carrying something with both hands. As he drew closer, I realized it was a large stone with a carved channel around its circumference, which he carefully placed inside the canoe. Then he tossed in what looked like a crudely fashioned rope.

He walked next to the chair and untied me. Then he picked me up, kicking and squirming, and carried me to the front of the SUV, opened the door and slid me into the passenger seat. His face like stone, he reached over and buckled my seatbelt.

"Thanks. Wouldn't want to go through the windshield or anything."

181

He grunted and shut the door. Grateful he hadn't noticed the tear in the tape, I leaned forward and continued to work on it.

A few minutes ticked by, and the tape gave a little more. The driver's door opened. I eased back in my seat. He climbed behind the wheel and started the engine.

We pulled out of the garage and drove past the house, toward the water.

"Where are we going?" I asked. Whether he told me or not was irrelevant. Although it was a long shot, establishing some kind of connection with him might humanize me to the point of creating guilt or remorse at what he planned to do.

Pretty obvious this wasn't going to be a romantic flotilla for two.

He stared ahead, his expression unreadable.

"You find out. Be patient."

"Patience has never been my strong suit." I glanced out the window, trying to gauge where we were. In case I got lucky. The stars glimmered brilliantly this time of night. It looked like someone had scattered a handful of white diamonds across inky black velvet. It occurred to me it could be the last time I'd see a starlit night.

"What's the significance of the statue? Couldn't you have Alek recreate the piece from photographs?"

Alek's uncle shook his head and muttered, "Stupid Haole."

"Yes, I'm ignorant. Enlighten me. Obviously, your secret will be safe."

Especially if he succeeded in my death.

He tapped a finger on the steering wheel, apparently considering if he should answer. Then he sighed deeply.

"Old stories say we must use original carving. Has powers reproductions do not possess."

"Did you have to kill the volunteer? What was her name, Sonja?"

"A blood sacrifice was needed. Her soul is now at peace."

"Didn't sound like a real peaceful way to die. In fact, it appeared to be especially brutal."

He glanced at me. Even in the dim light of the dashboard, I could see anger flash in his eyes.

"How you know how she died? It wasn't reported. Even Alek doesn't know details."

I shrugged, not wanting to implicate Gabby or the night guard. "I heard it from someone."

He grew silent, his mouth set in a firm line. Good. Maybe now he had a small, niggling doubt about who knew what.

Not that I had any illusions it would prolong my life.

The truck broke through brush on each side as the road ended and we rolled onto a sandy beach. The smell of the sea air that once brought peace now held an element of threat. He maneuvered the truck so the trailer was as near to the water as possible, then climbed out and shut the door.

Again, I leaned forward to wrestle with the tape around my wrists. Alek had wrapped them several times which made it difficult to rip through each layer. I glanced out the back window to watch what the uncle was doing. The red glow from the taillights gave him a demonic look.

The hand crank clanked as he slid the canoe off the trailer. I knew he'd finished when the back of the truck jacked upward. I leaned into the seat as he opened the rear door to grab the dry cleaning bag. He walked to the front of the truck and stood in the headlights with his back to me and slipped the plastic off, letting it fall to the ground. He pulled off his shirt and wrapped himself with what looked like an ornate, floor-length cape with a hood. When he turned, my breath caught in my throat.

The headlights acted like floods, throwing their light upward, illuminating the powerfully built man, completely swathed in multicolored feathers. The hood obscured most of his upper face and had a kind of a wooden beak projecting from the top.

It was like being in a bad Indiana Jones movie. Only he was no Harrison Ford.

He walked to the passenger door and opened it, reaching across me to unbuckle the seatbelt and lifted me out of the truck.

I wasn't about to make it easy for him and started to scream, kicking and squirming. He lost his grip with one hand and my feet hit sand, but he recovered quickly and grabbed my legs. I kept fighting him, but his hold on me wouldn't break. The cloak opened, exposing skin. I leaned forward and bit down hard on his left pectoral, drawing blood.

He grunted and dropped me. The blow from his fist felt like the business end of a baseball bat. I may have seen stars earlier, but it was nothing compared to this.

He lifted me again and continued down the beach to the canoe, depositing me in the bow. Vaguely aware of my surroundings, I watched as he reached between my legs for the end of the fiber rope, which he tied around my waist. The boat swayed and jerked as he pushed the outrigger into the Pacific and jumped in as we cleared the sand. Still close to shore, I considered throwing myself overboard, but thought better of it. I didn't know what the other end of the rope was tied to. If it was the boat, I'd be dragged underwater. Not a pretty death.

Alek's uncle faced forward, picked up a large paddle from the side and pointed us out to sea.

Death Rites

The waves buffeted us with spray until we cut through the break. The ocean rose and fell in large swells, but the canoe rode them gracefully. The fog in my brain began to lift and I slid my feet across the floor, trying to find the end of the rope. My toe came up against the large rock he'd put in earlier.

Shit.

He was going to throw me over the side. Weighted down by the rock, I'd sink straight to the bottom.

While I watched him retreat into a semi-hypnotic state from the rhythm of paddling, I worked at the tape with renewed panic, trying to keep from alerting him by moving too much. I didn't know how far from shore he intended to go, and glanced at the sky to memorize the position of the constellations to fix the location of the beach in my mind, but I couldn't see much.

The lap of the waves against the hull drowned out the ripping sound of the tape as one side of it finally gave way. I didn't dare peel the rest of it off my wrists, sure he would notice. I'd just have to finish in the water. My ankles would need to stay taped for now.

I'd lost track of time. Fifteen minutes or an hour could have passed. All I knew was that we were far from shore when he laid the paddle down. I tried to relax so my muscles wouldn't cramp when I went over the side.

Easier said than done.

Alek's uncle stood to his full height and spread his arms wide, lifting his face to the sky. An unearthly, guttural sound was followed by chanting in a language I couldn't identify.

The boat moved in a seesaw rhythm from the swells. The cloak looked top heavy.

Timing the next wave, I lunged forward and caught him at the knees. He lost his balance and fell backward over the seat, toward the stern. I misjudged the angle, intending to shove him overboard. His hand clamped down on my shoulder and I felt a sharp pain as I crashed into a brace. We both struggled to our knees.

He didn't look happy.

I fought to rip the rest of the tape off my wrists, but he had me by the throat before I succeeded.

"Fucking Haole, you're going to DIE." He spit out the words, the force of his anger rolling off him in waves. I twisted and jerked, trying to shake him off, but I was losing strength from oxygen deprivation. Desperate, I opened and closed my mouth, my lungs screaming, but couldn't take a breath.

Then, the pressure eased. I sucked in a gulp of air and sank back. Alek's uncle bent down and grabbed first the stone and then a chunk of my hair and yanked us both upward.

The canoe crested a swell and dropped into the trough. Behind him, a dark wave materialized, growing in size and height until it dwarfed the outrigger. The dark mass hovered for an instant before crashing over the gunwales.

The water was a shock. I surfaced outside the canoe sputtering, tasting salt. My flesh stung as I ripped the last of the tape off my left arm. I waited for the weight of the rock to pull me under, but nothing happened. The fibrous rope lay draped over the edge and disappeared into the boat. Apparently the boulder stayed put when we were washed overboard. Flipping onto my front, I started to breast-stroke toward the outrigger.

Behind me, the sound of splashing and sputtering told me Alek's uncle was nearby. I put more force into my stroke to create a larger gap between us, hoping the feathered cape would drag him the hell under.

Death Rites

My progress was slow with my ankles taped together, and it worked against me. He seized my left foot and I screamed. With no time to take a breath before my head went under, I clamped my mouth shut and kicked. My heel connected with something solid, and he released his grip. Adrenaline punched through me and I carved into the water, propelling myself forward. I swam to the outrigger and gripped one of the spars, leaning backwards in the water to lift my bound feet to the first rung.

Using what upper body strength I had remaining, I hoisted myself to sit on the lower brace. Alek's uncle sounded close. His breathing came in explosive puffs, punctuated by excessive splashing. Panicking, I slid my feet under me and gripped the next rung, leveraging myself upward.

The top edge was within reach when I felt the boat tilt. He'd lifted himself onto the lower rung, his face a mask of fury. He no longer struggled with the weight of the cape, having evidently discarded it. I threw myself forward, but he grabbed my legs and dragged me down. I fell on top of him and both of us hit the water.

No match to his superior strength, dread spiraled through me as he gripped my hair and held me under.

Black spots crowded my periphery. Struggling to remain conscious, I clawed at him in panic, knowing it would use any remaining oxygen, but unable to stop. Every part of me screamed to open my mouth, my nose, to breathe.

He released his grip. I broke the surface with a deep gasp.

Wiping wet hair from my face in order to see, I realized his focus had shifted. The whites of his eyes gleamed in the moonlight as he tracked the dorsal fin now circling him. I froze, scarcely breathing, one hand on the outrigger. His head just above water, he began to chant in a low voice, the sound mixing with the gurgle of the waves.

Our panicked splashing must have attracted the predator, continually looking for prey.

The fin cut a second circle around him, then disappeared below the surface. Alek's uncle stopped chanting as he twisted 360 degrees, searching for the creature. Using strength I didn't know I possessed, I climbed out of the water, onto the outrigger and dragged myself up and over the side, into the boat. I peered over the edge and waited.

The first strike jerked him under like the float on a fishing line, cutting short his cries. The water roiled for a moment and then calmed. Seconds later, his arm shot up and hit the water with a slap. His head emerged, his mouth open in a scream.

The shark dragged him down a second time. I remained still, my heart pounding, and waited for him to resurface.

He didn't.

My fingers curled around the necklace I wore with the protective carving, and I offered a silent prayer of thanks.

My heartbeat now close to normal, I hinged forward to pick at the end of the tape around my ankles. Funny how much easier it was when I had the use of both hands. Weak from the loss of adrenaline, it took time and determination to unwind the tape and free myself.

The swaying of the canoe reminded me that I was at the mercy of the current, and it didn't look like I was headed for land. Wearily, I lifted the paddle and attempted to steer toward shore. If unsuccessful, there was no telling where the boat would end up. The most likely scenario would be several miles out to sea.

Death Rites

Or possibly Tahiti.

Sighting on a pinpoint of light, I struggled to bring the canoe about and head that direction. At first awkward, I eventually relaxed into a kind of a rhythmic stroke. Exhausted from my ordeal, I was in no condition to single-hand a power boat, much less an outrigger canoe, and I fatigued quickly. I stopped to take a break, resting the paddle on my knees.

I'd always felt insignificant when I looked at the stars. This was an entirely new kind of insignificant: adrift in the Pacific Ocean under a huge expanse of night sky. No one knew where I was, or even that I might be in trouble. The thought of hungry sharks gliding silently under the canoe filled me with anxiety.

Get ahold of yourself, Kate. Closing my eyes, I tried to imagine myself reaching shore. I remembered a technique that Sam taught me to calm the mind and took a few minutes to use it. Despair visited again at the thought of him lying in a hospital bed in Anchorage. His brush with death was the direct result of being assigned to protect me. He'd gotten in the way of Salazar's killers.

Never again would I feel his arms wrapped around me, or hear him whisper my name. Sam meant safety and I didn't get to be safe. Not unless and until I was able to rectify my past.

That was if I made it back to land.

Movement in the water caught my eye. Heart in my throat, at first I thought the shark had returned, but a turtle's head popped above the surface. He watched me a moment, then submerged and floated away, popping up again a few feet from me.

Honu.

Hawaiian legend said that friends and relatives long gone took Honu's form and often came to the aid of

189

someone familiar to them in a previous life. Crazy Ray's prediction popped into my head. "The headless corpse, Honu will show the way. Do not be afraid."

A fresh sorrow overwhelmed me at the thought of my old friend, Eduardo. They'd found him in the Sonoran desert, decapitated for his role in my rescue, and for implicating the two men I'd spent the last five years of my life trying to avoid. I mentally shook the thought away.

Everyone who tried to help me ended up dead or close to it. This was not a good way to make friends.

A few minutes later, the turtle's head and hard shell surfaced next to the canoe. I stopped paddling and watched. He ducked his head and turned the same direction he'd gone before—far to the right of the light I'd been using to guide me. He stopped a few feet away and raised his ET-like head above the water as if to say, "Follow me."

To my weary mind, it was as good a sign as any. With new resolve, I followed him toward shore with thoughts of Eduardo to keep me company.

EIGHT

Honu stayed with me until I was close to shore, then disappeared below the surface.

With my last shred of energy, I timed the canoe's landing on the beach so the waves wouldn't pulverize it, and me, to matchsticks. Exhausted, I dragged myself out of the boat onto the sand and remained still, breathing heavily from the exertion. Tempted to lie there for a week, I knew I needed to go to the police and tell them where to find the statue from the museum. Preferably before Alek or Calvin sobered up and realized Alek's uncle hadn't returned.

With a groan I rolled onto my hands and knees and stood. I attempted to brush the wet sand off my ass, but was only mildly successful. What the hell did it matter, anyway? I probably looked like a half-drowned hooker, wearing nothing but a ripped t-shirt and panties.

With a deep sigh, I headed across the beach toward the highway. The terrain altered from sand to tufted mounds and long, coastal grasses, but wasn't too difficult to navigate. Before long I reached blacktop.

Even though it was still dark, I recognized the stretch of highway as being within a mile of Gabby's place. I started to walk, staying on the road to avoid stepping on rocks with my bare feet.

I'd passed a couple of driveways and had just rounded a corner when headlights slid into view. Hoping they hadn't seen me, I slipped into the shadows. Sure that hours had passed since Alek's uncle took me for a cruise, I didn't trust that Alek and Calvin weren't out looking for him.

The car drove past a little too slowly for my peace of mind. I stayed in the shadows the rest of the way to Gabby's.

About twenty minutes later, I reached the iron gate leading to Gabby and Henry's ultra-modern waterfront mansion. It took longer than it should have, but I'd been paranoid about letting anyone see me. I thought there wouldn't be much traffic this time of night, but I'd seen several cars. The same dark sedan passed me more than once.

I pressed the buzzer on the entry box and stood where the camera could see me.

"Kate? Is that you? Oh my God. Get in here."

I'd never been so glad to hear Gabby's voice as at that moment. There was a click and the gate swung open. I walked through and headed down the driveway.

Gabby met me halfway with a blanket in his arms, wrapping it around my shoulders. He hugged me to him as we walked the rest of the way to the house.

"What the hell happened? How did you get so wet?" He glanced at my bare legs. "And so naked?"

I sighed. "Long story. Suffice it to say, I know who stole the statue."

For once, Gabby was at a loss for words.

"What? How?"

"I'll fill you in on the way to the police station. Better yet, can I use your phone? I want to make sure they arrive at the scene before Alek wakes up."

"The guy who was stalking you is involved?"

"Yeah. He kidnapped me and his uncle tried to drown me in some freaky ritual."

"Are you hurt?"

"Nothing that a good night's sleep and a couple dozen Piña Coladas wouldn't take care of."

Arriving at the huge portico, we climbed the steps to the front door and entered through the tall, etched glass double doors. The dull pink of dawn was visible through the floor to ceiling windows directly in front of us.

I sat on one of his white Danish Modern couches, realizing too late I probably should get a towel to sit on. "Sorry about the leather."

Gabby waved my concern away. "Forget it."

Drained, I leaned my head back and closed my eyes for a moment, relaxing into the soft leather.

I was safe now.

"Did you see the statue?" he asked.

"The one from the museum, yes. Along with three life-sized wooden tiki gods and some other pieces, although I didn't see anything that looked like the carving you described stolen." I lifted my head and gave Gabby a look. "Probably should have gone to the police about Alek the second time he showed up unannounced."

"What happened to his uncle? How did you get away?"

"I'm pretty sure he's dead, although I didn't see the body." I stopped, the effort to speak too difficult. Better save it for the statement to police. "Can we talk about this later? I'm exhausted."

"Of course. I'll call the police. They should be here in less than ten minutes. You need to rest and figure out what you want to say to them. Besides," he nodded at me, "you're in no condition to go out in public."

I didn't have the strength to argue with him. He was probably right. A see-through t-shirt and panties would undoubtedly distract from the message.

"How's Henry?" I felt a momentary pang of guilt for not asking earlier.

"He's doing fine. Be as good as new in a matter of weeks. I'll tell him you're here and get you something to wear."

He climbed the stairs, leaving me alone with my thoughts.

If my luck held, Alek and Calvin most likely passed out from the party last night, and wouldn't notice if Alek's uncle didn't show up right away. The police visit would surprise them before they realized they'd need to get rid of the evidence.

The only question remaining was where they put the statue. I doubted Alek's uncle would have taken it with him when he took me for the boat ride. The risk of loss was too high. It had to be somewhere in the house or the garage.

I waited a few more minutes, but when Gabby didn't return, I went over to the phone on the side table behind the couch, picked up the receiver and hit the call button. There was no dial tone. I set the handset down.

At that moment, Gabby walked in the room carrying an armful of clothes which he put down on the couch.

"Your phone doesn't work," I said.

"A previous guest ran up a huge long distance bill, so I disconnected that one. Don't worry, I already called police. They should be here soon."

"Can I see Henry?"

Gabby frowned and shook his head. "He's pretty groggy from the drugs. In fact, he's probably already asleep again. You're going to stay here, right? You can see him after he wakes up."

I considered changing into the pair of running shorts and button down men's dress shirt, but decided against it before the police showed up. I wanted to make sure I didn't mess with any evidence they might need.

Gabby walked outside onto the patio. The sky had turned an orange-hued pink.

"Kate, come out here. You need to see this."

I crossed the living room and joined him on the patio. He pointed to a spot several yards out on the beach. I didn't see anything unusual.

"What?"

"Can't you see it? Here." He guided me so I stood in front of him. I stepped back when I noticed a deep, freshly dug hole in front of me.

"What are you going to use that for?"

"It's for roasting game. I'm hosting a celebration later."

And then he pushed me.

***

I came to as something struck my face.

The taste of dirt made me gag. I tried to draw in a breath, but inhaled soil. My ankle throbbed with pain. Disoriented, I tried to move my arms.

They wouldn't budge.

I opened my eyes. Horrified, I realized I was covered with dirt.

Someone is trying to bury me alive.

I screamed for Gabby.

His face appeared over the edge of the deep pit, a silhouette against the deep glow of the sunrise.

"Gabby, thank God, they're trying to bury me alive. Help me—" The plea died in my throat as he disappeared.

A clod of dirt rained down on my head. I closed my mouth. Another followed. I shook my head, trying to dislodge the clumps.

"What the fuck are you doing?" I shouted, panic flooding me. Frantically, I tried to rock back and forth to free myself.

He peered over the edge.

"Things have gone too far." Gabby leaned against the shovel and stared down at me. "There's no other option. I wish there was."

"Henry," I yelled, "Help!"

Gabby shook his head. "He can't hear you. I gave him an elephant's dose of nighty-night drops. He wouldn't understand."

"Your neighbors will hear me." Fear morphed into confusion and anger. Why did he want to kill me?

More dirt. I shook it off and blew at the soil next to my face.

And screamed again.

Larger clumps of dirt fell onto my face. Apparently he'd decided to push it in, rather than use the shovel.

I screamed until my voice grew hoarse.

As the earth rose around me, I closed my mouth and stretched my neck to the breaking point, straining to keep my nose clear so I could breathe.

Gabby's elaborate front door chimes echoed through the back yard.

"Fuck." He poked his head over the side again.

"Apparently, we have a visitor. You just sit tight while I get rid of them. Probably some fucking religious groupies," he muttered. The shovel hit the ground with a clang and he disappeared.

Never before had I hoped so fervently for the followers of Jehovah to be at the door. Twisting my head and shoulders, I continued trying to create space around me Eventually, I was able to rock my upper chest free and sit up. I dug the rest of the way out of the dirt, flipped onto my hands and knees and, favoring my swollen ankle, stood on one leg.

To my left and about three feet above me, a thick root jutted from the vertical wall of dirt. I hobbled over, grabbed onto it and pulled myself upward. Using the toes of my good foot, I kicked at the dirt, creating a toehold to boost me closer to the top. The pit was narrow enough that I could brace my back against one side with my good leg against the other and slide upward.

Digging my fingers into the side of the pit, I inched toward the top, praying whoever was at the door would keep Gabby busy for a few minutes longer.

I stretched my hand over my head and grabbed hold of the edge, hoisting myself up and over onto my stomach. I stood and stumbled past the outdoor table and chairs with their bright red cushions, and hobbled around the side of the house, desperate to catch Gabby's visitors before they left.

The front corner was close. Just a few more feet and I'd be in full view of anyone parked in the circular driveway.

A hand clamped down on my shoulder and Gabby spun me to face him. I ducked, pivoting on my good leg, and landed an elbow to his solar plexus. He doubled over with a groan. I turned away, but he grabbed my wrist.

Struggling to wrench free, I stopped short when I saw the gun in his hand. In all the years I'd known Gabby, I'd never before seen the raw emotion now visible on his face.

"Why, Gabby?" I choked out the words, despair ripping a hole through me.

"I couldn't let them destroy the island, Kate. Don't you see? The only way to save her is to return to the old ways. To bring back the balance with the ancient death rites.

"I can't let you go to the police." He raised the gun, pointing it at my head. "I'm sorry, Kate."

I squeezed my eyes shut, tensing my body for the agony that would come.

Gunfire split the early morning stillness. I felt no pain and opened my eyes in time to see Gabby fall to his knees and drop, face forward, to the ground. Behind him stood the dark haired man with the tattoos I'd seen at the hospital. He walked over to where Gabby now lay, and leaned over to feel for a pulse. Apparently finding none, he rose from the body and holstered his gun.

"Who are you?" My voice shook.

"A friend of a friend who asked me to look out for you." He glanced down at the body then back at me. "Sorry I didn't get here sooner. You're a hard woman to track. I wouldn't have known where you were except I saw you walking on the highway. But when I turned around, you'd disappeared. I knew you and this guy were friends, so it was the logical destination. It took a while to get through the gate. It has some kind of scrambler and wouldn't open right away."

He moved to the side with my bad ankle and wrapped my arm around his shoulders. I'd been wrong about the tats. They were Hawaiian, not prison art.

"You okay to walk?"

I nodded. "Yeah. I need to call the police."

"Already done. Let's get you back inside and off that foot while we wait."

With his help, I managed to make it into the living room and sink gratefully into a couch.

Henry.

"There should be a big guy asleep upstairs. His name's Henry. He's been drugged. Would you mind checking on him?" Even with what just happened, I couldn't believe Gabby would do anything to hurt him. My heart broke when I thought about how Henry would react to Gabby's death.

And why he died.

"Sure." Tattoo Man raised my feet and slid a footstool under them.

"Can I ask you a question first?"

He nodded, waiting.

"You said you were a friend of a friend. Can you tell me who? I don't know that many people in Hawaii."

A slight smile curved his lips as he turned toward the stairs.

"He said to tell you 'mile marker fifty-eight.' That you'd know."

Sam.

NINE

Dozens of travelers milled past as Henry enveloped me in a bear hug. We were standing on the sidewalk outside the airport. It was busier than I'd seen it in a long time, as if everybody chose that day to leave paradise.

He stepped back, holding me at arm's length.

"Are you sure you can't tell me where you're gonna end up? I might want to leave this place, see another part of the country." Henry smiled his easy, friendly smile, but his eyes lacked the usual sparkle.

He'd taken Gabby's death hard, but his betrayal harder. Everything he'd come to know and love about the man had been shattered. Gabby hadn't meant for Henry to get hurt when he'd paid Alek's uncle to rob the house and take the carving; somehow, though, he'd mixed up the date and he and Henry didn't go out for the evening as planned.

None of that mattered to Henry. Gabby's role in Sonya Farnsworth's murder, albeit by proxy, tore a hole through Henry's gentle heart. The worst part in his mind was that Gabby was willing to kill me to keep his role in the murder/robbery quiet.

The same day Gabby was killed, the police arrested Alek and recovered the statue, returning it to the museum to be restored. As for Alek's uncle, there had been no report of a body washing up on shore. Someone had, however, fished a strange-looking cape made of rare bird feathers out of the ocean while diving. A lab was conducting tests on it in case it held any significant historical value.

"God, Henry, I'm going to miss you. I promise I'll keep in touch, send a postcard, maybe." I wiped at a tear threatening to slide down my cheek. "I wish I could tell you where I was going, but I can't. I just know I don't feel the same way about this place. I need to move on."

"All the bad guys are either dead or in jail. Why leave now?"

"It's more a feeling I have. I've learned to trust my instincts, and they're telling me it's time to leave."

"If you weren't safe out in the middle of Nowhere, Alaska, where can you go?"

"Exactly." Little soldiers of despair began their painful march through my brain, tearing apart my resolve. It took concentrated effort to push past the ache, to focus on the here and now and what was possible.

"Well, then. The way forward is clear." Henry drew himself up to his full, impressive height.

"Oh?"

"We'll have to have them all killed."

It took several minutes for my laughter to subside.

"Oh, Henry, thank you. I needed that more than you know."

"I'm here for you, babe."

We hugged once more before I walked through the doors into the airport. I turned left and headed for the first ticket counter I came to. The woman behind the counter smiled.

"May I help you?"

"I need a ticket."

"No problem. Where would you like to go?"

I scanned the destinations listed on the reader board behind her. What the hell, I thought. I'd never have any peace until I confronted my past.

"One way ticket to Phoenix, please."

THE END

Touring for Death

ONE

Getting up at the crack of dawn shouldn't be in anyone's job description.

At least, not anyone who has a life.

I guess that says a lot about me, since I was at the crest of Black Top Mesa waiting for the sun to rise.

My name is Kate and I guide Jeep tours in the high desert of northern Arizona. Of all the jobs I'd had in the years since Mexico, being a tour guide in red rock country fit.

I'd just finished telling an old Navajo legend to the two couples on the tour – a retired Army Colonel and his wife, their daughter and her husband—when the sun reached the summit on the far side of the canyon. The intense colors bled into the landscape, and the gnarled mesquite trees and dusty jojoba bushes surrounding us morphed into ancient beings come to life.

The Colonel and his wife snapped some last minute photographs while I stowed leftover Danishes and the remaining coffee in the Jeep, and everyone piled back in to continue the tour.

"Where to now?" the daughter asked.

"Now we head back down the trail and follow along the dry creek bed. Keep your eyes open for wildlife."

I turned the Jeep around and started down the steep grade, avoiding the largest ruts.

"Everybody belted in?" I glanced in the rear view mirror.

"Ma'am, yes ma'am," came the reply. I smiled. Ya gotta love the armed forces.

We started to gather speed and I shifted into low. We'd traveled a few yards when an ear-splitting screech severed the early morning quiet. The Jeep shuddered.

I pumped the brakes—my foot hit the floor. Confused, I tried again.

Nothing.

The Jeep dropped into a free fall.

Panicked, I grabbed the gear shift and tried to ram it into low. The shriek of metal on metal pierced the air. I tried second.

Third.

We hurtled downhill like a rodeo clown on a pissed off bull. The Jeep hit a rut and tore the steering wheel from my hands.

The Colonel lunged across the console to grab the wheel. I held on with my left hand and used my right to haul on the emergency brake. No luck. The Jeep careened down the almost vertical trail.

We hit something big and rocketed sideways onto two wheels. Someone in the back screamed.

I steered to the left to angle the path of the Jeep, missing boulders and barreling between piñon pines. Branches slashed at the sides. I tore through every bush I could find, trying to slow us down.

The Jeep jerked to a stop about fifty yards from the base of the trail.

"Everyone out!"

I didn't have to say it twice. The group scrambled clear.

"Is everyone all right?" I checked to see if any of the passengers had sustained contusions or broken bones. Aside from being badly shaken, the Colonel's wife and daughter and her husband appeared to be okay. The Colonel, on the other hand, looked furious. His red face and flashing eyes told me I'd better damn well be ready to explain what happened.

I didn't know what to tell him.

"What the hell kind of half-baked outfit is this? Who does the maintenance on your fleet? I want their names, now." His voice ricocheted across the canyon. He glanced at his family and then back to me. Anxiety radiated off him in waves.

"I understand your concern, Colonel, but our maintenance schedule is the best in the business. I'm as confused as you are. I need to see if I can locate what caused the failure." My voice sounded a lot calmer than I felt.

The Colonel took a deep breath and gave me a stiff nod. The color in his face started to fade. "I used to work on these things in the service. Let me have a look."

We walked over to the Jeep and I popped the hood. Both of us began to search for the source of the problem.

It wasn't hard to find.

***

My boss, Art arrived in his Hummer forty-five minutes later, followed by Sandra Simpson of Simpson's Fuel driving the tow truck. Sandra walked over to the

Jeep to look at the damage while Art saw to the passengers.

The Colonel's family climbed into the Hummer. By now they were over their fright and hadn't said anything about suing us, so I figured I'd done a good job calming everyone down. Art promised to refund their money and offered them all gift certificates for a future tour.

The Colonel took me aside and leaned in close.

"You'd best be careful, Kate. I don't know what you've gotten yourself into, and don't want to know." His gray eyes were riveted to mine. "Those sliced brake lines and the leak in the tranny were no accident." A small shiver tracked up my spine.

The Colonel walked back to the Hummer to join his family. He stopped and said something to Art before he got in. As soon as Art made sure everyone was secure, he headed my direction, his mouth set in a grim line.

"You doing okay?" he asked. The frown on his face combined with his thick neck and bristly crew cut reminded me of a bulldog. I nodded.

"I called Cole and he's on his way." He gave me a look. "Come by the office when you're finished." He didn't wait for a reply and strode back to the Humvee.

They left and a few minutes later Sheriff Cole Anderson pulled up in his SUV. The seriousness of the situation wasn't lost on me. I'm nothing if not good at denial but this went way beyond even my abilities. Cole walked over to where Sandra and I waited by the disabled Jeep.

"Tell me what happened."

I started from when I got to the office that morning and ended at the point where the Colonel and I found the sliced brake lines and the punctured transmission. He listened in silence.

"How are you holding up?"

"Pretty well, considering. No one was hurt and the Jeep's still in one piece." And my knees were shaking. Other than that, I was golden.

Cole peered under the Jeep. Sandra pointed out the cut in the lines and the small hole where the tranny fluid had leaked out. He worked his way around the vehicle and shot several pictures with a digital camera, stopping at intervals to take notes. After he'd gone over the entire Jeep, he stood up and brushed the dirt off his jeans.

He turned to Sandra. "Once you get this towed back to town, let Jason know it's down at the shop so he can check things over. I don't want to miss anything." Jason was the Deputy Sheriff and the town's resident computer geek.

"Sure thing, Sheriff." Sandra gave me a look loaded with questions as she walked over to get the tow truck.

"You want a ride back?" he asked.

I'd normally jump at the chance to be alone with Cole, get to know him better, but I needed time to regroup. The possibility that Mexico may have caught up with me had me fighting a panic attack.

"Thanks, but I'm going to stay with the Jeep."

"Stop by when you get back."

I said I would, and he climbed into his truck and left.

This couldn't be good. I didn't need any trouble. Years ago I'd testified against two drug lords and a corrupt DEA agent in Mexico. I'd changed my name and address so many times since then, it was hard to remember who I was supposed to be. The way I figured it, anonymity was way better than dead. This kind of attention could lead to some serious problems.

Like being found.

Unless it already happened.

As far as I knew, no one had been released from prison yet. There'd been no indication they even knew where I was since I left Alaska. I'd almost stopped looking over my shoulder.

Almost.

Sandra lay underneath the Jeep, working the tow hook. I leaned against the door and waited. My heart rate slowed as I worked to calm myself. Finished, she slid out and I gave her a hand up. She frowned as she wiped her hands on her coveralls. Nervous, I cracked a joke about my bad driving habits, but she didn't laugh.

"Kate, you know as well as I do that you're in some kind of shit if someone deliberately cut your brake lines."

"Hey—it could have happened to any of the guides. There are a lot of rigs to choose from. We need to check the other Jeeps to see if they were vandalized. It was probably some stupid, messed up kid."

Even I didn't believe me.

Sandra shook her head. "Art had Armand do a quick check of the fleet before we left, just to be sure. None of them had a problem." She hit the button for the winch. The motor whined as the Jeep's front end started to rise. "It's not like it's a secret that this ride is your personal favorite. Even I know it, for chissake. The creep didn't just slice your brakes. They punched a hole in your tranny. Whoever did this wanted you dead and didn't care who else came along for the ride."

She was right. But what could I do? Sure, from now on, I'd make it a point to check every vehicle I used, but if someone wanted me dead, I doubted they'd hit my vehicle again. That wasn't the only way to kill someone, and certainly not the most efficient.

Explosives or decapitation were more their style.

Sandra got into the tow truck and started the engine. I climbed in the passenger side and put on the seatbelt, making sure it clicked close.

"You okay?" she asked.

I nodded and took a deep breath. Why let a little thing like a sabotaged vehicle bother me? Besides, the people I worried about wouldn't know which name I was using now.

Right?

Sandra shoved the truck into gear and we headed for town. Something told me my old friend denial wouldn't work this time.

***

After Sandra dropped me off in town, I stopped in at Wilma's Café for a coffee to go. I should have ordered something calming, like chamomile tea, but I'd never been one to do what I should. As I waited for my order, I caught a glimpse of Dave Sinclair in the mirror behind the register.

Durm's neighborhood banker sat in a booth next to the front door, deep in conversation with a well-dressed guy I didn't recognize. Dave glanced up and gave me a look that said I'm having an important conversation, so don't even think about approaching me, then returned to talking with the other man.

In his mid-fifties and overweight, Dave chain smoked and drank like a fish, wore a crappy toupee and had delusions of being a player. He helped negotiate a sale of private land east of town for a big developer, and, as a result, turned into quite an asshole. Most of the folks in town decided to take their business elsewhere. I usually didn't let a chance go by to give him a hard time. Mainly because he annoyed me, but also because I'm not that fond of bankers.

Today I ignored him, paid for my coffee and walked out, headed for the Sheriff's office.

The possibility the sabotaged brake lines and transmission could be a remnant from my past had me on hyper alert. I glanced down every side street and registered the driver of each car that passed by. Old habits die hard.

Especially with old friends like mine.

I walked into the Sheriff's office and Cole's receptionist, Cecelia, took one look at me, announced my arrival on the intercom and buzzed me through to the back. When I reached Cole's office, he'd already pulled out a chair. I walked in and sat down.

He leaned back on the edge of his desk, arms folded across his chest.

"You don't look so good."

"Thanks for that."

"Do you have any idea why someone would do this?"

I considered the question. I'd never told anyone in Durm about my past and I didn't want to start now. The habit of deception had become too ingrained and I'd been safe here, so far. I opted for brevity.

"Not that I know of. All I can think is maybe somebody didn't like one of my tours." Humor had its uses. Especially when fear was the dominant emotion.

"I'm asking because a woman who took one of your tours yesterday was found dead in her hotel room this morning."

My heart rate kicked up a notch and I leaned forward.

"Who?" It didn't make sense. The people who'd most likely come after me wouldn't waste their time on a civilian. Unless they were in the way.

Cole picked up a spiral notebook from on top of the pile of papers on his desk. "Her name was Roxanne Greensborough. A biologist out of Oklahoma freelancing for somebody local."

"She was on my early tour."

"That's why I wanted you to come down, see if you noticed anything unusual." He tapped the notebook, adding, "This is hers. We found it taped under a shelf in the closet in her room. The circumstances surrounding her death are suspicious. We'll know more after the autopsy report but we're treating it as a homicide." His gaze felt like a burn. "Right now, I have two links between the dead woman and your cut brake lines—the tour company and you."

A shiver danced down my back as I tried to think. "There wasn't anything weird that I can remember." I went over the tour in my mind, but only came up with one thing even remotely unusual.

"She did get pretty excited when we spotted a bird down by that tributary off the HoHoKam River. You know, the area with all the cottonwoods?"

Cole nodded. "Yeah." He flipped to a page in the biologist's notebook. "The Speckled Pygmy Twitter?"

"That's the one. An older couple in the Jeep saw it first and shot a bunch of pictures. Roxanne got a few, too. They said it was on the Endangered Species list, so her reaction didn't seem unusual. I know I'd never seen it before."

Cole leafed through a couple of pages in the notebook.

"How many passengers?"

"Seven. Roxanne, the older folks, and a family of four. Eight people signed up, but Roxanne's boyfriend never showed. She said he wasn't feeling well. How's he taking it?"

"We haven't been able to locate him yet. Jason tried the hotel earlier, but no luck. We're running both their names to see if there's anything to go on. Art's going to fax me a passenger list, along with where everyone is staying. We'll need to talk to them, too."

"I'm supposed to meet the older couple for lunch later. Do you want me to ask them to stop by?"

"That would be great."

He took a pen and one of his business cards out of his shirt pocket, wrote on the back, and handed it to me. "Here's my cell. If you remember anything you think might be useful, call me. Anytime," he added.

"I will." I slid the card in my back pocket. Too bad it wouldn't be a social call. He was a divorced father of two girls. Stable. Not my type. There was just something about him that made me think of quiet evenings by the fire.

Quiet evenings by the fire? Where the hell did that come from?

"You should take some time off until we can figure out what's going on, whether there's a connection between Roxanne's death and the incident with your Jeep." Cole chewed on his lower lip. I caught myself staring and shook it off. "You're pretty isolated out at Art and Barb's. Why don't you consider moving closer to town, so we can keep a better eye on you?"

I lived in a 30-foot trailer next to the HoHoKam River down the hill from my boss and his wife. It was safe enough, especially with Art and his weapon fetish.

"Do you think that's necessary?" I said. "Barb's always in her studio when she isn't at an art show, and Rudy barks at anything. Besides, Art's got a frigging arsenal in that house. I should be fine." I hoped, anyway. I didn't want to move closer in. There's no way I could afford to rent something if I cut back on my hours at work. I had to finish out the season or I didn't get to go somewhere tropical for the winter. In Kate's Religion, that's a Cardinal Sin.

I'd also found that moving targets were harder to track.

"Do you at least have a gun?" he asked.

Not a registered one. "No. But I suppose it would be a good idea." Okay. So I get a demerit for flat-out lying. It was complicated.

"I'd feel better if you did. Do you know how to shoot?"

This one I thought I could cop to. "Yeah. It's been awhile, but I think I can still handle one."

Cole moved to the other side of his desk, selected a key from his key ring and unlocked a desk drawer. He pulled out a 9mm Glock and handed it to me.

"You're able to legally have a gun in your possession, right? Any felonies I'm not aware of?" He half-smiled but I noticed intensity in his expression.

"No, no felonies. And yes, I can legally have a gun." We both knew he already ran my name to see if I had a criminal history.

He walked to a metal cabinet, unlocked the doors and removed a box of ammo, then carried it back to where I sat. I gave him the gun. He hit the release on the clip and started to load the magazine.

"Keep this one as long as you need to—it's mine. You know how to load?"

I did, but I let him show me. He moved closer so I could watch. The scent of his aftershave enveloped me like a coastal fog, and I found myself distracted by something other than the pistol. The snap of the magazine into the grip jolted me back to the present. Cole held it out to me. I started to bring it around to the back of my jeans, but thought better of it and instead placed it on the desk.

"You free later? I thought we could take a drive, go somewhere to test it out."

My heart did a tiny flip. Warning signals started going off in my brain. I did my best to ignore them.

"I'm booked solid with tours the rest of the week. How about Saturday morning?"

"That works. Meet me here at eight."

He got no argument from me. Maybe he'd show me how to hold something other than the gun.

***

Later that day, I walked into the lobby at Mulligan's Golf Resort, looking for Jack and Alice, the older couple from my tour. We were supposed to meet for lunch, but I waited for half an hour and they never came. My friend Deirdre stood at the concierge table, writing something down on a sticky note. She looked up at the sound of my approach and smiled.

"Well, if it isn't my favorite tour guide. How's business?"

She narrowed her eyes at me. I must have looked like shit.

"Exciting," I replied.

Deirdre gave me one of her WTF looks.

"Don't ask," I said. "Do you know if Jack and Alice Mason are still here? I was supposed to meet them, but they never showed."

"They were on your tour yesterday, right? I gave them directions for the hike up to Mount Delight earlier this morning. I hope they're all right."

"I'll run out to the trailhead, see if I can catch them. Do you know when they're supposed to check out?"

Deirdre typed something into her computer and waited a couple of seconds.

"Tomorrow."

"What time did they leave for the hike?"

"About six. They said they were going to Wilma's for breakfast, then to the trailhead." Her frown deepened. "I'll bet they just misjudged the length of the hike. You'll probably meet them on the trail. I'll put a message in their folder, though, in case you miss them."

"Thanks, Deirdre. I appreciate it."

My next tour wasn't until three, so I had plenty of time. My gut told me something wasn't right. They should have been back by now. I got in my beat up yellow Jeep and pulled out of the resort's parking lot.

Just outside of town, I turned down the gravel road that led to the trailhead, arriving at the parking lot a few minutes later. Jack and Alice's rented white Subaru sat in the shade of a mesquite. I parked the Jeep and decided against locking my wallet in the dash. Trailhead parking lots weren't the safest areas to leave valuables. Leaving my Jeep out in the open in a deserted lot didn't sit very well with me, either, but I had no choice if I was going to look for Jack and Alice. I'd just have to do a fast check when I got back.

The deep turquoise sky held the promise of a warm spring day. The temperature gauge read seventy-five and rising, so I pulled off my long sleeved shirt and tied it around my waist, leaving me in a blue sports bra. I grabbed my hat and the first aid kit from the backseat and snapped on a fanny pack with a bottle of water in the holder. I learned early on never to go anywhere in Arizona without water, especially hiking. Then I felt under the front seat and pulled out the gun Cole had given me and shoved it into the pack.

The winter had been mild and there were few trees down. I kept to the shade of the junipers, refreshing my memory on the steepness of the trail, where the large boulders were and where it might get a little tricky for less able-bodied folks. Jeep tours often included hiking segments and this trail was one of the most popular. The climb was well worth the effort, ending with a spectacular view of Sinagua Canyon.

As I neared the end of the trail with no sign of Jack or Alice, my concern turned to anxiety. The trail itself didn't take that long to hike. I wondered if they'd gone exploring. In rugged country like this, hiking off-trail without the necessary equipment and experience was a big no-no. I didn't have a clue if they knew what they were doing, but in my experience as a guide more often than not most people's idea of hiking didn't include a compass or even drinking water.

I called their names every few minutes as I scouted for footprints. There were few distinct ones and I was able to pick out what looked like the treads of the gear Jack and Alice had bought the other day; Jack's traditional hiking sole, size twelve, and the newer, amphibious style hikers with the squiggly tracks that Alice had shown me before the tour.

The prints headed off into the underbrush, around the crest of the ridge and angled downward. The drop to the canyon floor was steep and had no clear routes. I followed the tracks around the ridge, aware of another faint set of prints with an indistinct tread headed back toward the parking lot that at times obscured the ones I followed. What I assumed were Jack and Alice's footprints didn't have a match coming back, so either they were still somewhere nearby or had found another way to hike out.

I racked my brain, trying to think of lesser-used trails that led out of the canyon. I couldn't think of any. It was dangerous terrain for anyone, much less a couple of healthy eighty-year-olds.

The tracks veered right and moved lower into the canyon. I rounded a corner and decided to stop and rest in the shadow of a large rock. I slid the water bottle out of its holder and drank about a quarter of it, then wiped the sweat off my face with my forearm.

As I scanned the area, I caught a glimpse of something bright blue further down the canyon. I kept an eye on it to make sure it wasn't some brightly colored bird or a butterfly. It didn't move, so I put the water bottle back and started to work my way toward it through the thick undergrowth.

It turned out to be a square of satiny fabric snagged on the spiky branch of a cactus. Maybe one of them left it there to mark the way back. I eased around the sharp spines and moved through the brush, careful to stay clear of a nearby prickly pear.

The terrain grew steeper and I had to hold onto tree roots and branches to keep from sliding. I'd begun to wonder if this was such a good idea when the dirt shifted under my feet. I lost my balance and started skidding toward the bottom. Dropping onto my back, I spread my arms, trying to slow the slide.

I squeezed my eyes shut as sharp rocks tore my skin and branches whipped at my face. Blindly, I grabbed onto the trunk of what I thought was a small tree.

It wasn't.

The slide was over before I had a chance to think. Groaning, I sat up and checked to make sure I hadn't sustained any serious damage. Aside from my neck feeling like it was caught in a vise, I had a few painful scratches along with a handful of cholla spines.

The cholla cactus produces long, sharp spikes that have the habit of embedding themselves into anything they touch, especially exposed flesh. I wouldn't go near a cholla with full body armor on, much less bare skin. I'd seen them sink deep into steel-toed boots and thick horseflesh without trying hard. Funny thing is, the more you try to pull at them to get them to come out, the more they dig into whatever's available—a hand, a leg, an arm.

I proceeded to twist them out with a utility knife from my pack, sucking at the small holes they left in my skin. Then I finger combed my hair, dislodging the leaves and dead twigs I'd picked up during the death slide, and brushed off as much of the dirt on my clothes as I could. I'd ripped a hole in my jeans and my watch was broken, but otherwise everything else appeared to be intact.

Wincing, I dragged myself to my feet and glanced at the sky, trying to gauge what time it was. I didn't know how long it would take me to climb out of the canyon or even if I could, and I still had to find Jack and Alice.

The bottom of Sinagua canyon was a dried up creek bed, also known as an arroyo. Arroyos were dangerous during the unpredictable squalls that blew through the area. Because of the underlying hard-packed earth, small trickles turned to raging torrents in a matter of minutes, especially now during the spring rains. Lucky today was dry with no hint of weather. I decided my best bet would be to follow it out. I still had my cell phone with me, but it didn't do me a lot of good. Reception at the bottom of the canyon was nonexistent. Good thing I still had water.

Picking my way to the bottom, I started to walk. I'd gone about thirty yards when I stopped dead in my tracks.

I'd found Jack and Alice.

TWO

The helicopter lifted the second body out of the canyon with a *thwap thwap thwap* of the rotors. The sun arced high overhead and the temperature had spiked. I sat in the shade of a *palo verde* and watched Cole as he walked over to join me.

It had taken me over an hour to hike out of the canyon and then another forty-five minutes to get back to my Jeep, check for signs of sabotage and drive into town.

I'd found Jack and Alice where they'd fallen at the bottom of the steep canyon. Their ripped clothes revealed cuts and bruises over their arms and faces and they appeared to have broken several bones. I'd noticed the bright green of one of Alice's new amphibious hiking sandals a few yards from her body. A deep sadness washed over me. They'd been such vibrant, lovely people.

Confusion clouded my mind. What was happening here? One dead body wasn't good, but it didn't suggest a pattern. A sabotaged Jeep and three people from the same tour found dead? Coincidence was a long shot.

Cole broke into my thoughts. "Okay, so let's work with what we know. Three people are dead. One thing that connects them is that they took a tour of yours a few

222

days ago. One of the company's Jeeps had been tampered with, which just happened to be one you always use with a good chance that you'd take it out for your next scheduled tour. It's common knowledge all the guides have favorite vehicles, right?"

"Yeah, it's kind of a thing with us."

"Okay, so we can make a connection between four people on the same tour—Roxanne, Jack and Alice, and you. The difference being, you're not dead."

Was that supposed to make me feel better? Or did he think I might have had something to do with the deaths?

"What was the name of the family on the tour?" Cole glanced at me to fill in the blanks.

"The Harrisons."

"Right. The Harrisons. I never did get a chance to talk to them. They left town the day after the tour. I waited before I called, but I got an answering machine. They could still be on the road." He looked up as Jason walked toward us, holding a clipboard. "Jason, you need to try the Harrisons again when you get back to the office."

"Sure. What do you want me to tell them?"

"If you get a hold of them, transfer the call to me. I'll be on my cell if I'm not in the office."

Jason nodded. "What do you want to do here?"

"I'm requesting autopsies on both of these bodies. The possibility of this being accidental seems slim." Cole turned back to me. "Looks like something else is going on here, Kate. Any ideas?"

I gave him an innocent look. "Nothing's coming to me at the moment, Sheriff, but I promise I'll call you if I think of something."

I was afraid to tell him my suspicions. I had too much to lose. Once I let that cat out of the bag, there was no stuffing it back in. Besides, I still wasn't convinced the dead bodies had anything to do with Mexico. They wanted me dead, not innocent bystanders. What if I said something, it turned out to be wrong and my sordid past ended up becoming common knowledge in town? Word would spread and then I'd have to leave. Once that happened, I'd be easy prey. Rumors had a bad habit of reaching the wrong people.

I stood and dusted myself off. "I need to go. Armand offered to take my three o'clock tour, so if you need me for anything, I'll be in range until later this afternoon."

"You okay to drive?"

"Yeah. I'm fine." I picked up my fanny pack and fished out the keys to my Jeep. "Let me know if you guys hear anything else, okay?"

"Sure, Kate."

I walked back to my car, checked under the hood and headed to town.

***

"Ham and Swiss on rye, please."

"Sure thing, hon." The deli clerk smiled and busied herself with my order. I hadn't eaten anything since early morning so I stopped for a sandwich before going back to work. As I perused the bags of chips on a rack in front of me, I sensed someone standing behind me.

"Ah. A classic sandwich for a classic lady." His smile almost blinded me by its whiteness. I recognized him as the guy Banker Dave had been speaking to that morning at Wilma's Café.

He wore pressed chinos and a starched white oxford shirt, with a navy blue sweater casually draped across his shoulders. I glanced at his shoes. Loafers with tassels. I had the urge to tell him it was no longer the eighties and we weren't anywhere near Martha's Vineyard, but Jack and Alice's death had put me in a pensive mood, so I kept quiet. He had a container of cottage cheese in his hands. I figured him for some kind of bean counter or investment banker. I smiled politely and turned back to the chips, hoping he'd go away.

"Isn't your name Kate?"

I tried not to sigh as I turned to him and nodded.

"That's me. Have we met?"

He extended his hand. "Simon Boudreaux, Vice President of development for M.B. West."

Oh yeah. The corporation who bought all that land east of town. Like Durm needed another golf resort.

When I didn't respond, he smiled again.

"You're a guide for Hard Rock Country Jeep Tours, right?"

I stiffened. An automatic response when someone knew more about me than I did about them. It didn't happen often.

"I realize that this is a small town, but even I don't know everyone. How do you know me?"

"Dave Sinclair. I was having breakfast with him when you walked into Wilma's and I asked who you were."

I felt my shoulders relax a little. *Give the guy a break, Kate. He's probably new in town.*

The clerk placed my wrapped sandwich on top of the deli counter. I thanked her and picked it up, turning to go.

"Well, give Dave my love, would you? It's been such a long time since we've spoken." I knew the message would annoy Dave. The last time I'd seen him, we hadn't parted as friends. Maybe it was the ruthless way he made decisions about money owed to Durm Fidelity & Trust. I'd spoken to at least three hard working folks in the past few months that had lost either their home or business when the bank called the notes early. Dave could have intervened, but didn't.

"I've got a better idea. Why don't you come to our big party Saturday evening to celebrate phase one of Wild Horse Ridge?" He smiled his hundred-watt smile. "Dave will be there—you can tell him yourself." He pulled a card out of his wallet and handed it to me. It had Wild Horse Ridge Gala Event—Admit One printed on it. "Please come. The food's going to be great and it's open bar."

"Thanks, Simon. I'll think about it." I put the card in my pocket and walked to the front of the store to pay, Simon dogging my steps. I glanced out the window as I handed my sandwich to the cashier. A tan, late model four-door sedan parked in the lot outside caught my eye as she rang me up. I'd seen the same car down the block from the Sheriff's office when I'd gone to meet with Cole. I took my sandwich and started to walk out the door, keeping an eye on the car.

"Kate wait—"

I turned and waited for Simon to catch up to me. He handed me another ticket.

"I know you'll enjoy the party. Bring a friend."

He seemed so earnest. I glanced at the second ticket. Maybe I'd ask Cole to come along.

"All right, Simon, I'll see what I can do." As I said goodbye, I glanced over to see if anyone was sitting in the driver's seat of the sedan.

The car was gone.

Touring for Death

***

It was dark by the time I'd finished my last tour. I checked my Jeep and, finding nothing out of the ordinary, got in and stashed the gun Cole gave me under the front seat. Art had insisted that Armand and I do tandem tours until things calmed down. I couldn't blame him. Hard Rock Country Jeep Tours represented fifteen years of Art's sweat and blood. Even the hint of scandal could ruin business. Other companies in the area would be only too happy to pick up the slack.

The sliced brake lines, the dead bodies and what they might represent played at the edges of my brain like an annoying mosquito. The collateral damage the additional deaths represented wasn't my old acquaintances' style. All three individuals had reasons to want me dead. It was a good bet that two of them would prefer to do the honors personally.

I'd learned firsthand how one lousy choice can shape a lifetime.

With no discernible problems for years, I'd developed a false sense of security. I should have known better than to stay in one place so long. If I dwelled on it, I'd be a basket case. I did my best Scarlet O'Hara impersonation and told myself I'd think about it tomorrow.

I took a left onto the deserted highway and headed for home. I loved this place. The peace and quiet had a calming effect on me. Several of the people I'd met in the time I'd lived here were more like family than my actual family. I couldn't imagine having to pack up and leave. Not again. But I had that old, nagging feeling, the one that whispered I'd better move on, keep a step ahead.

Scarlet wasn't working too well tonight.

As I mulled over my options, I glanced in my rearview mirror and noticed a pair of headlights a little distance behind me. I wouldn't have given it a second thought, but tonight everything looked menacing. At first I couldn't decide if I should speed up to stay ahead or slow down and let them pass me. I didn't want to be paranoid and keep watching the mirror all the way home, so I allowed them to catch up.

The other vehicle's left turn signal came on and the late model SUV passed me and I resumed breathing. I couldn't tell through the smoked windows who was driving. I hoped no one else came along, or I'd be a wreck by the time I reached my place. I brought the Jeep back up to speed. The truck's taillights disappeared around the next bend.

I'd gone about a quarter of a mile when I caught a flash of headlights out of the corner of my eye. I glanced in the rearview mirror as the vehicle pulled in behind me from the side of the road. It looked like the same vehicle that passed me before. My heart rate skyrocketed. Panicked, I ran through a list of evasive maneuvers in my head.

One. Drive as fast as I could and hope I knew the roads better than the driver of the truck, giving me enough of a lead.

Two. Go off road at the first opportunity and lose them in the dark.

Three. I couldn't think of a three.

I opted for one, followed by two if I couldn't outrun them. I reached under the seat for the gun, put it in my lap and floored it. After a slight pause, the truck regained its position behind me.

I kept my foot on the pedal and pulled out my cell phone, praying for a signal.

No service.

They kept pace. That's the one problem with a Jeep. It's not exactly what I'd call a speed demon. The ability to outrun killers wasn't part of the criteria I'd used when I'd bought it. My lack of foresight would probably get me killed.

The SUV swerved into the outside lane and pulled alongside me. I slammed on the brakes, my body tensed for impact.

The truck clipped the front end of the Jeep with enough force to throw it into a tailspin. I gripped the steering wheel as I fought to turn into the spin, heading straight for the metal road barrier.

At the last second, the Jeep stopped short of busting through and hurtling off the cliff into the river below. I shifted into gear and skidded back onto the road, going the opposite direction. The other truck slid into a U-turn and accelerated after me. As my foot forced the accelerator to the floor, I experienced a laser-like focus from the adrenaline pumping through my veins.

Think, Kate. Where could I turn off and lose the son of a bitch? There were several scenic pull-offs on this section of highway, but they didn't do me any good. The entrance to Tsina Trailhead lay a hundred yards ahead to my left. I might be able to lose them on one of the dirt tracks that branched off of the main gravel road.

I could just make out the reflective sign that marked the entrance to the trail. I kept my speed steady until I was almost level with the turnoff, then I hit the brakes and skidded into the turn. The SUV raced past, the squeal of rubber telling me it wouldn't be long before they were on my ass again.

I gripped the steering wheel and floored it again, kicking up dust and rocks behind me.

The first of three feeder roads came into view. I blew past it, knowing it was only a short jog to its end. The second turn would take me deep into a twisting canyon where I had the best chance of losing the other vehicle. I just had to make the corner before they got close enough to see my taillights through the dust.

The turn came faster than I expected. I stomped on the brakes and swerved left, drove a few yards past an ancient, twisted pine and stopped, switching off my lights. A minute later, the other truck screamed past. Without turning the lights back on, I put the Jeep into first gear and followed the rutted road further into the canyon. I didn't stop until I came to a long forgotten prospector's shack I'd discovered during a hike the year before. I pulled in behind the piñon pines next to the disintegrating wood and stone structure, switched off the ignition and listened. Not hearing anything, I leaned my head back and closed my eyes, taking slow, deep breaths to calm my galloping heart.

I wouldn't last if this kept happening.

With a shaky hand I smoothed my hair back, and climbed out of the Jeep to search the dark trail behind me. No lights followed me into the canyon. My heart rate almost returned to normal, I waited a while longer, then got back into the Jeep and started the engine. A little-used outlet on the other side of the canyon would deposit me back onto a secondary road that led home.

I couldn't deny it any longer.

Someone wanted me dead.

THREE

The next day, I told Cole what happened. He called Art and after a short discussion, it was decided that I would stay at Art's until Cole deemed it safe for me to go back home to my trailer. I was leery and voiced my concerns about whether my staying at Art and Barb's house would put them in danger. A bemused expression flickered across Cole's face.

"He replaced all the windows with bullet-proof glass last year and the doors are reinforced steel. A tank wouldn't be able to penetrate the perimeter. If one tried, the security cameras would digitally capture the assault."

Art was ready for something.

"Do you have any idea why?" I asked.

Cole shrugged. "I've got my suspicions, but can't say for sure."

I left it at that. Maybe I didn't want to know. I counted Art as a friend, but even friends have their secrets.

I should know.

Cole accompanied me to my trailer so I could pick up clothes and my laptop. The silver Airstream wasn't anything special, but it was home. And, I could lock it and leave in the winter when I left for the tropics. Perfect.

231

I had a serious hankering to head south, now.

As we were walking out the door to bring my things back to Art and Barb's house, I decided to test the waters.

"So, are you busy Saturday?" I'd never been accused of being subtle.

Cole's expression could only be described as surprised. I couldn't tell if he was also pleased. I hoped so.

"Why?"

Part of me tried to stop what I was going to say next, to keep myself from getting too close. The last time I'd allowed that to happen, the other person almost died. I pushed the thought of Sam away and let the other part of me win.

"Actually, I just happen to have two tickets to the hottest event this side of the White Mountains: the blowout for Wild Horse Ridge." I locked the trailer door behind us and we piled my things in the back of my Jeep. "It's Saturday night, if you're interested."

Something registered in his eyes. "Ah. By Saturday you'll have cabin fever and, knowing Art, he won't let you go out alone. What better way to escape than to go somewhere with the sheriff?"

"I hadn't thought that far ahead, but you're right. He's like a Rottweiler." The idea of staying with Art made me wonder how far he'd go to protect me, but I knew I had to do it. He'd be fine with me going out, if Cole was along.

"So, is it a date?" I asked.

Cole's smile came easy. "Why yes, ma'am, I believe it is."

***

232

Touring for Death

Saturday evening couldn't have come too soon. Cole's prediction had been spot on. Art was driving me bat-shit crazy with his overprotective nature. Yes, I knew it was because he cared, but damn, he reminded me of a stalag commander from a World War II movie. The saving grace in the situation was his wife, Barb. A successful artist with a sensitive nature, she had a way with the commandant, speaking to him in her gentle, lilting tone. Art's demeanor softened, emerging from his razor focused role as designated Kate-protector.

That evening found me in front of the full length mirror for the tenth time, checking to make sure I looked as good as possible. I wore a clingy black, off the shoulder dress, strappy heels and just enough turquoise jewelry to set off my green eyes. Granted, jeans and a tee shirt were more my style, but Cole had already seen me in that. Seduction was all about the small things, and I meant to seduce him until he begged for mercy. The possibility of another opportunity seemed slim.

Especially if I wound up dead.

A small dab of my favorite French perfume, and I was ready to go. Funny how all caution got tossed out the window at the prospect of my untimely demise.

Cole arrived right on time. I grabbed my wrap, said goodbye to Art and Barb and headed out the door. Cole opened the passenger door of the SUV and I climbed in.

"You look beautiful tonight, Kate."

I felt my face grow warm from the compliment. "Thank you. You're looking pretty good yourself." He had on a pair of jeans that had evidently fallen in love with him, white shirt, no tie, and a tailored black sports coat. The exotic scent of his aftershave worked its way into my brain, and I had to fight the impulse to grab him by the lapels and devour him.

Down, girl.

I took a deep breath and gave him a demure smile as he closed the door.

Apparently, my sex-by date had passed its expiration.

We pulled into a slot in The Rocks' parking lot, then followed the winding slate path to the elegant bronze and glass front doors.

The concierge directed us down a hallway and through the large, carved double doors into a cavernous room filled with animated, well-dressed people. Waiters in cream and black floated by, bearing trays filled with flutes of champagne and mouth-watering hors d'oeuvres.

My stomach rumbled, demanding attention. I latched onto a glass of champagne and an hors d'oeuvre from a passing tray. The waiter stopped to offer something to Cole. He shook his head. The waiter nodded and swooped over to another group of folks who looked parched.

"I need a beer," he said, by way of explanation.

Several movers and shakers from Arizona politics and entertainment were in attendance. I recognized a state senator in the corner deep in conversation with a local environmental activist. A five-piece jazz ensemble played on one side of the room, while a famous pop star, rumored to be working on a new CD at her ranch near Sedona, commiserated with a news anchor from Phoenix. Here and there I recognized a handful of other bigwigs.

Cole let out a low whistle. "Lot of players here."

"Looks like it. Let's get you a refreshment."

As soon as Cole had a beer in hand, we headed for the food.

A cascading crystal fountain sat nestled next to the well-stocked spread. Lit from below, an elaborate ice sculpture of a golfer in mid-swing rested in the middle of the fountain, surrounded by little ice golf balls.

Simon Boudreaux intercepted us before we reached the table. He looked impeccable in a tailored tuxedo. His shoes gleamed, he'd had a manicure and his hair was perfect.

"Kate. So glad you could come. Who's your friend?" Simon asked, looking Cole over.

Cole held out his hand, sizing him up, as well. "I'm Cole Anderson. And you are?"

"Simon Boudreaux, V.P for M.B. West." A thoughtful look crossed his face. "Cole Anderson," he repeated, frowning. "Why do I know that name?" Then he smiled. "Sheriff Cole Anderson?"

"The same."

"I'm glad to meet you. Good to see Kate's in capable hands." Simon turned to me. "And a pleasure to see you again, Kate." He brought my hand to his lips and never once broke eye contact. I glanced at Cole, but he appeared unfazed.

"Thank you, Simon. Quite a spread you have here." I nodded toward the food. "We were on our way to sample some."

Simon smiled, his perfect teeth gleaming in the low room light. "Don't let me keep you. I need to run through a couple of things before the presentation, so if you'll excuse me?"

Simon moved off to the stage in the center of the room to speak with someone working the microphone and flat screen. A scale model of Wild Horse Ridge stood nearby. Cole and I each got ourselves a plate of food and wandered over to take a look. Several people milled around, waiting for the presentation.

A generously proportioned woman dressed in a black sequined gown and about half a million dollars' worth of diamonds walked to the microphone. She tapped it with her manicured fingernail to make sure it was working.

Clearing her throat, she intoned, "Ladies and gentlemen."

At first no one paid any attention, most deep in conversation or queuing up to the bar for drinks. The woman spoke into the microphone again, this time gaining everyone's attention. A hush settled over the room.

"Thank you for coming this evening. I hope you all had the opportunity to enjoy the refreshments." A general murmur of approval traveled through the crowd.

"Tonight is about vision." She gazed at the audience, pausing for emphasis. "A vision that will soon become reality." I stifled a yawn as she went on about how Wild Horse Ridge was the largest resort ever attempted in Northern Arizona, etcetera.

"I'm honored tonight," she continued, "to present the man behind the vision; a man without whom this extraordinary enterprise would not have come to pass. M.B. West's own visionary, Simon Boudreaux."

Applause erupted as Simon took the stage, I would guess more from the free alcohol rather than from his popularity. The guy behind me did a wolf whistle. Simon smiled and waited for the applause to die down before speaking. He was clearly at home on a stage—he worked the crowd like a pro.

I caught a glimpse of Dave Sinclair standing in the front row. He looked quite pleased with himself. Durm Fidelity and Trust was a major player in the project, and his obvious sense of superiority showed in the way he stood apart from the milling crowd.

That was my take, anyway.

The lights dimmed and Simon turned toward the large monitor as the first strains of the theme from The Magnificent Seven boomed through the speakers. Bright, colorful images of sunny, happy people living the Southwestern lifestyle flashed across the screen and Simon's commanding voice-over narrative recounted the beginnings of Wild Horse Ridge.

After what seemed like hours, but was probably closer to twenty minutes, the program ended with a musical crescendo. The screen went dark. Scattered applause accompanied the crowd's migration to view the model.

"Pretty impressive," Cole said, reading the information off a placard placed next to the model. "Says here it's a professionally rated 36-hole course, surrounded by a water park, a movie theater, and riding stables."

"It's all very nice," I said, "but they're messing with one of the best areas I know for wildlife spotting."

Cole shook his head. "Progress."

I excused myself and went in search of the ladies room. Afterward, I gave myself a once over in the mirror and left the restroom, all but colliding with Simon in the hallway.

"Sorry," I said with a laugh.

Simon's eyes lit up.

"Just the person I wanted to see." He waited until two women exited the restroom behind me and had walked back down the hall to the party.

"I don't want this to be general knowledge, since I can't accommodate everyone, but I've invited you and Cole on an exclusive tour of Phase One of Wild Horse Ridge. He'll meet up with us shortly. Shall we go to my office to wait?" He indicated a closed door at the end of the hallway.

"Oh. Sure. Fine." Damn. Just as I was going to suggest to Cole that we leave. It looked like my plan to seduce him would have to wait.

Simon led the way, unlocking the heavy wooden door with a key from his pocket. Silence descended as he closed the door and the party noise receded into the background.

"Help me celebrate?" Simon poured two glasses of champagne from a bottle on his desk and handed me one.

"Sure. Thanks." I raised the crystal flute in a toast and took a small sip.

"Please, have a seat," he said, indicating one of two chairs positioned in front of a blazing gas fireplace.

I sat down and took in my surroundings. The thick carpet added to the luxurious, insulated feel of the room. A massive bookshelf lined one wall. Floor to ceiling windows covered another. Simon sat on the arm of the other chair and smiled.

"So Kate. Why don't you tell me a little about what brought you to Durm?"

As usual, my cover story slid out with ease. "Nothing too interesting, Simon. I came here on vacation about five years ago and fell in love with the place. Applied at Hard Rock Country Jeep Tours and the rest is history."

He set his glass down, his dark eyes focused on me.

"What about before you came here? I'll bet there's an interesting story there."

"I'm afraid not." I shrugged, keeping my expression as neutral as possible. What was he driving at? "I grew up in Minnesota. Nothing exceptional about that." I took another, larger sip of champagne.

"Are you sure you've never lived anywhere else?"

His intense gaze started to make me feel uncomfortable. I shifted in my chair, the impulse to leave growing.

"No, can't say as I have. Why do you ask?" The last word came out as 'athk'. My tongue tasted like wool. Odd. I hadn't had that much to drink.

"You don't remember me, do you?" His eyes narrowed when I shook my head.

"No. Should I?" *We'd met before?* I searched my memory, but couldn't come up with anything. I'd never met Simon before, I was sure of it. Klaxon horns started going off in my brain.

I tried to stand. "Where's Cole?"

Simon pushed me back into the chair.

"He's not coming. It's just you and me, Kate."

My heart beat double time. *What was he doing?* His features started to blur and I felt nauseous.

He circled me, trailing his fingers across my hand and up my arm to caress my cheek. I jerked my head away, and the room started to spin.

"Now is that any way to treat an old friend?" He ran his fingertips along my collar bone, giving me chills, and not the good kind.

"Old friend? What are you talking about?" The words came out thick and slurred. My brain kept telling me I was in trouble and needed to leave but my body wouldn't respond. My arms and legs felt like dead weights and my peripheral vision faded in and out. Simon wavered like the flame from a candle in a gentle breeze.

"Are you feeling all right?" Simon bent down so I could see his face. There was no trace of concern. It was too difficult to form words, so I didn't try.

"I'll refresh your memory. We met at one of Roberto Salazar's bashes several years ago."

239

I tried to speak, but only managed to turn my head in his direction.

"I remember." He lifted the hair off my neck, letting it fall through his fingers. "You wore a backless red dress and drank champagne. Salazar couldn't take his eyes off you. No one could." He moved behind me, where I couldn't see him. The voice in my head screamed Run! Now!

I couldn't move.

He chuckled, but it lacked mirth. "I thought you were a damsel in distress and needed saving. I slipped a note under your wine glass, telling you I'd be waiting outside the compound in my car and we'd drive to safety. You didn't come. Instead, three large men did and made it very clear I wasn't to come near you or anyone associated with Salazar's operation." Simon's face was like stone. "I had to leave everything, start from scratch. Believe me, Kate, I won't make that mistake again."

I tried to speak, tried to tell him I never got the note, but it was no use.

He grabbed a handful of hair and wrenched my head back. The pain seemed far away but important. I wondered if anyone would hear me scream. I opened my mouth to try but the attempt died in my throat.

He brought his face next to mine, breath hot against my cheek.

"You gave me up to those sadistic thugs. Now I'm going to return the favor."

The faint realization hit me that I'd been drugged and was now in grave danger, but then the idea skated away and all I knew was that I couldn't hold myself upright anymore.

As I slid to the floor, my last thought was of Cole.

FOUR

Cold. Damp.
Dark.

The pain wrenched me from the void, spiraling down my neck and shoulders. I was curled in a fetal position, my hands and ankles bound. It took a minute to realize I was being transported somewhere. The air around me smelled like rust and dirt, and whatever was below me emitted a *screek! screek!* sound. Each jolt brought the pain back, sending a shudder from my head to my cold, bare feet.

I made myself focus on the pain as I struggled against the lure of oblivion.

Opening my eyelids to slits, I kept my head down and tried to get a glimpse of my surroundings. Intermittent, strobe-like light splayed across my bent legs from a single, bobbing light, revealing details one moment, plunging everything into darkness the next.

I was in a wheelbarrow being pushed by a tall, broad-shouldered silhouette of a man wearing a headlamp, his breathing labored. It wasn't Simon. Too tall. The shadows created by the lamp obscured his features, but something about the way he carried himself seemed resolute and vaguely familiar.

We slowed to a crawl and stopped. The pain receded, leaving my mouth dry and head throbbing like some horrible hangover from my twenties.

Water dripped, echoing in the stillness and penetrated the fog surrounding my brain. The man coughed and reached inside his pocket, pulling out a pair of leather gloves. He struggled to yank them on, flexing and jamming his fingers together to make them fit.

Where was I? The last I remembered, I'd been waiting for Cole in Simon's office. My confusion began to clear and it was just enough to scare the crap out of me. Things were way better unconscious.

He turned and walked out of my field of vision and I raised my head to get my bearings. Between flickers from the headlamp, I recognized the rock walls and dirt floor of an abandoned mine, similar to one of hundreds scarring the high desert of Arizona. The man stood near a metal contraption the miners called a "honey wagon." Historically used by miners to relieve themselves during grueling, sixteen hour days, it had two square lids that opened to reveal a pair of buckets.

I'd been around enough mines to know this was not a great place for a first date. If the bad air or hidden shafts didn't kill you, then the support timbers, rotted through from years of moisture and neglect, would give way if you so much as sneezed on them. There was also the distinct possibility of stumbling across an unstable, long-forgotten cache of dynamite.

The man picked a canvas bag up off the ground and loosened the drawstring, glancing inside. I blinked hard. It must have been the drugs – I could have sworn the bag was writhing. He turned. I dropped my head back and closed my eyes.

The sound of his footsteps signaled he was nearby. I felt his hands slide underneath my knees as he lifted me out of the wheelbarrow. I willed my body to go slack. Any rigidity and he'd know I was awake. I let my head fall back and kept my breathing steady. I opened my eyes to slits again and tried to get a glimpse of who I was up against.

I didn't have to wait long.

He dropped me onto the ground. I hit hard. Gasping for air, I rolled onto my side and propped myself up on my elbow.

"You're awake." The mine wasn't the only thing that brought a chill.

I'd know John Sterling's gravelly voice anywhere. Anyone else and I might have been able to talk or fight my way out of whatever might be in store. Not Sterling. I was pretty sure I'd made the top of his shit list and that wasn't about to change with some amiable conversation.

"When'd you get out?" Last I'd heard, he was going on an extended vacation - for ten years. And, from what my DEA contact told me, the prison he'd been assigned to in Tucson wasn't exactly spa-like.

"A week ago. Surprised?"

Though vaguely defined from the indirect light of the headlamp, the familiar facial features stood out: square jaw, aquiline nose, high forehead. He hadn't changed much from ten years in prison, except the nose had an unfamiliar jog to it, like it had been broken. Probably from the accident. He crouched in front of me and pulled out a length of rope.

"Sit up."

I slid backwards and leaned against the cold steel of the ancient porta-potty. He wrapped the rope around my chest and arms, and then looped it through a bar on the honey wagon, cinching it tight behind me.

"How do you know Simon?" Did Simon know Sterling wanted to kill me? If so, then his anger ran deeper than I imagined.

"Simon was a stroke of luck. He was happy to accept the finder's fee I offered. After I saw the two of you together and did a little research, I was able to play on his need for revenge."

Where had Sterling seen Simon and me together?

Sterling checked the rope for slack. "I know a little bit about revenge, you see. When I got released I hooked up with Enrique, and the rest was easy. Just took a little persuasion. Did you know he'd been keeping tabs on you for Salazar?" Sterling leaned back with a thin smile. "Knowing where the rot is hidden *¿es muy importante, si?*"

Salazar knew where I was all along? Why hadn't he come after me? He wouldn't have wasted resources keeping track of my whereabouts for no reason. It wasn't his style. His style was slice a throat now, ask questions later.

The money. That was it. He was waiting to see if I went back to Mexico to get the money I'd stashed. It'd be a long wait. I had no idea if the money was still where I'd left it. It had been ten years. I sure as hell wasn't going to find out.

Not yet, anyway.

I assumed Enrique was dead, knowing Sterling's fanatical need to tie up loose ends. Salazar would have to find someone else to take his place.

"If anyone could be described as rot, Sterling, it's you. You were the bad seed in all of this, not me."

His laughter ricocheted off the walls. Small stones skittered down the rock wall beside me, bouncing across the dirt floor. I braced myself and hoped the tunnel was sturdier than it looked.

"And you were little Miss Innocent, right? You would never steal from the great Salazar. You'd have to look over your shoulder the rest of your natural life."

"I didn't steal from Salazar," I lied. "Only you were that stupid."

Sterling had played both sides. One of the DEA's best field agents, he worked undercover in Salazar's illegal drug world. Boredom or vanity took over and he decided to use his connections for real, and ran his own operation under the ruse of undercover work. The sweet side deal lasted for years, until his luck ran out. He hadn't been pleased with my role in that.

"No, you did me one better. You betrayed both Salazar and Anaya." He stood up, reached behind his back and pulled out a gun, aiming it at me. "Where's the money, Kate?"

He wouldn't fire it. We'd both die when the mine collapsed. He was trying to intimidate me.

"I don't have it."

"I don't believe you." He slid an old wooden box over with his foot and sat. "I got time, Kate. And, to help you in this little exercise—" He grabbed the canvas bag and slid it between us, "I brought your favorite." He opened it and indicated I should take a look.

God, the thing was moving. Whatever was inside was alive—ominous hissing sounds erupted from the interior. Nauseous, I leaned back, but he shoved the bag in my face, lighting the interior with his flashlight. I had no choice but to peer in at the mass of coiled, slithering snakes.

Visceral fear washed over me. I glimpsed orange and white sliding among the familiar diamond pattern. Corals and rattlers. He didn't stint on quality. Not that there wouldn't have been enough ways to off someone in an old mine—throw them down a dark shaft, rig a timer on some old explosives, drown them in a slurry pool. No, Sterling brought snakes.

I hated snakes.

I'd always had an aversion to the things, even the harmless ones. I leaned back again, keeping my face impassive. I refused to let him see my fear.

"That's sweet. How did you know rattlesnakes were my favorite?"

"I didn't. That's why I got all different kinds. Now, where's the money?"

"I told you, I don't have it."

"Wrong answer." He grabbed my wrists and yanked me forward. His glittering eyes bored holes into mine. "I hear death from snake venom is slow and painful."

I swallowed but my throat went dry. He pushed my hands toward the bag.

My fingers retracted and I turned my face away. My voice ratcheted up an octave. "God, Sterling, don't do this. Yes, I had it." He eased off a bit and I added, "But it's gone."

His lips curled into a thin line and he pulled my hands back toward the bag.

"No. Stop. I lost it. I'm not lying to you. It's gone." I squeezed my eyes shut and held my breath, waiting for the pain. *Please, God, let it be fast.*

I was surprised when Sterling let me go and dropped the bag to the ground. "If you're not going to tell me where it is, its location dies with you. Unless—" He turned to look at me. "You let someone else in on it, like maybe that sheriff friend of yours?"

Now he was bringing another innocent person into his twisted act of revenge. I had to do something, fast, or he'd go after Cole.

He pulled out his cell phone and came in for a close up with the camera. "Turn to the right, the light's better." I stared ahead, not moving. He took the picture and stood.

"I hear Anaya's got a reward out for the person who finds and kills you. I know you have the money, Kate, and I want to make sure he knows I was the last one to see you alive." He slipped the camera back into his pocket. "I'll take the post-mortem afterwards. It's so much more gratifying this way." I didn't think Vincent Anaya, the other drug lord I'd testified against, would be pleased Sterling had let me die before recovering the money, and I said as much.

His laughter had a brittle ring. "I need...what'd they call it in group?" He frowned, then snapped his fingers. "Closure. I need closure. Fuck Anaya."

Sterling must have realized he'd been standing next to the snakes. He moved past me to get out of the way and I thrust out my feet. I was fast and he was unprepared. He lost his balance and grabbed for something to hold onto, but caught air. His body slammed into the half-rotted wooden support beam and six-and-a-half feet of angry landed on the ground with a thud. Dirt and small rocks rained down around us. I shielded my head with my bound hands, expecting the whole thing to collapse and bury us alive.

The mini landslide came to a standstill. Sterling and I both let out audible sighs. He stood and dusted himself off.

"Good try, but luck's with me this time. It'll be nice to hear you beg me to put you out of your misery." He slid off his gloves and tucked them back in his pocket. "Ten years is a long time to wait. Watching will be the best entertainment I've had in a while." He glanced at the canvas bag at my feet. "Looks like you don't have much time left." One of the snakes had crawled free of the others and was now tasting the air with its tongue.

A couple of small rocks fell from the ceiling and hit Sterling on the head. He shook them off and looked up. More started to fall.

The rumble started low, reverberating deep within the mine. The ground started to shake. Sterling caught himself as he fell against the wall. Rocks, dirt and debris fell to the ground. I flattened myself against the honey wagon, trying to become as small as possible. Pieces of the tunnel glanced off my shoulders and arms. The sound of splintering beams cracked through the chaos. The mine was collapsing on itself. Sterling and his headlamp staggered back the way we came, arms raised over his head.

One minute, the sky was falling. The next, total stillness. I tried to take a breath, but ended up coughing from the dust.

I'd been plunged into a darkness so complete, there were no reference points, not even a trace of light. Sterling's headlamp had been the only source of light in the mine. I looked down, but couldn't see my hands. The mine's icy temperature crawled up my spine like a caress from a corpse.

I thought fleetingly of Cole and whether anyone would find my body. The possibility was grim. Chances of survival were dismal. There was no reason for anyone to investigate the mine. No one knew I was here. Hell, I didn't even know where I was. For all I knew Sterling could have taken me across the border into Mexico.

Prrrrrrrrrrrrrrttttt! The snake's rattle got my attention. I'd forgotten about them in the collapse. I imagined the snakes escaping the bag, coiled and strike-ready, close to my bare feet. Alarmed, I raised my knees, dragging my bound ankles away from the invisible threat.

I felt no bite, no pain. Panic rode high in my throat and I began to work my hands back and forth, trying to loosen the ropes. Sterling had tied them tight and it wasn't easy. At the same time, I twisted my body from side to side and back and forth, trying to fray the rope around the metal edges of the honey wagon.

The stillness of the mine amplified my ragged breathing and every so often a rattle pierced through the darkness, ramping up my panic. I tried to calm myself, not knowing how much oxygen I had. Running out of air was a distinct possibility. Probably better than snake venom, but still, not a great way to die.

I worked the ropes hard, my fear of the snakes edging close to hysteria. I wrenched a hand free and bent to the ropes that bound my ankles. Like a dog worrying a bone, I kept at the knot; easing, pushing, picking. Not easy with fingers clumsy from the cold.

One more try and the rope came free. Now all that remained was the one around my chest. That, and find a way to dig out of a collapsed mine tunnel with no light source and no tools.

Easy.

The snakes had cooperated up to this point, but I think they had become attracted to my body heat. The sound of slithering over loose gravel grew closer. In my mind's eye, I saw the others poking their elongated heads out of the canvas bag, curious where their buddy had gone.

Perspiration dripped down my face and back as I ratcheted up my activity, slouching and straining against the rope, trying to stretch it enough so that it would either snap or I'd be able to slip underneath it. My pulse slammed in my ears as fear threatened to overwhelm me.

The rope loosened enough for me to slide out from under it. Scrambling on hands and knees, I moved as far away from the slithering noises as I could get.

Antarctica would be too close.

I felt my way around the honey wagon and along the damp rock wall, tripping over rocks, hunting for an opening. Nothing but sticky cobwebs. Half-expecting to disturb a Brown Recluse or some other death-spider, I continued to grope my way along the wall.

Disoriented, I raised my hand in front of my face, but couldn't even make out a silhouette. I wasn't sure where I stood in relation to the tunnel and the way out. Sticking close to the wall, I fumbled along until another wall stopped me. This time it was loose rubble, not solid stone.

On the off chance that it was debris from the collapse, I moved along its face and pushed at the rock, searching for an opening. Before long, I came up against the impenetrable rock wall on the other side of the mine. At least now I knew where I stood in relation to the entrance.

A long fucking way.

Panic threatened to take the lead, and once again I fought it back down to where I could function. I calmed myself with deep breaths and went through my options. I had one. Dig, and dig fast. The air smelled musty and stagnant and I didn't know how much time I had.

I reached down and felt along the ground for something dense. My hand closed around a rock that I thought might work. It had heft and was pointed at one end. I chose a section of the loose rock wall and climbed upward, cursing the sharp rocks jabbing into my cold, bare feet. The wall should be thinner near the top, making it easier to break through to the other side. That was my theory, at least.

With every step I slid back when loose debris gave way. It was like the Stair Master from hell. I stopped to catch my breath and it occurred to me Sterling's body was somewhere beneath all this rubble.

He did say he wanted closure.

I continued my battle upward and reached the top of the pile after what seemed like hours. I knew it was the top because I hit my head on the solid roof of the mine. I slammed the rock in my hand against the loose rubble. The sound of cascading debris tumbling down to the floor of the mine gave me hope.

To try and dig rock with another rock is slow and painful. I scraped my knuckles raw, but kept working, despite inhaling dust. Stories about being buried alive kept popping up in my mind, but I didn't allow myself to go into detail. I'd had first-hand experience five years before in Hawaii and didn't want to relive the fear and claustrophobia I'd felt. I forced myself to focus on getting out. At least I had room to move.

And then my rock hit air.

I shoved my hand through the small hole and began to pull away more debris. Sweet, cold air flowed toward me from the opening. It took me a while to enlarge the space enough for me to squeeze through. Exhilarated, I shimmied through and half-climbed, half slid down the large pile of rubble to the other side. Once I'd hit bottom, I sat for a moment, waiting to get my bearings.

It was still pitch dark. I inched over to the wall of the mine, using it as my lifeline.

Then I started to walk. Shivering, I swung my arms, trying to generate some warmth. My feet were like bricks and I stumbled, becoming less coordinated with each step. At least hypothermia was a better death than snake venom. I'd just go to sleep.

I had no idea how long the tunnel was, or if the collapse had blocked it further up. I put one foot in front of the other, counting the steps to keep my mind from wandering. When that got old, I started singing hit songs from the seventies.

My calves strained from the pressure of walking at an upward slant and my breath came out in hard gasps. My body temperature had begun to reverse its downward trend and I started to sweat.

After walking at a steady pace for what seemed like miles, I noticed I could make out simple shapes. I brought my hand in front of my face and saw the faint outline of my fingers. An eternity later, I stumbled out of the mine, relieved beyond words to see stars in the night sky.

I needed to figure out where I was and find a main road. I scanned the area for Sterling's vehicle and wasn't surprised when I didn't see it. He'd leave it well hidden.

Leaning against the hard rock of the entrance to the mine, I closed my eyes, the urge to lie down overwhelming. I had to get to a phone to call Cole. There was no way around it. I'd have to tell him about Sterling and Mexico.

At least he'd have a good lead on the murders. I wondered why Sterling felt the need to kill innocent bystanders. Had he become so warped during his time in prison that he killed folks for effect? Too bad I couldn't ask.

I banged the back of my head against the rock until it hurt. Things with Cole had been going so well. Couldn't a girl just put the past behind her and move on to live a normal life?

An old shaman once told me I had bad spirits following me. Apparently, they were back from vacation.

As I put distance between me and the mine, walking along a gritty mule trail, a profound weariness settled deep in my bones. My numb feet muted the pain of the sharp stones.

I'm not sure when I reached the forest service road. The sky was still dark, and I had no idea which way to go. There were no lights in the distance, no warm, welcoming homesteads with hot coffee and something to eat. If I made the wrong choice, I could be wandering out here for days. Shadows of nameless mountains were almost visible in the distance. It didn't matter. I didn't recognize any of them. Sterling made sure he'd executed his little plan miles from anywhere. He wasn't one to take chances. I was sure he anticipated the possibility of my escape. He'd been trained to leave nothing to chance.

I picked a direction and started to walk.

The gravel road did a number on my bare feet, and the sexy little dress I'd been so careful to wear for Cole turned out to be the worst kind of insulation from the desert evening's chill. But I kept moving. To stop would be giving up.

The sound of a motor startled me out of my zombie-march. I turned to watch, too exhausted to move out of the way.

The headlights reminded me of one of those bouncing karaoke lights, the kind that points to the words you're supposed to sing on a screen. The lights drew closer. Still, I didn't move. The vehicle slowed and pulled to a stop a few feet away. I squinted against the glare of the headlights, waiting for some kind of acknowledgment. I figured folks in these parts didn't take kindly to being approached by strangers.

"Need a ride?" The voice was like a chain saw sliding over wet gravel.

I nodded.

"C'mon then, git in. I ain't got all night."

I moved to the side of the car and opened the door. An empty can of Rolling Rock bounced onto the road. I left it and climbed in, glancing at the old man behind the wheel as I closed the door against the harsh night. I leaned my head back, thankful to be somewhere warm, with someone other than Sterling.

"Thanks for the ride." A spring poked through the seat. I shifted, trying to get comfortable and took a long look at my rescuer.

His bushy gray hair and beard looked like he hadn't run a comb through them in years. His pants were caked with dirt, and he wore several layers of ancient, long sleeved flannel shirts. A khaki-colored field vest with every pocket bulging completed the outfit. He smelled like Sunday night at a polka festival; boiled sausage, sauerkraut and beer. A worn leather cowboy hat took up prime real estate on the front seat.

"What're you doing way out here? Ain't nothing but coyotes and crazy old men." He chuckled, setting off a round of explosive coughing. He hammered on the dash like the phlegm was in the car instead of his lungs.

"Dinner date gone bad. How far am I from Durm?"

"Be a damned long walk, 'specially the way you was goin'." The old guy shook his head and spit tobacco into a can as he maneuvered the car around and headed the opposite direction I'd been walking. "Lady like yerself shouldn't be foolin' around with the kind of feller who'd take you out here and dump you in the middle of the night, plain as you please. No sir, that ain't no way to treat a woman. Why, when I had my Mary—" Clearing his throat, he pawed at his eyes. It took him a moment to regain control.

"When my Mary was still alive, I worshipped the ground she walked on. Made the best rabbit stew you ever had the chance to eat." He gave me a sidelong glance and nodded. "You hold out for a good one, hear? Not some shit bag who leaves you wanderin' alone in the wilderness. Life's too damned short."

I didn't tell him my track record hadn't been too good. Instead, I gave him directions to Art and Barb's place. Leaning back in the seat, I closed my eyes.

Despair hung thick and stagnant in the car, and it wasn't only from memories of Mary.

FIVE

The car lurched to a stop and I bolted awake. The old man had pulled over to the side of the road, next to Art and Barb's driveway. I reached for the door handle, but before I could get out he placed a gnarled, arthritic hand on my arm. His fingernails were black with dirt.

"Don't ever let something like that happen agin, hear? You look like a smart woman."

"Wish I could agree with your assessment. Thanks again for the ride. I owe you."

He snorted. "Hell, I'd do the same for anybody out there in the middle of the night. You just take care of yerself, and remember what I said about waitin' on the right one."

"Is it really that easy?"

He shrugged and smiled, revealing gapped and yellowed teeth. I dragged myself out of the car, let the door swing shut and watched the glowing tail lights fade away as he drove off into the early dawn. A lone coyote yipped somewhere in the distance, unanswered. I wrapped my arms around my waist and walked down the drive to the house.

The lights were on, inside and out. I had no idea what time it was, or even if it was still the same night.

Art and Barb were waiting for me as I walked into the living room. Their dog, Rudy, barked happily and scampered over for pets. I reached down, but stopped short when I saw the look on their faces.

Barb crossed the room in two strides, took my elbow and led me to the couch. She grabbed a blanket off the back of a chair and wrapped it around me.

"What happened? You look awful."

"Long story. I need to call Cole."

Art's face was dark with anger but another emotion played at the edges of his eyes. "Cole's already been here. Said you left him at the party to go along with some other guy."

With a sigh, I leaned my head back. I didn't have the energy to explain.

Barb sighed. "Look at her, Art. She's filthy, half frozen and doesn't have any shoes on. You tell me she's had a good evening."

Art nodded as he looked me over. His expression softened. "He came by to see if you got home all right. Where have you been?"

I tried to frame my answer so it didn't sound made up, but couldn't figure out a way to describe my evening.

"I need to call Cole."

Barb went into the kitchen and returned with the phone. I took it from her and punched in Cole's number.

***

Cole pulled into the driveway within the hour. I dreaded talking to him, but knew I had to tell him about the mine incident and testifying against Sterling. The trial records had been sealed, so I didn't think I was in any danger of the rest of my story getting out.

Art let him in and murmured something to him that I couldn't hear. Then he walked out of the room, leaving the two of us alone.

I sat on the couch. Cole chose the armchair across from me. He leaned forward, elbows on his knees, his mouth set in a hard line.

"What happened, Kate?"

This was going to be hard. I drew the blanket tighter around my body. "I'll explain everything. But first, I have to tell you something and it's going to be difficult for me to do, so please let me get through it before you say anything."

"I'm listening."

The look on his face held a mixture of anger and something else—hurt? Betrayal? Mainly anger. I took a deep breath and explained about Sterling, how I'd been the cause of his incarceration, and that he'd been planning my death for years.

I skirted around the issue of my drug cartel association, leaving out the parts I didn't think he needed to know, like stealing Salazar's money. There was no reason to tell him everything. Even though I'd felt justified taking the money to get out of the situation I was in, it was not my finest hour.

"How did Sterling get to you?"

"That's where it gets a little complicated. Simon told me he knew me when I lived in Mexico and although I've tried, I can't remember ever meeting him. Sterling said he saw Simon and me together, although I'm sure I'd never met him before the day he gave me the tickets to the party." I paused, remembering the tan sedan outside the grocery store and the sheriff's office.

"Simon told me he set up a private tour of Phase One of the project for the two of us, and that you were on your way to meet me. While I waited for you in his office, he must have drugged my champagne because I blacked out. The next thing I knew, I woke up in the abandoned mine with Sterling."

"An abandoned mine?" he repeated. Disbelief skated across his features. "And why would Simon drug you and hand you over to a convicted criminal?"

Now that I'd said it, I realized it sounded farfetched. I struggled forward with my story, hoping he'd believe me.

"He thinks I was responsible for some things that happened to him and when I didn't remember him, I guess he decided to teach me a lesson."

"Were you?"

"What?"

"Responsible."

I shook my head. "I had no idea what happened to him. The man I was with at that time threw a lot of parties to flaunt his wealth. There were hundreds of people in and out of the place, and I imagine Simon was one of many who hung around, hoping to get a piece of whatever he threw their way. I don't know what I did to give Simon the impression that I was interested, but it wouldn't have been the first time." Being from the Midwest, I was raised to be polite and respectful to everybody. In the drug cartel world that was a rare thing and often construed as interest.

"Apparently, some people decided that Simon was out of line and remedied the situation." I couldn't imagine what Salazar's men did to him. Simon made the mistake of messing with one of his possessions—me.

Cole nodded once, as though my response answered some question in his mind.

"Then what?"

"The mine collapsed. Sterling didn't make it. I dug my way out and got a ride into town."

"Tell me who gave you the ride and I'll contact them."

My heart sank as the realization hit me that the old guy was the only witness who could corroborate my story.

"I didn't get his name." Anguish replaced exhaustion. Cole had to believe me. I opened the blanket to show him the rope burns and the cuts and scrapes on my hands and feet.

He leaned forward, his eyes darkening. "Would you be able to find the mine again?"

"I think so. I was so exhausted, I fell asleep on the way home, but I paid attention to the road signs up to that point. If you give me a map, I can work backwards and try to pinpoint the area."

"Simon's explanation's a little different than yours."

"Oh?"

"When you didn't come back from the powder room, I went looking for you. I found Simon. Or more likely, he found me. He told me he hadn't seen you." Cole's eyes narrowed. "We need to get you in for a blood and urine analysis. There will be traces of the drug Simon used in your system." He reached over and took my hands in his. His warmth radiated into my body, along with a trace of something that might have been me feeling hopeful. He searched my face. "I'm sorry I wasn't there."

"You couldn't have known." I gave him a tentative smile. I almost added, *and you believe me. That's all that matters.*

"Once you figure the location, I'll contact search and rescue and have them go into the mine if it's stable, see if they can recover the body." He shook his head. "You should have told me about Sterling when everything started going sideways. I might have been able to prevent him from getting to you."

"I know. I was afraid."

"Afraid of what? I think you'd be afraid of a guy like Sterling and would want all the help you could get."

"I was afraid to tell you about my past. I've been doing all right to this point. There hasn't been any trouble. And to be honest with you, I didn't think it was him." I didn't bother to tell him I was more afraid of losing the life I'd built in Durm than being scared of the bad guys. Bad guys I could deal with. It's a tangible threat; some guy wants you dead, you run away and hide or fight back. The fear of losing my sense of belonging somewhere, of not having to live like a ghost, was difficult to explain.

"Do you believe Sterling killed the passengers and sabotaged your Jeep?"

"I didn't get a chance to ask, but it's possible. The Jeep, yes. I'm not sure what his reasons were for killing, though, other than to send me a message."

I watched him process this new information about the murders, about me, as though with his whole body, not just his mind. He appeared to pull into himself, arms still crossed in front of him. I'd spent so many years not being able to trust anyone it had become ingrained and to my addled, sleep-deprived brain, it looked like he was going into lockdown. I didn't know how to keep him from pulling away.

"I'm exhausted. Can we meet later, after I've had a chance to rest? I'm feeling a little overwhelmed at the moment and I'm not sure I'm making sense."

"Yeah," he nodded, "of course. But first we need to get you in for a blood draw. After that, I'll have to take your statement about what happened while it's still fresh. Then you can sleep for as long as you need to." He'd gone into sheriff mode, efficient and gruff.

Cole brought me back to Art and Barb's after the blood draw and filing the report. I tried to pinpoint where I thought the mine was and thought I came pretty close, but we wouldn't know until Search and Rescue had gone in and located the body, or at least found Sterling's car.

I fell into bed, exhausted, and didn't wake up until late afternoon. After thinking it through and against Art and Barb's protests, I decided to move back to my trailer. With Sterling out of the picture, I was no longer in any danger. Even Art agreed there wasn't any reason I couldn't start leading tours without Armand along to babysit.

I needed my life back.

When Cole found out, he advised against me moving until they found Sterling's body. I argued that I was certain Sterling hadn't made it out of the mine alive and that my staying at Art's put an undue burden on my boss and his wife. Cole didn't agree.

"Until we find the body, you could still be in danger."

"I appreciate your concern, but Sterling's dead, Cole. No more danger. I'll keep checking the vehicles and keep my eyes open for anything suspicious, but there isn't any reason for someone to kill me. Not now."

To tell the truth, I was too damned tired of living in fear, waiting for something to go wrong. That was no way to live. Cole might think otherwise, but I knew the truth. Sterling was dead. Anaya was still in prison, and Salazar would have killed me already if he wanted to.

I just wanted to get on with living out whatever time I had left.

SIX

A few days later, I was back to my old life, leading tours and living on my own. Cole called to tell me the initial lab results were in and asked if I'd stop by and meet with him.

I arrived at the Sheriff's office and said a quick hello to Cecelia. She buzzed me into the back and I walked down the hallway, stopping at the entrance to Cole's office. He looked up and said hello, and waved me into the chair across from him.

I dropped my backpack on the floor next to me and sat down.

"How are things going?" he asked.

"Good. Business picked up. I'm back on the job. Art's a happy man."

He shuffled through the papers on his desk and pulled one out, placing it on top of the pile. Then he cleared his throat.

"First things first. The lab results came back and it looks like Simon used Rohypnol."

"Rohypnol. You mean ruffies? The date rape drug?"

He nodded. "We got a warrant and searched his office, but didn't find anything. His home, on the other hand, was a different story. We found a bottle that contained several tablets in a wall safe. We arrested him this morning."

Relief flowed through me. Another problem solved. I'd been worried Simon might try something once he'd found out I'd survived Sterling. The look on Cole's face told me that finding the ruffies wasn't everything.

"And?" I asked.

Cole cleared his throat again. His expression sharpened. "There's one more thing." He leaned forward, his hands clasped in front of him on the desk. "Who are you, Kate?"

My smile froze. A microsecond later I recovered and cocked my head to the side.

"What do you mean? You know full well who I am."

He shook his head. "I ran your social and you've got no work history before Hard Rock Country Jeep Tours. That seemed odd, so I ran your credit history. Nothing. No passport, no utility bills, nada. I checked several other states. It's like you didn't exist before you came to Durm. You need to tell me what's going on, Kate. If that's even your name." He sat back in his chair and crossed his arms.

What was I going to tell him? My mind raced for something plausible, something that didn't start with I was incredibly stupid and end with goodbye.

A tiny, insistent thought came to me that maybe I could trust him. That maybe we could keep this between us and I wouldn't have to leave again.

I was tired. Tired of living a lie with everyone I met. Tired of looking over my shoulder, of doing everything on my own. Maybe, just this once, I could actually let someone in on my secrets. The idea engulfed me like a bonfire and I could feel the walls I'd built around myself start to crumble.

Cole sat quietly, watching my face. I searched his eyes for an answer. Then, something inside of me cracked. I took a deep breath.

"My name isn't Kate Evans. Or actually, it is at the moment. I've had others. Jones was the first one." I watched him, but his expression didn't change. "The person I told you about that I knew in Mexico? Let's just say he was not a good romantic choice for me. I ended up on his bad side and he tried to kill me. I made a deal with the DEA and testified against him, his boss and Sterling. In exchange, the DEA got me out of Mexico and helped me start a new life. I've been moving from place to place ever since, changing my name, trying to stay a step ahead." My mouth had gone dry. I pulled a water bottle from my pack and took a drink.

"So you're in the Witness Protection program? Don't they usually set you up somewhere with a new identity and a job?"

I shook my head. "I opted against it. Salazar or Anaya had an informant in the Mexican government or the DEA field office. They never found out which."

"Why didn't you tell me before? This isn't something a person should carry on their own." He sat forward in his chair, concern evident on his face. "When's the last time you contacted your family?"

Memories of an emotional phone call ten years earlier from a payphone in Mexico to my sister, Lisa, clouded my mind. It was the last time I'd spoken with anyone from my family in Minnesota. It didn't end well. I couldn't contact any of them. I'd never forgive myself if I put them in danger. I told myself it was part of the price I had to pay for my sins.

"It's been a while," I said.

Cole studied me for a moment. His features softened. "What are you doing tomorrow night?"

Surprised, I shifted in my chair. "I'm booked until five. Why?"

"How would you like to come over for dinner? I'm a pretty good cook and I'd be eating alone since the kids are at their mother's in Phoenix."

Another piece of the wall fell away.

"I'd love to. What time?"

***

I took a wrong turn trying to find Cole's house, but finally got it on the second try. I'd stopped at Wilma's Café to pick up a nice bottle of red that she assured me would go with anything.

Cole lived a few miles out of town in a well-kept neighborhood located along Rattlesnake Ridge with a great view of town and Mount Delight. It was a clear night with plenty of stars visible already. The house stood near the top of the ridge, nestled among the pines and had an Asian influence combined with rough-hewn timber accents. It looked rustic but elegant at the same time. I went to the front door and rang the bell.

Somewhere inside I heard Cole yell, "Come on in. The door's open."

The slate entrance opened onto a large living room with an open beam cathedral ceiling and gleaming hardwood floors. A fireplace stood at one end, with a cozy fire already lit. Soft music played in the background and something smelled wonderful. I breathed in deeply and my stomach growled. I pulled off my coat and placed it on a chair by the hall table and slipped off my shoes.

"I'm in here." His voice came from the back.

Carrying the bottle of wine I walked toward his voice, checking out the art on the walls. His taste definitely ran toward well-crafted landscapes, but every now and then was something surprising; a surrealist portrait of a woman here, a colorful modern piece there. He had a couple of bronzes and some Native American pottery along with hundreds of books on shelves and tables. Pretty impressive. It looked like Cole wasn't your average, beer guzzling, sports watching kind of guy.

But then, I knew that.

The hallway veered to the left and opened onto the kitchen. Cole was over by the stove, basting a chicken that looked close to done. He'd set two small plates, wine glasses, napkins and silverware on the center island. He turned and smiled at me.

"Have a seat. I'll be done in a second."

I sidled up to one of the bar stools and set the bottle of wine on the counter. Taking the chance to observe the back of Cole's neck and broad shoulders, my gaze travelled down along his tapered waist to his narrow hips, fine ass...

He turned around and I snapped back to attention, a little too late. His eyes danced as he moved over to the sink to wash his hands.

"I hope you're hungry, because I made a lot of food."

"I was born hungry."

Opening the lower of the two ovens, he slid the chicken onto a rack and closed the door with his foot. He pulled a corkscrew out of a drawer and proceeded to open the bottle of wine. After pouring some for each of us, he set the bottle on the counter and raised his glass.

"To the start of a beautiful evening."

I smiled and touched my glass to his. His eyes were the same shade of blue as the Atlantic Ocean and so intense I had to look away. Damn, he made me nervous. Good thing the timer on the stove went off.

Cole reached for a hot pad, opened the upper oven and pulled out crisp brown quesadillas. He sliced them and retrieved bowls of sour cream, salsa and guacamole from the refrigerator, placing them on the island. Then he came around and sat beside me.

"Great wine," he said, pulling the bottle closer so he could read the label.

That old familiar feeling switched on as I got a whiff of his aftershave. A tingle of anticipation started in my toes and spread rapidly. I willed myself to say something witty, but my brain wouldn't cooperate.

"It was Wilma's recommendation. I wasn't sure what you were making, so I hope it works." I took a bite of the quesadilla. You could never go wrong with melted cheese. It also took my mind off of the image of Cole, naked.

"It's good."

We both reached for a napkin and our fingers brushed. An electric jolt shot up my arm.

Cole picked up his wine and turned to look at me, his eyes half lidded in that sexy, bedroom way. Evidently we were both thinking the same thing. He cleared his throat and got up to check the chicken. I mentally shook myself and decided on a safe conversation.

"The quesadilla's great."

He turned and smiled, obviously relieved to talk about something harmless. "Thanks. They're pretty easy to make."

I laughed. "Believe me, I can't cook much of anything—to my mother's horror."

"What did your parents do? You're from Minnesota, right?"

"Yeah. Mom taught at a junior college and Dad sold insurance." Uncomfortable, I changed the subject. "So what about you? I'll bet your folks were law enforcement, right?"

"Not exactly. Mom was a civil rights attorney in Seattle and Dad was career military."

"That must have been an interesting combination. Did you move a lot?"

"My mother decided she didn't want to move my brother and me around, so whenever Dad was stationed somewhere other than Seattle, he'd go alone. We'd visit him when we could."

"So you got to travel quite a bit? That sounds like heaven."

"You know, it didn't seem like a big deal; that's just the way it was. Dad would come and visit us when he had leave and we'd go to visit him on school breaks. It worked for us, although he missed a lot of our growing up stuff. That's why I fought so hard for custody of my two girls. I didn't want to miss that." Cole took another bite of quesadilla.

"Dad came back to Seattle when he retired. Now he and Mom do a lot of sailing. In fact, they're somewhere in the Caribbean as we speak."

"Mmmm. Now that's what I call living."

"I take it you like the tropics?"

"Complete beach bum. I'm a sucker for warm sand, cool water and little umbrellas in my drinks."

"So that's where you were last winter?"

Surprise. He was keeping track. I didn't think I'd made that much of an impression on him. At least, he hadn't shown any real interest as far as I could tell.

"I'm flattered you noticed."

"It's my job to notice." Cole got up and opened the oven to check on the chicken, then took a bowl of salad out of the fridge, brought it into the dining room and set it on the table.

I followed, noticing that the table had already been set, complete with tapered candles and a small bouquet of tulips in the center. How romantic. This evening just kept getting better and better.

"So tell me about where you like to go." I studied him for a moment. "I'll bet you like active vacations-skiing or hiking, right?"

"You're good," he said, walking back into the kitchen. "I am not real fond of lying out by the pool all day." He topped off the wine in both of our glasses. "My favorite trips have been where I combined things—like camping and rafting, or sailing to somewhere remote and hiking."

Now this was a man I could spend time with. I didn't enjoy sitting in a beach chair drinking all day, either. Not that napping in a hammock was out of the question, but I needed something else.

And he knew his way around a firearm.

The timer for the oven went off. Cole waved me into the dining room while he got everything together. He came back out with the roasted chicken, sun dried tomato and wild rice dressing and a big, steaming bowl of asparagus.

The conversation was effortless as we ate. Time flew off somewhere and did its own thing, and I could feel myself relaxing, forgetting about the events of the last few days. By the time we'd finished eating, the other bottle of wine was close to empty. We took the dishes into the kitchen and put them in the sink

"What do you say we go outside and look at the stars?"

He didn't have to ask me twice.

He grabbed the bottle of wine and I followed him with our glasses, past the living room and through a pair of French doors onto the patio.

The evening was mild and clear. I could hear the low hum of a hot tub off to my left, and directly in front of me stood an outdoor fireplace with a loveseat and two chairs surrounding a low table. The patio itself was a continuation of the slate from inside, and here and there low voltage lights illuminated the trees and plants.

Cole sat on the loveseat and patted the cushion beside him. I obliged. He picked up a remote and pointed it at the fireplace. Flames sprang to life, instantly transforming the patio into an outdoor living room. He put his arm across the back of the loveseat and I leaned my head back, turning a little so I could see him.

The light of the flames danced in his eyes. He reached up to stroke my cheek. I closed my eyes and sighed contentedly. He brushed a kiss across my neck, my nose, my eyes, my lips. I kissed him back, softly. The food and wine had mellowed us a bit, so the earlier lust was less prevalent, although that appeared to be changing rapidly.

Cole's voice had taken on a husky quality. "How do you feel about hot tubs?"

"They're my favorite."

He got up, pulling me after him and led me over to the hot tub. The underwater lights cast a bluish glow onto a mesquite tree growing beside it. The water looked inviting and it would so give me a chance to see more of Cole. I figured he probably had thoughts along those same lines.

He disappeared inside the house to get some towels and I seized the advantage and took off my clothes, laying them on the rock wall beside the tub. Naked, I slipped into the warm water while I searched for the button that would turn on the bubbles. I found it and the tub erupted as the jets surged to life.

Cole reappeared through the doors and, seeing me already in the tub, dropped the towels on a chair and started to take off his clothes.

His body was lean and his muscles well defined—he obviously took care of himself. The tingling started at my toes again and headed north. He slipped into the tub and floated his way over to my side. I smiled and moved a little farther away from him.

Enjoying the game, he moved closer. I slid to his right and just out of reach. He grinned and faked a move to his right. I fell for it, laughing and he promptly caught me, wrapping his arms around my waist as he pulled me toward him.

We kissed again and I wrapped my legs around him. He let out a groan and grabbed my hips, pulling me closer. He planted little kisses over my neck and breasts and I impatiently but gently took him in hand.

It wasn't long before we were both oblivious to anything but each other. The warm water swirled around our bodies in a sensual dance. I looked up at the sky at one point and the stars exploded before my eyes.

Okay, maybe not, but it was probably one of the best orgasms I'd ever experienced, bar none.

The intensity subsided and we relaxed against the side of the tub in each other's arms. Stroking my now damp hair, he kissed me as I snuggled into the crook of his arm.

"Kate," he murmured, "I don't think I've ever met anyone quite like you."

I smiled as I looked up at him. He kissed me on the mouth, this time with such tenderness it took my breath away.

My fight or flight instinct kicked into "flight" and I pulled away. Memories of Sam, a cop assigned to protect me years earlier in Alaska, flooded my mind. He'd almost died because of me. Every time I got close to someone, something awful happened.

God, I was tired of those fucking bad spirits. They had no place here. Not tonight.

"I'm thirsty. I think I should go get us a glass of water." I climbed out of the hot tub and grabbed a towel off the back of the chair as I walked toward the house. I looked over my shoulder at him and lifted a corner of the towel to give him a peek, prompting him to whistle softly.

Laughing, I went into the kitchen and started to open cupboards.

"Where do you keep the glasses?"

"They're in that cupboard."

The voice came from a lot closer than the patio and nearer to the floor. I looked down and let out a yell, dropping my towel.

A pint-sized girl with light brown hair stood in the doorway leading from the hall to the kitchen. She pointed matter-of-factly at a cupboard to my left.

Another voice came from behind her.

"Who are you talking to, Abby?" The voice rounded the corner, attached to a tanned, beautifully dressed, perfectly coiffed platinum blonde woman about my age.

She stopped short in the doorway and leveled a cool gaze at me, arms folded across her chest.

Momentarily flustered, I retrieved the towel from near my feet and wrapped it around my now exceptionally naked body. The stony silence was interrupted by the sound of Cole on his way in from the patio, and I could tell without turning around when he reached the doorway that he'd neglected to put on his towel.

There was a pause in conversation as he took in the situation.

"Hey, Abby," he said.

Abby's face lit up and she looked like she was about to run to him, but the woman restrained her.

Cole quickly recovered his composure and moved a little behind me as he wrapped his towel around his waist. Once that was accomplished he moved forward and put himself between the ice queen and me.

Abby looked curiously from Cole to her mother back to Cole. She craned her neck, trying to catch a glimpse of me around her father. I tilted my head to the side so she could see my face. Our eyes met and I winked at her. She grinned and leaned back into her mother who at this moment was speaking in a cool, clipped and rather icy tone.

"Lauren wasn't feeling well and she asked me to bring them both home tonight. It appears she doesn't want to miss school on Tuesday and she was afraid if she stayed in Scottsdale I wouldn't let her come home until she was completely well." Her light blue eyes had a wintry glint. She appraised me, devoid of emotion. "Aren't you going to introduce me to your...friend?"

I straightened up from making faces at Abby and stood at attention. She'd make a good drill sergeant, I thought. Abby mimicked my move and comically stood at attention, too. I stifled a laugh.

"Abby, go to your room," the woman snapped. I winced at her sharp tone.

Abby's face fell, wondering what she'd done now to get into trouble. I made another face at her and she giggled as she turned and ran down the hallway to her room. Her mother waited until the door to the bedroom clicked closed.

"Lorna, we made a deal—" Cole began.

"To what? Expose our children to strange naked women?" Her voice rising, she raked me with a glare I assumed was intended to make mere humans quail. Unperturbed, I debated whether I should make a comment about not being so strange, but bit my tongue.

"And what kind of an impression do you think that makes on them, hmmm?" she said, as she eyed the empty bottle of wine sitting on the counter.

"You could've called to tell me you were coming. That's another part of the deal, remember?" The anger in Cole's voice sliced through the room. "And Kate is not some strange naked woman. We've been seeing each other for a while now."

That was news to me, but what the hell, it pissed Lorna off when he said it and I was all for anything that'd piss her off.

Lorna's face turned a fierce shade of red beneath her dark tan as I stepped out from behind Cole and adjusted my towel.

Her eyes followed me with cold calculation. She was predatory, on the lookout for some sign of weakness where she'd be able to press whatever advantage she thought she might have.

I had a lot of experience with predators.

Granted, she was fully dressed and the mother of their children, but I had the distinct advantage of having recently had sex with Cole and that trumped bitchy ex-wife any day, at least in my book. Besides, she was the one that brought the girls back early.

I held out my hand and said, "Hi. I'm Kate. You must be Lorna." I couldn't quite bring myself to spit out the "pleased to meet you" part.

Lorna ignored my extended hand and glared at me.

I let it drop to my side. I didn't play that way. With a sympathetic look at Cole, I slipped back out to the patio to put on my clothes.

As the fresh night air cooled my body, I let out a deep sigh. Well, it had been a good evening up to that point. I could hear the heated conversation going on in the house. I felt so sorry for Cole and especially the girls. It couldn't be easy being the children of a divorce. Hell, it couldn't be easy being the children of that woman. I shook my head. I thought my life was complicated. I only had people trying to kill me.

A raspy, whistling sound came from one of the windows near the back of the house. Curious, I walked around the big mesquite tree in the corner of the yard toward the noise. It didn't sound dangerous, but I picked my way carefully around the low growing succulents.

As I drew near the window, I could see a lamp on in the room, illuminating Abby. She had her little face pressed to the screen and her lips puckered up, trying to whistle.

I walked over to see what she wanted.

A loud whisper came through the screen. "I don't know how to whistle yet, but my Daddy's going to teach me, real soon." Abby paused, as if in thought, and then said, "Do you know how to whistle?"

"Yeah, but it's pretty loud. I don't think your Mom or Dad would appreciate my doing it right now."

Abby decided to try a different tack. "Why were you and Daddy naked?"

In my experience, honesty had always been the best policy when dealing with kids. "We were in the hot tub."

"Really?" Abby's voice was breathless. "We have to wear our swimming suits when we go in. You wanna see mine? It's got fish all over it."

I didn't have time to answer. She'd already run over to her dresser and pulled the bottom drawer open and was digging through her clothes. Triumphantly pulling out her little one-piece swimsuit with colorful fish on it, she ran back to the window to show me.

"That's really cool, Abby."

"Do you have one?"

"Yes, I do. It's back at home, though."

"Oh. Is that why you didn't have one on?"

"Yeah. I forgot to bring it with me."

A soft cough issued from the hallway near her bedroom door. Abby turned to see who it was. A lithesome young girl with blonde hair who I guessed must be Lauren walked in, wrapped in a blanket. She came over to the window and looked out at me. She had a lot of her mother in her, minus the frigidity. Abby was more like Cole.

"Who are you?" she asked.

"My name is Kate. What's yours?"

"I'm Lauren. Are you the reason Mommy and Daddy are fighting?"

That put things into perspective.

"I'm afraid so," I said.

Lauren nodded gravely. Then she looked up at me and said in a most serious tone, "Don't worry about

278

Mommy. She gets mad about everything." Abby nodded her head vigorously.

Lauren cocked her head to one side, looking at me through the screen.

"You're pretty."

"Why thank you, Lauren, so are you."

I looked over at Abby. "And you are too, Abby."

They both beamed. They were sweet kids.

We all heard it at the same time and looked toward the partially closed door. Lorna was coming down the hall, calling for both of them. They drew in their breath and looked at each other in a panic, then turned toward me. I put my finger to my lips and crouched down, out of sight.

They let out a collective sigh and said in unison, "We're in here, Mommy." I didn't wait to hear what she was going to say to them—I wasn't in the mood. Silently I slipped back to the patio.

Cole was dressed and outside looking for me. When he caught sight of me, he shook his head, raised his hands and rolled his eyes.

I smiled to let him know it wasn't a big deal.

"God, Kate, I'm so sorry this all happened." He still looked angry.

"Hey, there's nothing you could've done to change it. A tiny glitch." I grinned. "At least I got to meet your daughters." Abby may have met more of me than I'd intended, but hey, no harm done.

"Yeah. You know, Lorna was never like this when we were married." He paused. "At least I don't think she was."

I moved closer, wrapped my arms around him and kissed him. He kissed me back, passionately. I stepped back, fanning myself.

"You are one great kisser, I'll give you that," I said.

He took my hand and led me back into the house. I started for the front door.

Cole held me back. "She's going to be gone soon. She has a long drive back to Scottsdale. You could stay, you know."

I shook my head. "I think I should go. It was a wonderful dinner, Cole. Thank you for everything." I emphasized the word everything. He grinned.

I slipped on my shoes and he walked me out through the front door and down the steps to my Jeep. He opened the door for me and I got in and started the engine. He leaned in to kiss me again. It was lovely and soft and it made my lips tingle.

I put the Jeep into gear and he stepped back as I pulled out of the drive. All in all, not a bad beginning.

SEVEN

My eyes shot open and I was instantly awake. Something was different, but I couldn't put my finger on what. I checked the clock on my nightstand: two-thirty. Bright light streamed in through the gaps in the trailer's curtains.

That meant one thing. Something set off the motion sensor lights outside. I figured it was either Art's dog, Rudy, sniffing around or one of the other critters that frequented this neck of the woods. I sat up and reached over to move aside the curtain so I could get a better look.

Everything appeared fine. I padded out to the kitchen and peeked through the curtains at the window over the sink. Nothing out there, either.

I cracked the window and listened. The sound of the river booming down the canyon behind the trailer drowned out all other sounds.

It occurred to me that I should probably go out and check to see how high the water had risen in case I needed to move to higher ground. Art told me when I'd moved in that it hadn't overflowed its banks in the fifteen years he'd been there, but it had been an unusually wet spring.

I walked back into my bedroom to put on some clothes and grab a Maglite. As I passed my purse lying on the table, I reached in and slid out the 9mm before I stepped outside. Black bears were common in these mountains and having a gun made me feel better.

The lights in front were still on, so I didn't need the flashlight right away. I moved around to the back of the trailer, holding the gun in front of me. The rear motion sensor lights popped on, illuminating a bright-eyed thief in the middle of my garbage can scrounging for dinner. Relieved, I lowered the gun.

"Shoo! Go on. You're making a mess." I waved my flashlight at the raccoon. He stood up on his hind legs, clutching a chicken leg in his hands and chattered away, looking at me like I was some kind of entertainment provided for his dining enjoyment.

I took a step toward him, but a glove-covered hand clamped over my mouth. I tried to hit back at my assailant, but before I could, he pinned my arms to my sides. The gun fell from my hand and skipped across the gravel.

Struggling against the concrete-like grip, I attempted to bite through the leather glove, but it was too thick.

Panic raced through my body, threatening to paralyze me. This guy felt like all muscle.

He began to drag me away from the light of the trailer, heading for the woods near the river. That couldn't be good. I contorted my body, trying to break free, but then remembered an old self-defense instructor said to go limp, like a dead weight to make it more difficult for him to move.

I dropped. It barely slowed him down. With each attempt at escape, his grip tightened until I could hardly breathe. My ribs felt like they were about to crack.

He was eerily silent. No grunts, no threatening, nothing. It had a chilling effect.

I stood up and brought my heel down on his instep. It wasn't as effective as I'd hoped, but I did manage to get a grunt of sorts out of him. His grip loosened and I slipped out of his grasp, swinging the Maglite, hard.

It connected with a thud and I heard him groan. I ran toward the gun on the ground, my screams drowned out by the roar of the river.

A searing pain arced across my scalp as his hand clamped onto my hair and he wrenched me back.

Intense pain shot through my side as I connected with the ground. The flashlight flew out of my hand. I flailed my arms, trying to keep him from pinning me to the ground. He tried to straddle me, but was distracted by my kicking legs.

I grabbed a nearby rock with both hands and smashed it against his face.

He fell backward on the ground, shaking his head.

I scrambled to my feet. On his knees now, his huge frame blocked the door to the trailer. I sprinted toward the gun, a few yards to my left.

Bad move. I barely made it half way when his hand came down hard on my shoulder.

Something snapped inside of me. Anger from years of being afraid and looking over my shoulder roiled to the surface. An enormous surge of adrenaline coursed through me. I turned into him and delivered a sharp thrust to his groin with my knee.

He doubled over with a groan and grabbed for me, knocking me off balance. I fell over backward and he fell on top of me.

We both grunted with pain. It felt like I'd been trapped on my back by a refrigerator. I couldn't breathe. We were near the riverbank and the cold spray stung my skin. The water rumbled as it fought its way down the canyon. I turned my head to look at him.

I'd never encountered eyes that cold. They appeared black in the moonlight. He wasn't anyone I knew. A scar ran diagonally across his face from his forehead to his cheek. His neck and shoulders were thick, like a body builder. His expression held no emotion.

I stared back at him, struggling to break free.

"Why?" I practically screamed the word.

He didn't say anything. The next thing I knew, my head exploded in pain and a million stars with the impact of his fist.

I faked unconsciousness, my eyes opened to slits.

He pinned my arms down with his knees as he reached behind his back. In that instant I realized my legs were free. I raised them, hooked my heels around his shoulders and dragged him over backwards. The move caught him off guard and he lost his balance. He fell back, arms flailing. A knife flew from his hand.

I sprang to my feet and dove for the knife, but he recovered quickly and lunged for it at the same time.

I was faster and grabbed it before he did.

He eyed me warily, staying just out of reach.

Scared to death and running on pure adrenaline, I knew I had the advantage, however tenuous.

We circled each other.

Touring for Death

He feinted right, and I tracked his move. He came in fast using his left hand and I brought the knife down, slicing into his forearm.

A dark stain of blood appeared and spread. He sucked in a sharp breath and stared at his arm, then at me, surprise evident on his face.

Fury sprang to life in his eyes.

I held my ground, trying not to lose my nerve but I was petrified. I wanted to scream, but it wouldn't do any good; the noise from the river would swallow the sound.

He lunged at me and I took a step back, pivoting to the side. He overshot his mark, almost plunging over the edge of the cliff into the raging torrent below. He regained his balance, straightened and turned around.

Before I could react, he came at me with a roundhouse kick and knocked the knife out of my hand.

My arm went numb and a solid wall of muscle barreled toward me. Unable to support his weight we both hit the ground. A sharp pain swept through my body on contact.

His hands gripped my throat like an iron band.

I clawed at his fingers.

He squeezed harder. Blackness enveloped me. I continued to fight.

And lost.

***

I woke to the sound of tires crunching on gravel. I shook my head, trying to dissipate the fog. As my vision cleared, an avocado hued Hotpoint stove and ancient, clanking refrigerator came into focus.

Rug covered pinewood floors, painted to match the stove supported overstuffed Mohair furniture and a 1950s era maple coffee table. A small fire blazed in a rock fireplace at one end of the small cabin. A hard rain assaulted the roof.

All very cozy except for the fact that I was duct taped to a chair and my attacker sat on the couch, flipping through a magazine. I couldn't quite read the title, but figured it had something to do with how to kidnap someone in ten easy steps.

Why did he let me live? He had a knife and I'd been unconscious. But more importantly, how could I get out of here?

The door opened and Dave Sinclair walked in, carrying a paper grocery bag. A cigarette dangled from his lips.

"Dave, run!" I yelled, hoping to warn him before Psycho Boy tried anything.

He glanced at me, then at Psycho Boy. My happiness at seeing him dimmed when I realized his reaction didn't jibe with my expectations.

"She's awake."

Psycho Boy grunted and rose from the couch, cracking his knuckles as he walked toward me. I straightened in the chair, completely focused on his large hands.

Keeping an eye on the scary guy, I turned to Dave.

"What am I doing here, Dave? Playtime's over. Turn me loose and we'll call it a day."

Dave snorted as he pulled the cigarette from his mouth, using it to light another.

"Playtime. That's a good one." He took a deep draw from the cigarette and exhaled a plume of blue smoke. My eyes watered and I started to cough.

Psycho Boy's knuckle cracking distracted me. He looked like he was getting ready to put the hurt on someone duct taped to a kitchen chair.

"Wait, Roland," Dave said. He turned to me, his eyes glinting in the light of the lone bulb hanging from the ceiling. "Kate and I have business."

"And what kind of business would that be, Dave?" I asked. I didn't bother to keep the sarcasm from my voice. What kind of hell was I in to be this man's prisoner?

He dragged a chair over to sit across from me, wheezing as the exertion proved too much for his two-pack-a-day lungs.

"The business of seeing you die." He nodded his head at Roland. "It's hard to find good help these days."

"What do you mean?" I stared at Dave as I tumbled to his meaning.

"Surely you remember the morning your brakes failed? It wasn't that long ago." He tapped his cigarette into the ashtray on the table next to him. "And then Roland completely screwed up when he tried to run you off the road the other night. Didn't you, Roland?" Dave shook his head, making a *tsking* sound as he looked at Psycho Boy. "Repairs to the rental were an expense I hadn't anticipated."

Roland's scowl spoke volumes. It occurred to me that he might get pissed off enough at Dave to kill him. I certainly wouldn't get in his way.

"You did a good job with that biologist and the old couple, though, didn't you?" Dave turned back to me, his face flushed. His eyes narrowed. "But not her. What the fuck is so hard about getting rid of her?"

My reaction spiraled beyond stunned. The guy responsible for the murders turns out to be Dave?

Bankers weren't supposed to go out and have people killed. That was for sociopaths.

And shadow governments.

"What are you doing, Dave? I know we've had our differences, but Roxanne and that sweet old couple? They couldn't possibly have done anything to hurt you."

"Oh, but they could." Dave turned to face me as he inhaled deeply from his cigarette. He coughed wetly as he exhaled. "The other morning on one of your tours you, Roxanne and that sweet old couple saw something that could destroy everything. I won't let that happen. The projected profits from Wild Horse Ridge will put Durm Fidelity & Trust on terra firma for years to come. Not to mention the other, uh, let's call them revenue streams. Do you seriously think I'd let that stupid biologist submit her report?" He shook his head in disgust. "Another damned thorn in my side. She was principled." He practically spit the words. "My luck I get one that won't take a bribe, for fuck's sake."

Things started to click into place in my brain. "Is all this because of the bird? The Spreckled Pygmy Twatter, or whatever it's called?"

Dave nodded grimly. "Yeah. It's about the damned bird. Can you imagine? One little, insignificant bird and if anyone finds out, poof! The whole deal's dead in the water." He took another hit off the cigarette. If I was lucky, he'd keel over from a heart attack. "Not to mention my career. What the hell's the world coming to when a fucking bird can stop something as important as Wild Horse Ridge?"

I wasn't about to argue the merits of arbitration with crazy Dave. I was thinking more along the lines of getting out of the cabin, preferably with my life. Then the words he said registered. There were four other people on my tour that morning. The Harrisons. Had Rollie killed them, too? Is that why Cole hadn't been able to contact them? Think, Kate. Dave didn't mention that Rollie'd 'done a good job' with them. They might still be alive.

"You can't be serious, Dave. Having that family killed puts you and Rollie in monster territory. There were children, for God's sake."

Rollie looked up sharply. "I never killed them kids."

"Shut up!" Dave backhanded Rollie across the face. He winced and glared at Dave. I tensed for the bloodbath. It never came. Rollie must be waiting on his money.

Bankers.

A loud thump echoed from the far end of the cabin. Dave waved at Rollie.

"Check it out."

Rollie headed for the source of the sound, rubbing his cheek. I turned to Dave.

"They're in the back, aren't they?"

Dave frowned and didn't say anything as he stubbed out his cigarette.

He hadn't killed anyone yet. So far, Rollie'd done the dirty work. If I were a betting woman, I'd wager the banking mentality didn't generally predispose a person to violent acts, other than by proxy. That left Rollie as the main threat. I decided to wait and see if my odds for escape got any better.

Rollie walked back into the room. "It's nothing."

Dave lit his third cigarette and turned to me, squinting through the smoke. "This is going to hurt me more than it does you, Kate, believe me." He threw the roll of duct tape to Rollie.

"Get her out to the truck and strap her in good and tight. I'll be right behind you. We're going to take her out the back way, by the creek."

A puzzled look crossed Rollie's face as he looked at Dave. "The road's washed out from the storm and it's started raining again. We'll never get through."

Dave smiled. "Perfect."

***

Rollie hadn't been gentle cutting me out of the chair or dragging me outside into the woods. I didn't make it easy for him, but he was so much stronger than me that my attempts at immobilizing him weren't very effective. It was still raining hard, and soon we were both soaked through to our skin.

Panic overwhelmed me, certain "taking me out the back way" was some kind of lunatic banker jargon for "take her out in the woods and shoot her." It turned out he was parked out back with a tarp and a bunch of dead branches on top of the vehicle. The truck was an older model Dodge, maybe late seventies. He removed the camouflage and stuffed me into the front passenger seat, using the duct tape like a seat belt by taping it first around my upper body and then to the back of the seat.

There was no glass in the passenger side window. It was going to be a cold, wet ride.

Behind us, the headlights from Dave's SUV illuminated the interior of the truck. Rollie got behind the wheel and started the engine. We drove through the woods, the driving rain obscuring the narrow gravel road we followed. I had no idea where we were. That didn't stop me from planning my escape.

"You know what Dave's going to do?" I had to shout to be heard over the incessant drum of the rain and slap of the windshield wipers. Rollie stared straight ahead. He acted as if my voice didn't even register.

"What do you think Dave's going to do when he's through with you? Think he's going to just hand you a wad of money and send you on your way?" My laugh echoed across the cab. "Not likely. He'll probably kill you, too."

Rollie stared at me with a look that sent chills crawling down my back. I could barely hear him as he said, "I don't give a shit what you say, bitch. You're dead."

I took a deep breath. Psycho Boy was my one chance. "You think he's gonna let you live, knowing what you know?" I leaned my head back. "Just thought I should give you a heads up, Rollie. We're both in the same boat here."

Rollie drove on in stony silence. I hoped he was thinking about what I'd said.

We bounced uncomfortably along as the storm intensified. Water splashed up the doors and in through the window every time the truck hit a hole. Flashes of lightening split the sky as the rain beat relentlessly on the windshield. He set the wipers on high, but they barely kept up. Dave's headlights helped illuminate the way forward with a jarring, strobe-like effect. The old truck's own headlights were covered in mud, making them practically useless.

A short time later, we slowed to a stop. Dave's SUV pulled in behind us. Rollie looked tense. I didn't know if he'd let me go or if he'd still kill me, but anything was worth a try at this point. We watched in our side mirrors as Dave opened his door and got out, wearing a dark, hooded raincoat.

Rollie stepped out of the truck and slammed the door behind him. I twisted around to watch, but it was raining too hard to see anything. I tried wiggling my hands free. They were going numb and my shoulders ached. I tried rocking my torso back and forth, hoping the duct tape would stretch. It gave a little, but Rollie had wrapped it too many times to make it easy.

At this point desperation kicked in. I looked around the cab for something to cut through the tape and remembered my utility knife. The familiar feel of it in my front pocket gave me a tiny amount of hope. Neither of them had thought to go through my jeans. All I had to do was get to it.

The driver's side door opened and Rollie sat down heavily, slumping a little, not entirely on the seat. His legs moved as if they were made of rags. He didn't look too good as he leaned against the steering wheel. Dave was alongside him, trying to stuff him into the driver's side. Dread flowed through me.

Dave smiled at me and gave me a thumbs up. What the hell did that mean? I didn't have a lot of experience interpreting psychotic-banker hand signals.

Dave shouted through the rain. "It's all part of the plan, Kate. Rollie's dead."

No kidding. There went my bankers only kill by proxy theory. Dave fished in his coat pocket and produced an empty syringe. "Potassium. Found it on the Internet," he shouted over the rain. I assumed I was next. I hoped it wasn't painful. Dave shut the driver's door. I tried to look through the side windows to see where he was headed, but visibility was nil. Craning my neck, I turned toward the open window next to me.

And screamed.

Dave leaned in, his face nearly touching mine. He bent over to check the tape, making sure it was secure. Little rivulets of rain water flowed down the creases in his raincoat onto my leg.

"You scared the crap out of me." I shouted.

"Yeah? Well, then the rest should be easy." Looking satisfied with how the tape was holding out, he yelled, "See over there, where it looks like a steep drop off?" I looked. I could barely make out what he was pointing at. "It used to be an arroyo. Thanks to Mother Nature, now it's a river."

So that's why the headlights fell off in the distance. Usually, arroyos were dry. During rainstorms like this they became raging torrents. My throat tightened. I knew what he planned to do.

"I need to make it look like Rollie here was escaping with you in his truck and sadly you got stuck in the path of a flash flood. Both of you drowned, I'm sorry to report." He nodded over at Rollie. "When they find you, it'll look like he died of a heart attack. Since you were taped into the passenger seat you weren't able to escape."

Dave stepped away from the truck, but must have thought better of it and leaned in once more. "Any last words?" He grinned through the pouring rain.

"You can't be serious." Panic rose in my chest. His eyes had a disturbing luminosity to them, like someone else was in there along with Dave. I shuddered. Was he off his meds? Why did I care? He was going to kill me. I had to figure something out or I'd be coyote sushi.

"Goodbye, Kate." He put his hand underneath my chin and tilted my head back as if to kiss me. Oh dear God, please, no. His breath reeked of stale ashtray and bad gums. I turned my head away, gagging. I wasn't going to let my last human contact be a kiss from a jowly, delusional, out of shape banker with periodontal disease.

Dave let go of me and stepped back, evidently displeased. He went around to the driver's side, opened the door, reached across the steering wheel and Rollie's dead body, and shifted the truck into neutral. Leaning against the frame, he threw his body forward. The truck rolled a few inches, then returned to its original position. He tried again, and it rolled back again. The third try was the charm. We started to move. Dave leaned into it and we began to pick up speed. When he let go, the truck rolled over the drop off into the rushing water below.

I braced for the impact. Thanks to the tape, I didn't hit the windshield, although I couldn't say the same for Rollie. Good thing he was already dead. His body bounced sideways, his head close to my leg. The truck's back wheel slid along the gravel bed from the force of the water, then stopped.

You're going to die, Kate. The insistent voice in my head was annoying.

It wouldn't be long before we were either swept away or the truck was inundated with ice cold water. I didn't know if Dave was up on the bank watching or not and I didn't care. I worked my arms and upper body back and forth, straining at the tape until I was soaked with perspiration. It stretched, but not much.

I was not going to die in a freaking arroyo.

The water level rose high enough that it started seeping through the cracks in the door. I kept working the tape. It covered my shins before I finally started to see some progress. I wriggled my hands until they ached.

The truck slid sideways as the water pushed us further down the flooded gulch. I held my breath, praying it wouldn't flip onto its side. It shuddered to a stop as the truck hung up on something. I tried pulling my hands out of the tape. By this time, icy water streamed in through the open window and swirled around my waist. My teeth chattered and I could barely catch my breath. My legs were like blocks of ice. If I didn't drown, hypothermia was definitely next on the list. Rollie started to float and drift my way. I head butted him away once, but he kept coming back. I tried to ignore him and kept working.

Ignoring a floating dead body is harder than you'd think.

At last, I loosened the duct tape enough to tear one hand out. My upper arms and chest were still taped to the seat, but with my left hand free I was able to dig into the front pocket of my pants. Ignoring the pain, I pushed deeper into my pocket, searching for the knife. My fingers closed around it and I slid it out, inch by careful inch. I held my hand and the knife to my mouth and blew on them, trying to get some feeling back into my fingers. I managed to pull out the largest blade with my teeth and I worked to saw through the tape around my sternum, my fingers clumsy from the cold.

After several tries, the tape gave way. I ripped the rest from my arms and cut through what was left on my ankles. Then I pulled myself out through the side window and onto the hood. Water churned past the truck. The rain pelted me with such force, it felt like I was drowning. A big, uprooted tree in the middle of the arroyo stopped the Dodge from sliding. I squinted at the bank to see if I could make out where the truck went in, but we'd covered a lot of ground in the slide and nothing looked familiar. I was relieved to see no sign of Dave.

Both banks were too far from the truck. I'd never be able to jump that far. There was one thing left to do.

I slid off the hood into the icy, rushing water.

The force of the flow pinned me to the front fender and made it tough to move. I inched my way along the side of the truck, fighting the suction and paused at the front end. The next step might be my last.

I inhaled and exhaled several times. Then I sucked in one last, deep breath before I stepped into the raging torrent.

EIGHT

The force of the water swept me under. The frigid shock sucked the breath from my lungs. Closing my eyes, I ducked my head into my arms for protection. I smacked against something hard with my hip, but scraped past it. It felt like my chest was going to explode. Raging, swirling suffocation. I surfaced for a second, gasped for air, went down again.

The water dragged me along, tossing me like a plaything, a Raggedy Ann doll. I tensed, expecting more rocks, and was surprised by sharp branches stabbing, ripping at my sides. I tried to curl into a fetal position, offer less acreage for the debris, but I rotated, couldn't tell which way was up.

I reached out, hoping to snag a branch, something to pull me out of the spin cycle, and caught air. Flailing my arms, I bobbed to the surface and barely gulped another breath before being yanked down again.

I'd seen something ahead, some kind of shadow that looked like it might be part of the bank. With every last shred of strength, I kicked out and breast-stroked toward it, hoping for luck.

Sand.

I shoved my hand into the wet slurry, launched myself onto my front and dug in with my other fist, fighting the suction, kicking hard, not sure it would work.

Determined to defeat its morbid grip, I heaved my body upward until the raging, sucking river released its hold.

I gasped for air, coughing when I inhaled the last of the brackish water. I rolled onto my back and struggled to a sitting position.

The water roared past, dizzying in its force. The branches left a gash in my side. My shirt was ripped and when I brought my hand away, I felt something other than water. I shivered, teeth chattering uncontrollably, and rotated onto my hands and knees, pushing myself to stand. I'd landed on the same side of the arroyo as the cabin, but didn't have a clue how far I'd been dragged downriver.

I grabbed onto a handful of roots and a shrub barely clinging to the bank, and pulled myself upward, resolving to reach the top of the arroyo. I'd learned from previous bad situations to establish small, achievable victories or else the magnitude of what I needed to do would overwhelm me. I could figure out what to do once I passed the first step.

I'm not sure how long it took me, but I reached the top and stopped to get my bearings. A gray, watery light cast a gloomy net through the pines. The rain had stopped, for now. Branches bowed, dripping from the heavy downpour. The exertion had warmed me some, but my temperature soon dropped and I knew I had to keep moving or I'd die of exposure. I set out upriver, back toward the cabin. I didn't know how far it was from town, but figured there had to be a road nearby that led to a highway. Once I got to town, I wanted to be able tell Cole where I'd last seen Dave.

And maybe the Harrisons.

My mood plummeted at the thought of the family that had been on my tour—Blair and Charles and their two goofy kids, Dmitri and Heather. Dmitri had been a pain in my ass, but ten year olds tended to push their boundaries and I found that he grew on me. Heather was a sweet, bookish girl and she got along well with Roxanne the biologist and her scientific jargon.

I assumed the Harrisons had still been alive when I was at the cabin. The thought of what Dave might be capable of now that he'd killed Rollie filled me with grim resolve. I had to get back there, if only to be able to recover the bodies and secure evidence against Dave.

The smell of smoke jarred me out of my thoughts. I noticed a faint glow through the trees and guessed Dave had left the lights on in the cabin. I walked past a stand of pines and the cabin came into full view. Dave's SUV was parked outside. Surprised, I crouched behind the trees and watched for signs of movement.

He was still here? My heart raced with hope. Maybe he hadn't killed the Harrisons.

Yet.

Once I determined Dave wasn't outside, I crept over to his Lexus. Not my lucky day. There was no cell phone lying on the seat. I checked to see if he'd left the keys in the ignition. He hadn't. I eased the door open, freezing when the hinges creaked. No one came out to investigate. I started to breathe again.

I felt underneath the passenger seat and, finding nothing, laid on my stomach and felt under the driver's side. Again, nothing. I sat up and opened the console.

Dave's smart phone.

I searched the apps and found the GPS. Then I called Cole, glancing back at the cabin to watch for Dave. It rang twice, then silence. I checked the screen. No reception. I got out of the truck, easing the door closed with a slight click, and moved to another location in the yard. I was rewarded with two bars. I hit redial. Relief flooded through me when it started to ring.

"Cole Anderson."

"Cole- thank God. It's Kate. Dave's trying to kill—"

"Kate? Is that you? You're breaking up. Move... better reception..."

I walked closer to the cabin, careful to keep my voice low.

"Is this any better?" No answer.

Beyond frustrated, I redialed his number from several other locations, ready to duck if the cabin door opened. Nothing. I gave up and shoved the phone into the crotch of a pine tree.

Dave was still nowhere to be seen from my limited view of the interior of the cabin, so I crept underneath what I thought was the kitchen window. The sill stood about an inch too tall for me to have a clear view inside. I slid an old orange crate sitting nearby under the window.

The lone light bulb dangling from the kitchen ceiling was on and the fire in the fireplace had long since died. I'd about decided to try a different window when without warning, Dave's dark-blue suited bulk walked into the kitchen to my left. I ducked below the sill, certain he'd seen me. In a panic, I dove under the porch.

The door opened and the boards above my head groaned with his weight. Ancient particles of dust and dirt cascaded in clumps around me. I tried to quiet my breathing, certain he could hear my heart banging against my chest.

Touring for Death

His shadow spilled onto the ground next to the porch as he leaned against the handrail. A piece of ash floated to earth. I held my breath. Blue smoke billowed into the air. A few minutes later he flicked the still-lit cigarette butt into the yard. Then he turned and walked back into the cabin.

With control, I exhaled and closed my eyes. I couldn't wait for him to leave. The Harrisons might still be alive. I doubted he'd stay at the cabin once he killed them, but I couldn't be sure.

I crawled out from under the porch and kept to the shadows, skirting the perimeter of the cabin. The windows stood lower at the back and I could see inside. The first one I came to looked into an empty room. The second held the Harrisons.

They were alive. My spirits soared, but crashed soon after as I realized how dangerous rescue would be. Blair and Charles had been duct taped back to back in separate chairs, as had Dmitri and Heather. The bedroom door was closed. I tapped lightly on the glass. Dmitri's eyes grew large when he saw me. I quickly held my finger to my lips. He nodded that he understood. Blair looked at Dmitri, then at me. She shook her head, panic evident in her eyes and motioned toward the door. I pantomimed that I knew Dave was there. She closed her eyes and nodded.

I tried the window, but it wouldn't budge. I checked nearby for something that I could use to pry it open, but realized Dave would hear me before I could get the Harrisons out.

I had to go inside.

Giving them the 'ok' sign to let them know I was coming back, I continued around the outside of the cabin. I found the rear door on the other side. Someone had propped the screen against the outside wall. The rusty doorknob hung at an odd angle.

It came off in my hand and the door swung open. I left the knob on the step and carefully pushed the door wider, stepping inside the dark hallway.

My heart pounding in my ears and alert to any sign of movement from the interior of the cabin, I moved quickly to the Harrison's room. The sound of metal clanking against metal came from the direction of the kitchen.

The door to the bedroom opened easily and I slipped in, checking to see if it could be locked from the inside. It couldn't. I took out my utility knife and immediately set to work cutting through the tape wrapped around Charles and Blair's wrists. I worked methodically, moving to their ankles and then to Dmitri and Heather, until everyone was free. I walked to the door and listened before opening it and checking the hallway.

"He said he was going to blow the cabin. That we wouldn't feel a thing." Blair whispered, her dark eyes radiating anxiety.

That probably explained the clanking sound I heard. I pointed down the hall. "The back door is that way." I glanced at their feet. "Take off your shoes. Go outside and get as far away as you can. I'll be right behind you."

The Harrisons filed out, shoes in hand, moving like ghosts out the back door. I made it about half way down the hallway when I heard a sharp intake of breath.

"Well, fuck me."

I turned slowly. Dave stood in the hallway, cigarette burned to gravity defying ash in one hand, gun pointed at my skull in the other. His starched white button-down shirt was open at his flaccid neck and stained with perspiration. His loosened power tie fell limply across his chest. Toupee askew, it resembled road kill. All in all, not a great look for Dave.

"What, you got nine lives, like a fucking cat?" Dave's face was so red it was purple. Maybe if we waited long enough he'd have a stroke. "You're supposed to be dead." He poked at the air with the gun and dropped the cigarette butt on the floor, crushing it with his wingtip.

"It was all going to be so simple." He glared at me, his expression heavy with contempt. "You'd be dead, they'd be dead and I'd go back home and everything would be fine. But nooooo." He shook his head. "You changed everything. Now I have to leave the bank I worked so fucking hard to build. God I need a cigarette." He patted his chest with his free hand. "Fuck. FUCK."

I seized the moment and hurled myself at him. Both of us slammed to the floor. Dave's gun went off, but I kept moving, adrenaline galloping through my veins. My hand closed around the barrel of the gun and I gave it a vicious twist. It came free in my hand. He grabbed for it, but I slid off him, sprang to my feet and took aim.

He'd been struggling to sit upright, but at the sight of me with the gun pointed at him, he stopped.

"Well, shit." His shoulders heaved in a rhythmic motion as he wheezed, trying to catch his breath.

My left arm felt numb and was hard to lift. I kept the gun trained at his head, alert to any sudden movement. Dave turned toward me. A percussive sound like chopper blades beat the air somewhere in the distance.

Beads of sweat ran down Dave's pallid face. His eyes watered.

"A fucking bird." He looked down and shook his head. He started to sigh, but stopped, mid-breath.

"What's that smell?" I inhaled, trying to identify the odor. It had a hint of garlic and something else I couldn't quite place. I searched his face. A grin split his face as he reached in his shirt pocket and pulled out his disposable lighter. He held it up, like he was at a concert.

Propane.

I launched myself backward into the bedroom, crossed the floor in two strides, covered my head with my arms and hurled myself through the window.

The roar of the explosion drowned out the sound of shattering glass.

***

The medic finished wrapping where the bullet had entered and exited the fleshy part of my upper arm. All the cuts I received from the glass were treated and bandaged. Cole waited until she packed up her case and had walked around to the front of the ambulance.

He tucked the blanket she'd given me around my shoulders and sat down next to me on the bumper.

I leaned my head against his chest.

"How did you find me?"

Cole squeezed my good arm. "The GPS in Dave's phone. You left it on. One of the words I heard when you called was 'kill', and you were using someone else's phone. I tracked you."

"Thank God."

"Yeah."

I tilted my head so I could see Cole's face. He stared into the woods, his expression unreadable.

"Looks like we need to let Roxanne's boyfriend out of jail."

"You found him? Where?"

"Once he realized the entire State of Arizona was looking for him, he turned himself in."

"How'd he take the news about Roxanne?"

Cole shrugged. "Oh, you know. About as well as can be expected from a guy who was going to leave his relationship. He freaked out when I informed him he might be a suspect in her death."

"Did you find Sterling?"

Cole paused for a moment, as if searching for the right words.

"Search and Rescue went in, but the structure was so unstable they weren't able to continue. They made it to the area where you dug out, so we know we got the right mine. But—"

"But what?" I didn't like 'buts'. I needed absolutes, especially when it came to Sterling.

"We searched everywhere. There were no vehicles within miles of that mine."

I let the information sink in. Had Simon known Sterling's plans?

"Do you think Simon drove us there and waited for Sterling to kill me?"

Cole watched me, his gaze never leaving my face. "Maybe, but there is another possibility we have to consider."

At first I didn't get what he meant. Then, the light went on. I sat up.

"You mean that he made it out."

"Yes."

I stood, suddenly cold and clutched the blanket closed.

No.

I started to pace.

A dense throb began at my temples and worked its way around to the back of my neck. Sterling might still be alive. The threat to my life that I'd thought was gone could still be in play. It was too late to use the propane explosion to fake my death. Durm was a small town. Folks were probably already talking about what part I played in recent events.

My chest contracted. I couldn't breathe.

I'd have to leave.

Again.

Cole came over and took my hand, leading me back to the ambulance. Reluctantly, I followed. He reached out and swept a loose strand of hair back from my face, tucking it behind my ear. I fought the tears welling up in my eyes.

"I'll protect you, Kate."

The statement sounded so simple, I wanted to believe it could be true.

"You don't know these people, Cole. It's not just Sterling. Anaya won't let anything stand in his way. Especially when it comes to extracting vengeance. He once killed a man because he wore the wrong color shirt."

"I realize that. The difference is now we have Sterling's booking photos, known associates, family information. We also know he's probably at large. I called the DEA and they put me in contact with an agent who's familiar with both Salazar and Anaya. He also knew John Sterling. He's very interested in any information we might have."

"What's his name?"

"Chance Goodeve."

That's a name I hadn't heard in a long time. "I know him. He's one of the agents that helped get me out of Mexico."

"Your name came up in the conversation. He asked how you were doing. I told him what had been happening. He confirmed you testified against Sterling. He eventually told me about Salazar and Anaya."

"He lost men in an attack on a safe house in Mexico. I was the target." I closed my eyes. I could still see the flames.

Cole leaned in close. "The point is, people know what's happening. People who want to see justice done." He turned me to face him. "You have to let people help you, Kate. This isn't something you should deal with on your own." He leaned forward and rested his forehead against mine.

He was right. It was a lonely damn existence running from place to place. Time to take a stand. There was one small problem.

"What happens if they kill you? Or Jason? Or some other innocent? I'm bad luck, Cole. People end up dead when I'm around."

Cole pulled me to him and kissed me with that same tenderness he'd shown before. I kissed him back, believing for the moment that things would work out the way he said.

A girl can always hope.

THE END

ABOUT THE AUTHOR:

 **DV Berkom** is the award-winning author of two action-packed thriller series featuring strong female leads **(Leine Basso** and **Kate Jones**). Her love of creating resilient, kick-ass women characters stems from a lifelong addiction to reading spy novels, mysteries, and thrillers, and longing to find the female equivalent within those pages.

Raised in the Midwest, she earned a BA in political science and promptly moved to Mexico to live on a sailboat. Several years and a multitude of adventures later, she wrote her first novel and was hooked. The **Kate Jones adventure thriller**, *Bad Spirits*, was first published in 2010 as an online serial, and was immediately popular with Kindle and Nook fans. *Dead of Winter, Death Rites,* and *Touring for Death* soon followed before she began the far grittier **Leine Basso thriller** series in 2012 with *Serial Date*. Now, she tries to give equal time to both Kate's and Leine's stories, a must for her (happily) impatient readers.

DV currently lives in the Pacific Northwest with her husband, Mark, and several imaginary characters who love to tell her what to do. Her most recent books include *Vigilante Dead, A One Way Ticket to Dead, Yucatán Dead, A Killing Truth,* and *Cargo.*

To find out more, please visit **www.dvberkom.com** or DV's blog **dvberkom.wordpress.com**

To be the first to hear about new releases and receive special, subscriber-only offers, join DV's Readers' List here: **http://bit.ly/dvbNews**

More by DV Berkom:

Keep reading for an excerpt of the explosive thriller, Cruising for Death –Kate Jones Thriller #5:

CRUISING FOR

A KATE JONES THRILLER

DEATH

A MYSTERIOUS ARTIFACT. A RUTHLESS ENEMY.
PARADISE LOST.

DV BERKOM

ONE

MARCELA'S SHRIEKS SPLIT THE CALM evening air. I raced up the steps to the upper deck two at a time, with Cole close behind me.

She stood over a large, bulky shape on deck. As Cole and I approached the body, I recognized the jacket Karl wore to dinner earlier that evening.

Unfortunately, Karl was still in it.

We ran over to him and with some difficulty rolled him onto his back. I checked for a pulse but didn't find one, so I tilted his head and started CPR.

"You got this?" Cole asked.

I nodded my head between breaths.

"I'll find the doctor," Cole yelled over his shoulder as he disappeared down the stairwell.

Karl's breath smelled like after dinner mints and Amaretto. I stopped giving him mouth to mouth and continued with chest compressions willing his heart to start beating. From the illumination of the deck light his face appeared pasty white with a bluish tint around his mouth.

Marcela watched from the railing with a shocked look on her face. I continued the compressions until the ship's doctor touched me on the shoulder and indicated he would take over.

Gratefully, I sat back with dimming hope for Karl's resuscitation, watching as he unpacked a defibrillator. I pulled my shawl closer. Cole wrapped his arms around me while we waited. He had a calming presence I'd noticed competent law enforcement always seemed to possess. He'd had plenty of opportunities to hone that talent as the sheriff back home in Durm, Arizona.

Having no success, the doctor turned and shook his head, signifying he could do nothing more. Marcela burst into tears. I walked over to her and placed my shawl around her shoulders.

"What happened, Marcela? What did you see?"

She shook her head. "I don't know. I was searching for Gabriel and when I came up here, I found Karl..." She sobbed into her hand. "He was just lying there, not moving. I didn't know what to do." With this, she leaned her head on my shoulder, wet tears soaking through my thin blouse. A small crowd of passengers had grown around Karl.

I glanced at the doctor as he recorded the time of death in a small notebook. "What do you think?" I asked.

He stood and closed his notepad, sliding it into his shirt pocket. "It appears to be a heart attack. He is a very large man and is at the age for such a thing."

I looked at Karl's lifeless body. At least the wealthy manufacturer died on a Caribbean cruise, doing something he enjoyed. I only hoped I'd be so lucky.

With my track record, the chances of that were slim.

I'd learned things usually have a way of going sideways, especially when you don't expect it. It hadn't been easy, looking over my shoulder for years, waiting for my past to catch up with me. So far, I'd dodged killers hired by my ex, Roberto Salazar, and barely escaped with my life from disgraced DEA agent, John Sterling, both of whom I'd helped put in prison a decade before. The other man I'd testified against, Vincent Anaya, hadn't personally tried to recover the money I'd stolen. I assumed he preferred to leave that to his underling, Salazar.

A full year had passed since my run-in with Sterling, who I left buried deep in an abandoned mine in Arizona. With Sterling dead, that left Anaya and Salazar, neither of whom were members of my fan club. My contact in the DEA assured me Salazar's operation was quiet, having been absorbed into one of the larger drug cartels operating in Sonora, Mexico. Anaya had been released from prison the previous year and seemed to have slipped under everyone's radar. That had me worried.

When Cole surprised me with the ten-day trip onboard the exclusive cruise ship to the Caribbean, I had visions of snorkeling in jade-green water near deserted beaches and making love in the shade of a coconut palm, not giving CPR to a German industrialist.

Throughout the next day, as the ship sliced through the waves toward the next port of call, the usual chatter and antics of the cruisers were muted, the main topic of conversation being Karl's death. Cole and I decided to take a walk along the promenade deck in the balmy sea air after lunch and ran into an older gentleman named Harv, whom we'd met at dinner the evening before.

Harv hailed from Virginia and was on the cruise at the urging of his two sons, both of whom gifted him the luxury vacation in an effort to get him to move on with his life after the death of his beloved wife. Harv smiled when he spoke of the boys and shook his head wryly when he explained why he couldn't or wouldn't move on.

"Jeanne was the best woman a man could ever want. I'd never be able to replace her, and don't want to. Those boys," he shrugged. "I know they mean well, but they don't have a clue about true love." He looked off in the distance and sighed. "You can't replace perfection."

Cole ran his fingers through my hair, a smile on his lips. I smiled back, warming to his gesture.

It turned out Harv was somewhat of an expert on piracy, or, as he put it, nautical robbery. He kept us enthralled late into the afternoon with tales of historical Caribbean pirates and the ports of call they favored. One in particular intrigued me, a woman named Anne Bonny, who sailed the Caribbean as a pirate in the sixteenth century. There were other women who took to the life as well, and Harv regaled us with stories of several. I wondered at their courage, to defy convention in such restrictive times and live a life with a certain kind of freedom not afforded women then.

Of course, most met a violent end except for Anne, who apparently lived well into her dotage.

Later, after dinner, most of the passengers headed into the nightclub for the evening's show. Situated in the middle of the ship on an upper deck, the large room boasted a stage at one end and tiers with small tables surrounding a lighted dance floor. Cole, Gabe and I snagged a table near the stage, saving extra chairs for Marcela and Gabe's friend Stefano, who would join us later.

Gabe was Gabriel de la Vega, a well-known expert on sixteenth century Spanish shipwrecks hired by the cruise line as part of their onboard seminar lineup. Tall and lean, the Peruvian's demeanor suggested his intensely intellectual nature, and was in stark contrast to his assistant Marcela's overt sexuality. Cool and rational versus hot and impulsive; the two were a study in opposites.

We'd just ordered our drinks when Marcela showed up, exotic in a short red, off the shoulder dress with five-inch heels and fire-engine red lipstick. Gabe pulled out the chair for her to sit.

"Mind if I join you?" A tallish man in his early forties dressed in a tan sport coat placed his hand on the back of Marcela's chair, indicating the seat next to her.

"But of course." Marcela uncrossed her legs and smiled warmly at him. I checked Gabe to see his reaction, but he appeared unperturbed.

The man introduced himself as Larry, a restaurateur from British Columbia. I tried not to stare. A nagging sensation told me I knew him from somewhere, but I couldn't place him.

Stefano arrived moments later, apologizing profusely for his tardiness. A celebrated Brazilian football player and Gabe's best friend, he had a compact bearing, was a head shorter than Gabe and all I could say is that he smoldered. Women practically sustained whiplash when he walked by, whether they were with someone or not. He moved with a lucid grace and self-confidence that created throngs of adoring women blatantly offering themselves up for a possible tryst. I slipped my hand in Cole's, glad to be with a less volatile partner. My experiences hadn't been too positive with fiery Latin types.

The emcee took the stage and after a couple of jokes fell flat, introduced the band. I didn't quite catch the name, but it sounded like *The Party Hounds*. They played a mixture of calypso, Reggae and older rock and roll. It had been a while since Cole and I had gone dancing and we decided to let loose. Larry and Marcela seemed to hit it off, so I danced with Gabe, as well. Predictably, Stefano's dance card was full before the first song ended.

A couple of hours later, I was leaving the ladies room and walking back to our table when a staccato burst of machinegun fire erupted from within the club, followed by screams. Paralyzed, it took me a second to register what was happening.

Now completely sober with adrenaline pumping through my veins, I thought through various scenarios but couldn't think of one that made any sense. Images from long ago flashed through my mind.

Not again.

As I moved down the hallway in the direction of the gunfire, Cole was foremost in my mind. He was a professional, I told myself. He knew what to do in this kind of situation. He'd be fine.

Hyper alert, I made my way around the outside of the club to the back hallway and slipped through a door that opened to the backstage area. Then I moved closer to the stage. Someone wept softly on the other side of the curtain.

"Silence," a man's voice shouted. The weeping stopped.

"There will be no more outbursts of any kind. We will only remain until we find what we came for. If anyone tries to stop us we won't hesitate to use force."

I crept to an opening in the curtain and peered through.

The man had his back to me and wore a military style uniform with combat boots. He held a machinegun with the butt on his hip, barrel angled carelessly to the side.

Four other gunmen stood nearby, dressed similarly to the one on stage, all with automatic weapons pointed into the crowd.

I checked the rest of the room. At first relieved, fear slid to my stomach as I caught sight of Cole, Gabe and Marcela still seated at our table. Gabe and Marcela looked shell-shocked, while Cole's expression was a study in calm certainty. Stefano and Larry were nowhere in sight.

What the hell was going on? Who were these men? They were dressed like pseudo-militia, but why were they threatening cruise ship passengers? Were they looking for money? Valuables? I needed to do something. But what? I had no gun, no weapon of any kind. I didn't think I'd need it on a cruise.

Lesson learned.

I tore myself away from the curtain and moved along the back of the stage to another door that led to the main passageway. I had no idea what I was going to do, but inaction wasn't an option.

Removing my sandals, I ran barefoot along the carpeted hallway toward the stairwell. I needed to move up a level to get to the ship's bridge. If they hadn't yet taken control, there was still a chance to fight them off if I warned the captain in time. I reached the stairs and took two at a time, pushing through the panic.

How did they get onboard with their weapons? Had they boarded when the ship was in port and loading supplies?

I made it to the upper deck and hurried along the walkway, past the volleyball net and deck chairs. The bridge loomed in front of me with its full bank of windows. Lights from the ship's console glowed through the glass as I neared the outside door. It opened and a shadowy figure appeared. I ducked behind a stanchion. A gunman with an AK-47 walked out onto the deck.

Shit.

My breathing heavy from fear and exertion, I slipped behind the bridge to the other side of the ship. Sucking in deep gulps of salty air, I leaned against the railing.

Think, Kate. I could go back to the club and try to come up with a plan to subdue five machinegun toting militia men. That probably wouldn't be effective, since I had no weapon. All of the people in the club were in danger. Cole was in danger. There had to be something I could do.

I thought about checking the crew's quarters, but realized if they'd taken the bridge, they'd probably beaten me to it. The doctor would have some type of communication equipment in the infirmary; a satellite phone at least. It was possible they hadn't thought to secure that area.

Turning, I happened to glance down and noticed light glinting off the water. Puzzled, I tried to make out what it might be, but it was a dark night and dark water. I decided to get a closer look.

Not wanting to alert anyone to my presence, I moved silently to another set of stairs and peered through the steps. No one was below me and I quickly made my way down a level. Once on deck, I crossed to the railing and leaned over.

I'd found how the gunmen had boarded the ship.

TWO

I RAN DOWN ANOTHER LEVEL and stopped directly above where the smaller boat was tied to the ship. They'd thrown grappling hooks over the side and climbed aboard on ladders. There didn't appear to be anyone guarding the vessel. I'd heard of modern day pirates who boarded yachts and even an oil supertanker, but from what I knew, most of that kind of activity happened in the Gulf of Aden off the Somali coast, not the Caribbean. Then I figured, why not? It would be easy pickings. There were so many tourists with money floating around down here, how could a pirate lose?

I considered disabling their boat but discarded the idea. What would that accomplish? If they wanted to leave and it pissed them off, would it make them angry enough to kill? I wondered why the ship's radar hadn't tracked the vessel's arrival. Or, maybe it had. It was possible they planted a co-conspirator in the wheel house.

Realizing I was wasting time standing there, I hustled to the infirmary. The windows were dark. I tried the door, but it was locked.

Next, I tried the doctor's stateroom. There was no answer.

With nothing more I could do at the moment, I headed back to Cole and the gunmen, trying to think of some way to get him and the rest safely out of the club. It wouldn't be easy without weapons. I'd have to create a diversion. I moved through the door that led backstage, proceeded to the curtain and peeked through.

Relief replaced fear as I located Cole, Gabe, and Marcela standing on the dance floor. At least they hadn't shot anyone yet. It looked like the gunmen had rounded everyone up and herded them into the center of the room. They'd closed the three entrances to the club and posted a guard at each. One of the gunmen was collecting passenger's smartphones, Blackberries and iPhones. The guy I'd seen issuing demands earlier paced back and forth in front of the stage, glancing at his cell phone and smoking a cigarette which he abruptly dropped and ground into the floor.

Everybody except Cole looked scared and I knew from experience that when you had that many fearful people in one room, odds were someone would try something foolish. At that moment an alarm sounded and the disco lights started to flash. Over the loudspeaker, a woman's prerecorded voice intoned, "Do not panic. This is an emergency. Please refer to the evacuation manual located in the plastic sleeve on the back of your stateroom door. I repeat, do not panic."

Panic set in and frightened and confused people headed for the exits, only to be shoved back by men with guns. Cole worked the crowd, trying to calm folks, but there were too many of them.

I leaned back against the wall, feeling helpless.

A single gunshot filled the air and the room fell silent. A commanding voice floated over the prerecorded warning system.

"Quiet!"

The voice sounded familiar. I peered through the opening in the curtain. Everyone had turned toward one of the exits. A space had formed around a man with a forty-five in one hand, pointed in the air.

Larry.

Bringing a small walkie-talkie to his lips with his free hand he said something into the mouthpiece over the repeated warnings on the loudspeakers. The prerecorded voice abruptly stopped. The nagging feeling I knew him from somewhere continued to hammer at my brain.

Then it clicked.

I stopped breathing as the realization hit me. Things moved in slow motion as old memories flooded in.

Frank Lanzarotti. I mentally kicked myself for not recognizing him sooner. He'd had work done to his face and changed his hair color, but the eyes and his physique were essentially the same. What the hell was he doing here?

And, more importantly, had he recognized me? It had been over ten years since I left Mexico.

The cold sweat on my forehead told me he probably had. I would have to be even more careful now. I wondered if he kept in contact with Vincent Anaya. If not, then that might explain why he hadn't been more interested in me. Frank didn't have a bone to pick. Anaya did.

"I'm looking for Gabriel de la Vega." Frank pointed his gun at a woman nearby wearing gold lamé and a blonde wig. Harv stood rigidly by her side. She took one look at the barrel of the gun, her eyes rolled back in her head and her knees buckled. Harv caught her before she hit the floor.

Frank moved toward the stage and the crowd dropped away, clearing a path for him. He glanced toward the curtain and I shrank back, hoping the fabric hadn't moved.

He turned to face the crowd. "Where is Gabriel de la Vega?"

"I am he."

People scuttled to one side as Gabe moved front and center. I scanned the crowd and located Cole and Marcela standing a few feet behind him. I exhaled, not realizing I'd been holding my breath.

Frank nodded and motioned with his gun at one of his men.

"Tie him and gag him." He glanced at Marcela. "Her, too. And be careful; they are not to be damaged in any way." Frank and the first man I'd seen earlier walked near the curtain. I strained to hear their conversation.

"Go and find the tall blonde American woman. Keep her alive. She's valuable," Frank muttered. The man nodded and left.

If I'd been under any illusion he hadn't recognized me, I wasn't now.

Frank turned back to the crowd.

"If everyone will remain calm, this will all be over soon and you may go back to enjoying your vacation. But," Frank paused for dramatic effect. "If anyone decides to be a hero, they will be shot." By the look on most people's faces, I doubted he'd have any takers. I located Cole in the crowd again, eyes riveted on Frank, fists clenched, his knuckles bone white in the warm disco light.

I knew that look. Cole had a plan.

Cruising for Death

Stepping back from the curtain, I tried to figure out a way to divert their attention, give Cole some leeway to do whatever it was he planned to do.

A woman's scream came from somewhere on the other side of the club. I rushed to the curtain and looked through. Harv was on his knees with his back to one of the gunmen, a machinegun pressed to the back of his head. My heart leapt to my throat. *Not Harv.*

"What the hell is going on?" Frank demanded as he strode over to the two.

The gunman kept his weapon trained on Harv. "The guy came up behind me and tried to take my gun," he said, his voice a growl.

Harv's face hardened. "Almost got it, too."

I held my breath, hoping Frank didn't strike him.

Frank considered Harv for a moment, then said, "Get off your knees. Good try, old man."

With effort, Harv rose to his feet. His steely-eyed gaze surprised me. Harv didn't strike me as anything but a sweet older man whose sons had sent him on a cruise to help him move on from his wife's death. I wondered if I'd misjudged him.

Frank nodded at his gunman, who raised the butt of his weapon, aiming it at the back of Harv's head.

A disturbance broke out at the back of the club. People drew apart as Cole pushed through the crowd. He held one of the gunmen in a chokehold with a nine millimeter to his head.

"Drop it. Now." Cole's command echoed through the nightclub.

Frank turned, his eyes glittering. Then he smiled. I caught movement out of the corner of my eye and turned in time to see the gunman behind Harv raise his weapon and fire. At the same time, Harv threw himself at the man, knocking the gun to the side. The bullets missed Cole but not the man he held in front of him.

Two of Frank's other men trained their weapons on Cole from across the room. Realizing he was out-gunned, Cole dropped the nine and the dead man followed.

An adrenaline fueled, white-hot rage mixed with several shades of panic erupted from somewhere deep inside me. Without thinking, I launched myself through the curtains and off the stage, landed on top of Frank and knocked us both to the floor. The gun flew out of his hand and skittered away, coming to rest at the feet of one of the other goons.

Frank reacted like a coiled snake and whatever advantage I'd had abruptly disappeared as he writhed out from under me, flipped me onto my back and pinned me to the floor with his knees.

Cold recognition spread across his thin, perfectly tanned face. He reminded me of a member of the weasel family, although generally I don't like to be unkind to weasels.

"Just the person I wanted to see." Frank yelled for his man to throw his pistol to him. He caught it and pointed it toward Gabe and Marcela. "Get them in the boat. I can handle this one." Gabe's brown eyes grew large as the gunman jammed the barrel of his gun into his back, forcing him to move past us. Marcela kept her gaze trained on the floor as she followed quietly. Another of Frank's men took up position next to us, gun pointed at my head.

Frank glanced over to where Cole had been standing. I followed his gaze and was relieved to see he was no longer there.

"Where the hell is he?" Frank shouted. The gunmen looked at each other, the cold realization that they'd let Cole escape in the fracas dawning on their faces. When Frank received no response, his face flushed red. "Find him, now." His voice dripped menace. Two of the gunmen leaped into action and began to search the crowd while the ones remaining trained their weapons on the rest of the passengers.

Frank turned back to me, a cruel smile on his face.

"Well. If it isn't my old friend Kate. I never thought I'd see you again. Not after what you did to Anaya." He was close enough that my eyes watered from his aftershave. "It appears Fate has dealt me a full house. Not only will I deliver Gabriel de la Vega, expert on sixteenth century shipwrecks to Vincent Anaya, but as the *piéce de résistance*, I'll be able to hand over an old thorn in his side." Frank cocked his head. "Where've you been all these years?"

"Far away from people like you." I spit out the words.

"Now, now, is that any way to treat an old amigo?" Frank shook his head and smiled. "You never recognized me. I suppose that means the surgery was a success." He studied my face for a minute. "I knew you the moment you stepped on board. You don't look any older. I wonder what Anaya will do with you?"

I ignored the question and swiveled my head, straining to see if they'd found Cole. The two gunmen looking for him weren't visible.

Frank followed my gaze and his expression hardened. "You should be more worried about yourself." He climbed off and jerked me upright as his man grabbed my hands and slid a zip tie around my wrists, cinching it tight. Frank produced a roll of duct tape and tore off a piece, amusement evident on his face. "I always wanted to do this," he said, and slapped it over my mouth.

He grabbed me by the arm and pushed me up the ramp to the exit. I didn't blame the other passengers for falling back. I wouldn't want to get in Frank's way, either. He shoved me down the hall in front of him, his gunman following close behind.

My brain whirled. How the hell did I get into this, and, more importantly, how could I get out? I strained my neck, trying to find Cole, but saw only a crowd of strangers held at gunpoint. I hoped the gunmen hadn't received instructions to mow them all down as they left. If Frank got his orders from Vincent Anaya, there'd be no survivors. I didn't think Frank would be quite so cold blooded, but I'd been wrong before.

We moved toward the bow of the ship and took a left, then made our way to the place where I'd seen the smaller boat. Frank indicated I should go over the railing and climb down the ladder. I held up my zip tied hands and Frank shook his head.

Shrugging, I swung a leg over the side and grabbed onto the metal rungs of the ladder, then brought my other leg over. Everything moved. The bigger ship dipped with the waves, and the ladder slid side to side as I attempted to stay connected. My body swung the opposite way it should have as I tried to stabilize.

With a grunt, Frank reached over and clipped the zip tie apart. That made things easier. I took a couple of steps down and looked at the man ready to grab me once I made it to the deck. I needed to do something, now.

So I jumped.

END EXCERPT